WILD COW WEDDING

Wild Cow Ranch 5

Natalie Bright
Denise F. McAllister

Wild Cow Wedding
Natalie Bright
Denise F. McAllister

Paperback Edition
CKN Christian Publishing
An Imprint of Wolfpack Publishing
5130 S. Fort Apache Rd. 215-380
Las Vegas, NV 89148

Paperback ISBN: 978-1-63977-019-9
Ebook ISBN: 978-1-63977-018-2

WILD COW WEDDING

Dedication

Hats off to the readers who love the American West, cowboys, and romance. Of all the roads you travel in your life, make sure a few of them are dirt.
NB

Thank you to family and friends, some here and some who have moved on. Life's a journey. Thank God for being with us every step of the way.
DM

Chapter 1

Carli

Sunlight streamed through the dusty-paned window. Carli Jameson snuggled in bed with her arm stretched to the ceiling admiring the ring on her left hand. It sparkled, fire swirling deep within the stones. The engagement ring was understated with diamond nuggets clustered in a braided rope. It had been her fiancé's grandmother's ring. Her heart fluttered and a smile curved her mouth.

Engaged. To be married.

"Mrs. Carli Torres. Carli Jameson Torres. Carlotta Jean Jameson Torres," she muttered to the empty bedroom.

A knock on the front door broke her daydreaming and annoyed her, but maybe it was her fiancé. How strange to think of Lank in that way. She popped out of bed and rushed to the front of the house. Breathless, she swung the door wide only to find a neon purple-haired, stocky lady wearing the same-colored pant suit and holding a briefcase.

"Carli."

"Del?"

"You're being sued. I came right away."

A million things ran through Carli's mind at that moment. She needed to think about food, decorations, invitations, and a preacher. A dress! So many other things that went along with planning a wedding. Clean her house, for gosh sakes! She never noticed how filthy the windows were until this morning.

"Are you going to invite me in?" Del stood on the porch.

"Of course. I'm sorry. Come in."

"We have a lot of work to do." The attorney entered with a presence of bold authority and intelligence. "I brought my files and computer, if there's somewhere I can set up. We've got a case to build before we go to trial. Wowzer! Look at that on your finger. When's the wedding?" Del shot her a big toothy grin.

Carli remained in the entry hall, any comment caught in her throat while she watched Del place her briefcase and laptop satchel on the dining room table.

"Can I spread out here?" Not waiting for an answer, Del emptied the briefcase, making stacks of papers in neat rows.

"Sure," was all Carli could manage at the moment. "I'm being sued?"

"Hang on. I'll be back." Carli watched as Del walked outside to the car, the trunk lid still open. Hefting a file box, the attorney made another trip before Carli even thought to offer assistance.

"Is there anything I can help you with?"

"No, ma'am. This is the last of it. I would appreciate some breakfast though. I've been driving most of the night and haven't eaten." Del hauled a second box of papers across the living room to the dining room table. It landed with a thud.

"Breakfast. Yes. Okay." Carli tried to clear the fog from her mind to think if she had anything to cook. Maybe pancakes, but only two eggs. Definitely coffee. She padded to the kitchen in her bare feet, thinking she should change out of her nightshirt. But for now, it was warm and soft.

"Who is suing me?" she called out just before turning on the coffee grinder.

Del pulled up a stool at the tall counter with her briefcase. "Billy Broderick."

Carli spun around. "But the court already ruled on his protest. Almost a year ago. The judge said my grandfather's Will was legit and that I'm the legal heir to the Wild Cow Ranch."

"Billy believes otherwise and apparently he has convinced an attorney to take his case."

"What can we do?" Carli began pulling items from the refrigerator, hunting in the back to see what she had and for any ideas on what to cook.

"Here, let me." Del edged in front and studied the contents of the refrigerator.

Carli poured coffee and sat down on the stool Del had recently vacated. "I can't believe he's decided to raise his ugly head now. I have a wedding to plan."

"I know you have other things on your mind, Carli. But this is really important. You could lose this ranch if we don't present a solid case."

"Okay," Carli said. "Remind me about the Brodericks. Seems like a long time ago when I saw him in court the first time. That's when you found me in Georgia and then brought me to Texas for the ruling on grandpa's Will. I never wanted to think about the way Billy acted in the courtroom that day. He had such hatred for me. So much has happened since then."

Del stopped digging through the fridge and turned to sift through papers instead. Perched on the stool, she balanced a briefcase on her lap and gave a summary. "Here goes. Norwood Jameson, your great-grandfather, left his entire holdings to his only daughter, your grandmother Jean, instead of his wife Lottie. I'm assuming in a fit of rage, she signed over the Jameson ranch and guardianship of your grandma Jean to their friend and neighbor, Russell Broderick. That's how Billy's family got involved in this. The Jamesons and the Brodericks go way back."

"How could Lottie sign over something she didn't own? The ranch was not left to her." Carli poured their coffees and took a long sip of hers. She felt the beginnings of a headache. What a tangled mess this had become.

"I think in the beginning she duped the Brodericks. Maybe they thought Lottie did own it. The unique part is what she did to Jean. Lottie turned over her only daughter's guardianship, as a minor child, to Mr. Broderick and then she hightailed it back to her kin in Europe. Since Lottie didn't legally own anything, the ranch stayed with Jean. That part was ironclad which is why you own it now."

Carli could barely make any sense of it all. She only found out about the Wild Cow Ranch a year before. These people were just a list of names on paper, faceless, yet she shared the same blood. Her whole life she never knew her birth parents or any family on either side. The Fitzgeralds, who had raised her, did not have a large family either. She was on her own. Then, came to find out she had inherited a ranch in Texas from people she never knew. It was mind-boggling.

"For the record, your people found me and handed me a cattle ranch. While I'm forever grateful to live here and know more about the Jameson legacy, this Billy Broderick has got to move on with his life. I can't fix his issues and I don't see how a judge and lawyers can fix this either."

"It does seem to be clear cut. So, you see," Del continued, "your great-grandmother Lottie never owned the ranch legally. It had been willed to the daughter Jean, your grandmother, from her father. Their friends, the Brodericks, specifically Uncle Russell as he was known, took over operations of the ranch and raised Jean as his own."

"Women running away from their lives and abandoning daughters. That seems to be a recurring theme in my family," Carli said.

Del avoided her glance and cleared her throat. "Russell also had an only son, Fred Broderick. Fred and Jean were raised together. She married Ward Kimball but never changed her last name for some reason, maybe as a tribute to her father. Jean and Ward raised an only daughter on the ranch, your mother Michelle, who also kept the Jameson family name. We can't find any record that she ever legally married. The Jameson name was passed on to you. Your grandparents, Jean and Ward, continued the tradition, working alongside the Broderick family. Michelle and Billy were about the same age."

Carli took a breath. "You know, when I was

around ten years old my foster parents brought me to Texas on our way home after a vacation. I didn't remember for a long time but that's when I first met my grandparents. Grandma Jean was wearing the turquoise boots that I have now and she had hazel eyes like me...and my mother had the same eyes."

"I wonder why the Fitzgeralds never brought you back to see your grandparents again," Del said.

"Who knows? There are a lot of mysteries about my life." Carli's eyes lowered.

"I think you know the rest," Del said. "Your mother lived on the ranch until she was sixteen, then ran away. You were born in Amarillo at St. Anthony's Hospital and the nuns there handled your placement with a family. Your mother then got involved with drugs in California and overdosed. I was retained by a law firm in Amarillo to locate you in Atlanta. Billy Broderick is the only surviving heir in that family, and when he applied for a loan this other information about you popped up. Your grandfather Ward had changed his Last Will a month before he died after receiving a report from detectives. They finally found you."

"I wish I could have met him," Carli said.

"Upon confirming ownership of the acreage, we discovered that Billy's claim over the entire Jameson family ranch was incorrect. Your great-grandfather left everything to his daughter Jean. And since Jean's only daughter—your mother, Michelle—is dead, that leaves you, the only surviving heir of the Wild Cow Ranch."

"What a story," Carli said. "Sounds kind of like a soap opera. How about some oatmeal?"

"That would be fine," answered Del.

"And now we have to rehash that whole history again and dig up the past." Carli sighed. She just wanted to move forward. She had a future with a handsome cowboy to think about. "I hope it's cleared up before I get married. You'll be here long enough to come to the wedding, won't you?"

"Wouldn't miss it." Del smiled.

Chapter 2

Lola

Lola Wallace sat in the kitchen nook staring out the window of her second-floor apartment. A ranch horse nibbled, took one step, nibbled, and took two steps to eat in a new spot. A few in the group raised their heads to look around before getting back to the business of grazing. She loved this view, particularly early morning when the ranch was at peace.

She and Buck had lived in this space above the industrial ranch kitchen and dining hall since they were newlyweds, so many years ago she refused to do the math. So much in love, owning a lot of material things did not matter back then as long as they had each other. Actually, they barely had anything to fill up their space. But now it was her haven, her favorite place in the world. The walls and furnishings displayed the bright colors of her Mexican heritage. From the hand-painted blue Spanish tiles to the rugs and pillows with vivid pinks, bright oranges, and neon yellows, it was also reflective of her bubbly personality. Every room was painted a different color. Just walking into her home made her smile.

As the Wild Cow ranch cook, she was particular and grew her own herbs. A shelf over the sink bulged with the proof—dill, basil, chives, mint, and thyme— which added to the charm of her tiny kitchen. She got up from her seat and checked the soil, adding a bit of water to each before returning to the blank piece of paper.

"Whatcha doin'?" her husband and Wild Cow Ranch foreman Buck asked.

"Making a list." She picked up a pen and wrote "cake" in meticulous letters.

"What have you taken on now?" He bent and gave her a peck on the cheek.

"Carli's wedding. I'm sure Belinda will want to make the cake." The peace from the moment before, now gone as she scribbled more notes. "You need to talk to our pastor and make sure he's available, Buck. I don't know where we can go dress shopping, and have no idea about her colors. She needs to decide that today. We need floral arrangements and who knows what flowers will be available with this short notice. And, in this day and age, I guess we invite everyone by email because there's no time to order embossed invitations. A text seems too impersonal." The teapot on the stove whistled.

"Have they set a date?" her husband asked.

"Not yet, but it's never too soon to start planning. The date will be here before you know it."

"Hold up," Buck said as he placed a cup of herbal tea in front of her. "What if Carli doesn't want your help with her wedding? Have you talked to her or Lank to see what they want?"

"Of course, she'll need my help. She has no one else. Lank's mother has passed, God rest her soul.

That leaves me. I'm going to make sure those kids get the most beautiful wedding ever."

Lola added "flowers" with a question mark. "It will have to be fall colors. I can see orange and yellow mums, burgundy roses, maybe a few sunflowers. It's going to be just beautiful." She scribbled more notes. "Finding a caterer might be a problem."

"Aren't you cooking?" Buck sat down at his usual spot. He slathered two pieces of toast with homemade wild plum jam.

"I'd rather not. I'd like to be a guest for once. Of course, they'll want to get married at our church. Oh, but I think Lank's family is Catholic. We may need to talk to the priest over in Sunnyside. Lank may want a Catholic service. I'm sure they could use that church, but, on the other hand, I'm almost certain they'd want to have the ceremony at the ranch. I would, if I were them. Wild Cow Ranch headquarters will make a beautiful location for a wedding."

Buck could hardly get a word in because Lola didn't wait for his answer as she rambled.

"The stained glass at Sunnyside is just beautiful, stretching from floor to ceiling on both sides of the sanctuary," she said. "It reminds me of my hometown church in my family's village. My grandmother used to take me to services with her." She seemed to be all over the place in her thinking—first the church, then the ranch.

Lola closed her eyes and could practically smell the faint aroma of candle wax burning. The calm and quiet memory of the place rushed over her senses, a full heart and inner peace that only came from the Holy Spirit. How she loved that sanctuary.

Her one desire as a little girl was to be married in that church. She wanted a full lace dress, with a lace train that trailed all the way back to the entrance when she stepped up to the altar. She had always imagined white roses at the end of every pew, and more roses in arrangements across the entire front. Soft burning candles in every nook and cranny.

Buck laid a hand on her arm. "I'm sorry you never got the wedding of your dreams, sweetheart."

She smiled into his loving eyes. "It doesn't matter, dear. We're just as married."

"I'm heading out, but you do need Carli's input before you plan too much. I know how you are." He laughed.

"I'll go talk to her sometime this morning."

Buck shot her a questioning glance.

"I promise. We need to get on those invitations right away." She laughed too, but secretly her mind was buzzing. This was going to be the most talked about wedding for years to come.

From the back of hallway storage, she pulled out a stack of off-white lace tablecloths. Spreading them out on her bed, she admired the delicate patterns. Crocheted by her grandmother and aunts, they had been an engagement gift, but Lola never got to use them. She and Buck were married by a justice of the peace after a short, whirlwind engagement. The moment she had looked into his eyes, she knew. There had been no doubt. And of course, her parents had not approved. Her brothers were furious that she had chosen a gringo. That's why they ran away to get married. Everyone came around eventually though, and her family soon loved Buck as much as she did.

Lola loved her husband more than anything, but the desire to have a fancy church wedding had never completely gone away. Most of her family was passed now, and she hadn't been back to her grandmother's church in Mexico City since she was a young woman. Her chest tightened and she wiped a bit of moisture from her cheek. Straightening her shoulders, she stood and refolded the delicate lace, pausing in her work to admire the precise stitches. These would work just fine for the reception. If she just knew what colors she'd be working with.

What they needed was a wedding committee to make sure everything would go smoothly. No detail left unnoticed.

Lola sat back down at the table and picked up the pen. She stared at the wall calendar which hung next to the fridge. November fifteenth. It was a Saturday. Perfect. Maybe a mid-afternoon wedding and they could follow it with a reception here at the cookhouse. The neighbors would want to throw Carli and Lank an engagement party, and of course the church ladies would be excited to plan a bridal shower.

There was no reason a bride couldn't have the wedding of her dreams, and Lola was going to make sure that Carli had her big day. It would be perfect.

They had one month.

Chapter 3

Billy

Billy Broderick looked at his Rolex. That brat of a poser should have gotten word by now of the lawsuit he was filing. She wouldn't be living at the Wild Cow Ranch much longer. Not after his lawyers got done with her. And if he had anything to do with it, she'd be on the streets with only the clothes on her back, living in the gutter like her worthless mama.

He leaned his head back against the leather chair and propped both boots on the mahogany desk. Studded cowhide covered the front and both sides. An oak bookcase spanned one wall filled with unread leather-bound volumes and museum quality mineral specimens, all meticulously purchased and arranged to impress. His eyes wandered to the window. From the twenty-seventh floor of the office tower in downtown Amarillo, he scanned the horizon. He hadn't worked this hard and acquired this much only to have some second-rate, white trash female sashay to town and steal his birthright.

The Wild Cow Ranch belonged to him. His mother and Jean Jameson had been best friends.

His grandfather and father had worked at the Wild Cow for generations as the horse trainers. Billy had worked alongside his father, following Jean and Ward all over the country to roping events, hauling their horses, lugging tack in and out of show rings, tending to their every need. To heck with the Jameson family legacy. Billy loved the Wild Cow as much as any Jameson; he'd put his money on it.

No matter that dating the Jameson's only daughter, Michelle, had never worked out for him. His mother had been set on the match, but Michelle would have none of him. She was only out for a good time and he had plans for the future. She lived in the titillating moments with whatever cowboy she was sharing a pickup's backseat with on any given night. Her rejection and the anger he felt towards her had become a scalding fury.

He understood what owning a place like the Wild Cow could do for him. Driven to get ahead, he especially needed to prove himself to his father. Michelle didn't fit in his picture anymore. When she got hooked on drugs, he didn't want to put up with that bull crap. He didn't love her that much.

That's when his mother formulated Plan B. With the only heir out of the way as a homeless addict living on the streets, the sensible thing to do was to leave the Wild Cow Ranch to Billy. So, his mother convinced Jean to change her Last Will. It made sense. Jean wanted the ranch to stay in good hands and she was horrified at the thought of it being sold to strangers and having the land divided. His mother had been a force and always did what was best for her only baby boy. He missed her terribly.

Billy opened the bottom desk drawer and pulled

out a steel lockbox. Rising, he retrieved the key inside an antique tobacco jar on his bookcase which had belonged to Jean's father. He and his mom had once spent an entire morning helping Jean look for it.

Billy had always admired that leather-wrapped jar, but Jean told him once that she was saving it for her granddaughter if they ever located her. So, he took it. He promised himself that he'd return to their house one day, but he never did.

Jean and Ward got wind that Michelle had had a baby. They had spent untold amounts of money searching for her through detectives, but a newborn placed with foster parents, and not in the system, didn't leave much of a trail.

Billy unlocked the box and spread a dozen or so letters across the top of his desk. Letters from Michelle about her life in California, the myriad of aliases she used, the horse shows she'd won, the men who funded her lifestyle, and the beaches where she had lived. She made Billy swear to never reveal her location, only to let her parents know that she was alive and well. Michelle had trusted him with all of her secrets. He was the only one that knew anything about Michelle's life after she ran away from the Wild Cow. And he had said nothing to Jean or Ward. Ever.

Sifting through the pile, he tried to recall if Michelle had ever written about a daughter. To his recollection, there was nothing about a baby. He knew that she was pregnant and that she wanted to leave, but he never knew who the father was. He had agreed to Michelle's plan. Late one night, he picked her up on his motorcycle, drove her to Amarillo, and dropped her off where she'd live until the baby was born. She had decided at the very first that she was giving it up for adoption.

Billy leaned back in his chair again and picked up the first letter. He needed to read through them again to make sure. The case against Michelle's daughter, if Carli was in fact the granddaughter of Jean and Ward, had to be iron clad. There could be no heir and no question that Jean Jameson's Last Will had assigned all rights, title, and interest one hundred percent to Billy Broderick. They loved him like a son. Jean said so, and his mother had beamed with pride.

When they went to court, he would have a long list of character witnesses willing to vouch for him. He was an upstanding citizen and contributed much to the business community of Amarillo and to the little town of Dixon. His main office was in downtown Amarillo, but he maintained a smaller place in an old Victorian in Dixon where he met with clients and offered investment advice. He had a hand in most every project in town. Commercial properties, a string of automatic car washes, and oil drilling ventures. He ran a small herd of Angus on some leased grass, and he even had a racehorse that he funded. In fact, the Dixon Chamber of Commerce had named him Citizen of the Year in 2005. Everybody liked the Broderick family, pillars of the community, every one of them.

He needed the Wild Cow though. The main project he had poured his heart and soul into, never came to fruition because of the supposed Jameson heir. Ward had taken seriously ill so Billy began the process of finding money to build a lakefront community. People were standing in line to buy lots.

His wife had been coordinating that entire venture. Little did he know that Ward was still trying to find Michelle's daughter. But then they located Carli and Ward changed his Will.

Billy had been so furious he never went to the hospital during the last month Ward was alive. The Last Will stood, they located the long-lost granddaughter, and the judge ruled in her favor. Billy was tossed out like yesterday's meatloaf. But he was going to fight.

The only black mark against him had been his crazy ex-wife, Nicolette. She was a looker and ambitious too, just like him. But she failed to trust him to handle the situation. She had gone ape crazy when Carli moved into her grandparents' house.

Billy and his wife had talked and schemed for hours. Nicolette was obsessed with running Carli out of town, but she had no patience and wouldn't let him handle it. Burning down the horse barn had been her stupid idea. Carli's horse had escaped anyway, and then Nicolette had dropped her vape at the scene. There was nothing he could do but let them take her to prison. He sure did miss her though. She way outclassed him, that's for sure, and she turned every head in the room when she was on his arm. He had been lucky she fell for him. Rather, it was his money, but he didn't mind.

He turned to face his desk and glanced at his appointment calendar. Tee off at the country club was later this afternoon for a round with a friend. Best friend actually, since high school. Another solid citizen and businessman. He needed to read over Michelle's letters one more time.

"Shirley. Hold my calls," he spoke into the desk

phone.

"Yes, sir," came the reply.

Billy Broderick had big plans for the Wild Cow, mighty big plans, and one little lying girl from Georgia wasn't going to stand in his way. He couldn't even imagine where the lawyers had dug her up, but he was going to find out. His future depended on it.

Chapter 4

Taylor

Taylor Miller stared at the road ahead through Ray-Bans, watching the white clouds drift by, and made a conscious effort to think about the past. A time long ago that he had buried deep. More specifically, a particular girl.

Back then, he was a senior and the star quarterback, she a sophomore. Their attraction was immediate. He remembered her vividly, like it was yesterday, but over the decades he locked her memory in a special part of his heart and rarely brought it out to ponder. Such a pretty girl. A little wild. Seemed to him there was something lost about her, kind of sad. Always pushing the limit, she'd take anyone's dare. The first time he set eyes on her, she was wearing cut-off jeans, a halter top, holding a long-neck beer bottle in one hand, and dancing on the hood of a pickup truck at the after-game keg party.

He and his best friend were always on the lookout for a fun, wild time and Michelle Jameson was that girl. The life of the party, the first to arrive, the last to leave. Rotating from boyfriend to boyfriend on a weekly basis, until she laid eyes on Taylor. And they were the most beautiful eyes he'd ever seen. Sparkling with life, a deep hazel green that turned dark when she got angry or lighter when she was hungry.

Taylor talked to her father, Ward, at the Wild Cow Ranch and asked for a job just so he could get a chance to see her. But she was adamant that no one associated with the ranch know they were dating. The two snuck around a lot. Wherever they could be alone. She changed his life.

Before Michelle, he and his best friend, Billy sometimes got caught pulling the usual teenage shenanigans like egging or TPing houses. Their fathers were quick to whip their tails for those actions. Taylor's father worked at the Dixon hardware store and hardly ever smiled. He didn't stand for any nonsense from his son. Taylor's schoolteacher mom was sweet and subdued, followed anything her husband declared. And he was always laying down the law.

Those were Taylor's glory days. Football was his life, besides causing trouble with Billy. His senior year, the Dixon team could've won State when he threw an unprecedented pass of seventy-plus yards in the last quarter. If it hadn't been for that dimwit, Charlie Schneider, who fumbled the ball. Taylor heard that Charlie had moved away, sick of being the brunt of people's jokes. Slippery fingers. Blind as a bat. Almost grazed the tips of his fingers, but then the ball and the championship both vanished. The citizens of Dixon would never let poor Charlie forget it.

Plenty of girls flocked around Taylor Miller back then—J.T. they called him, John Taylor. He could have had any that he wanted. But he only wanted Michelle Jameson. He saw a future with her. He wanted to be better and more responsible. He wanted her to be proud of him. He still dreamt about her hazel-green eyes. He never thought he'd see those eyes again until he met the new owner of the Wild Cow Ranch. And darned if Carli Jameson wasn't the spitting image of her mother, Michelle.

An incoming call pinged on the dashboard. He pushed answer. "You got Taylor."

"Hey, darlin'." His wife Karissa. "Will you be home for dinner or are you working? I'm thinking maybe chicken fried steak, your favorite."

"No case work tonight but I am playing a round of golf. I'll grab a bite at the club. You should join us."

"No thanks. I've heard all the stories before," she laughed. "You have fun and I'll see you later this evening."

"All right, hon." He reached to tap END.

"You okay?" her question anxious.

"Yes. Fine."

"You sound sad. Something in your voice. Did you have a difficult day?"

"I've been thinking about some things is all." He needed to resolve this issue and come to terms with the emotions that the memory of Michelle had stirred up. Obviously, he wasn't good at hiding it.

"You sound like you're a million miles away, babe. Tell me." Her voice was tinged with sadness this time.

"Nothing for you to worry about. Just got some things on my mind." He forced a cheerfulness he didn't feel.

"I'll see you later then. Have a good game of golf."

"Bye, hon." He tapped "End Call" before she could say anything else.

He thought back to when he had gone with Agent McKinney to the Wild Cow Ranch to follow up on the rustling case. Introductions were made and Carli Jameson smiled. That face shook him to the core, which took him by surprise. He never imagined the feelings he had for Michelle would rise to the surface now, after all this time. But that was how strong their connection had been. Buried but never completely gone.

Since Carli was named heir of the Wild Cow Ranch, Michelle was obviously dead. Near tears and then anger, it pained him to think of the relationship they'd never had together. He should have done more to find her. He ached for the missed years with the love of his life. Anger burned through him that Michelle was gone forever. She was the most stubborn woman he had ever known.

Taylor shook himself. He was a grown man. He had to get a grip and stop dwelling on the past.

God help me. This third marriage had to stick. He and Karissa had been blessed with twenty-four years, but he was always on guard. Didn't want to throw it all away. He hated messing up his life. That's why he took his work so seriously and played by the rules. And he'd married above his pay grade, so to speak.

Karissa. Beautiful, smart, and, for some crazy reason, she loved him despite his flaws and past screw ups. She liked being a wife and homemaker and a mother to Hud. She also enjoyed staying busy and making a contribution to the community—as a fundraiser, president of her sorority, board member of every organization she joined—and, on top of everything, owned a decorating business.

Taylor had gotten involved with other girls after Michelle, even married them for a while. Those were mistakes. Well, not his son by the first marriage. Hudson. "Hud" they called him. He was a good kid, twenty-four years old, and lived with him and Karissa. Hud's mother was always on the skids—drinking, drugs. It was sad and Taylor refused to allow his son to grow up in that environment. He fought for, and won, full custody. There was another marriage in between that one and number three, but it was short-lived. Some floozy he met in a bar. No children from that liaison, thank goodness. Another one of his stupid mistakes.

Karissa was loving and patient. A devout Christian woman who never said a bad word about anybody. He had struck gold when he found her. But she had a strong will and an intolerance for the mistakes of his past. She loved Hud like her own, but she kept Taylor on a short leash.

Their daughter Shayla was twenty-two. Beautiful, smart, just like her mother. He believed his marriage had longevity. But still, he didn't want to become lazy and mess it up. He had a good thing and wanted to hold onto it. Sometimes he thought about his age, nearing fifty. He didn't want to be a jerk as in his younger years, and was determined to make his family proud.

Taylor Miller worked hard and had made a name for himself. He was respected around the area. Not only as a special agent but also a top-notch horse breeder. He'd made big money in that business. Most days did not have enough hours for him to get everything accomplished that he planned.

A deep guilt overwhelmed him. The thought of Michelle living on the streets all those years doing drugs. Why hadn't he done more to find her? She was the one who ended their relationship, without a hint that she was unhappy, by riding off with some guy in the middle of the night. Maybe in her mind their love was over, but it had never been over for him. Although he loved Karissa with all of his heart, he still reserved a place for Michelle even though they never saw each other again.

Taylor pulled into the parking lot of the Amarillo Country Club and immediately saw his high school friend raise an arm in greeting from under the front portico. In all the years he had known Billy Broderick, they shared many secrets. But Michelle Jameson had never been one of them. Taylor never told Billy about their relationship.

Back then, Billy had put in a good word with Michelle's father, Ward, to help Taylor get a job at the ranch. Billy lived and worked there with his mother and father. The Jamesons and Brodericks went way back for several generations.

Michelle had made Taylor promise that he would never tell anyone about their love. If there was one thing people said about Taylor Miller, it was that he always kept his word.

Chapter 5

Carli

Carli jerked open the front door following a loud knock that made the pictures on her wall rattle. Del burst in as if her pants were on fire. She walked straight to the dining room table and opened her briefcase.

"I met with your Amarillo attorneys this morning," she said. "We have a hearing date set with the judge."

"Have a seat," Carli offered. "I wondered where you were off to so early. Is that good?"

"You're darn right it's good," Del said.

"What's the next step?"

"Breakfast."

Carli laughed. "You are always hungry. As late as it is, I think we should call it brunch. I've got cereal and bananas. Is that okay?"

"Sounds perfect. Using your brain takes lots of calories. Keep the coffee pot going." Del seemed all business. "We've got lots of details to go over today."

"Food. Check. Now what?"

Del plopped her bulk into a chair. "The next

thing we have to do is establish your legitimacy as the rightful heir. We have your Grandpa Ward's Last Will, which was approved by the Probate Court Judge. I have a box full of files on your mother. We can go through it, if you want."

"I don't want to know anything about her." Carli pressed her lips together.

Del watched Carli's face. "I've been trying to piece her life together after she left you as a newborn at the hospital in Amarillo. It appears she was one little lady who did not want to be found."

"It's all in the past, Del. It doesn't matter to me. I'll never know why she hated life on the Wild Cow so much. What do you think happened between her and my grandparents?"

"That's something that may never be answered. I think she was a free spirit," Del said. "She didn't like anyone telling her what to do. I'm just glad we were able to track you to Atlanta. I'm sorry you didn't get to meet your grandfather."

Carli poured the coffee. "Fate sometimes doesn't like me very much. I can't believe he knew my name, but that I didn't make it back in time to see him before he died."

"That breaks my heart too, Carli. It's a very sad situation. But we have to focus on the lawsuit at hand. Mr. Broderick is great friends with the judge and that may be a problem for us."

Carli got bowls down for the cereal. "What can I do to help?"

"We will go over and over your story as it pertains to the case. Would you be willing to take a paternity test?" The attorney pulled more papers from her briefcase.

"You mean a blood test? DNA? Sure. I guess so," Carli answered as she grabbed a couple of bananas.

Del poured cereal into her bowl. "I don't think I'll need it as evidence, but, just in case, it would be good to have. We really need to know who your birth father is."

Carli stared at her bowl for a moment and then quietly said, "There is something you should know."

"What is it? You can tell me. We have attorney client privilege. I can't reveal anything that you don't want me to."

"Okay, give me a minute." Carli walked into the back study which now served as her office and returned holding a piece of paper. She hesitated a moment, wondering if she should reveal the name that was penciled on the document. It could have an impact on this man's life forever, and it would definitely change hers.

"I found this." Carli handed the paper to her attorney.

Del balanced a pair of neon green bifocals on her nose and studied the paper for a few minutes before replying. "Your birth certificate? Yes, I have a certi-fied copy from the county courthouse already."

"This one is different." Carli pointed to it.

"The father's name is penciled in." Del's brows scrunched. "That may be a problem or it may be just the piece of information we need. Do you know who this Taylor Miller is?"

"I've met him," Carli said. "He used to work summers at the Wild Cow for my grandfather. He's a supervisor and investigator with the Texas Cattle Raisers."

"He doesn't know about you, I'm assuming." Del

shoveled a spoonful of cereal into her mouth.

"No. I don't think he does."

"That makes it impossible to call him as a character witness. And then there is his family to consider, if he has a wife and kids. Do you know anything about him?"

"No," Carli said. "I haven't gotten that far yet."

Carli did not offer Del any further information, like the fact that she had been doing genealogy research on the man for most of the past year. She would really like to talk to him, have a relationship with him. If everything fell into place, he could walk her down the aisle on her wedding day. The possibility of knowing her birth father made her heart thump, but she remained silent. She knew that just because you wished for something and wanted it more than anything else in the world, life rarely did anybody any favors.

"I need to study this and research the case file on Texas law. This is good to have, but I'm not sure how much weight a penciled in name would have." Del cleared off a clean spot on the table, picked up her pad and pen, and began making notes.

"Who do you think wrote his name? I've thought about that a lot." Carli leaned over Del's shoulder and studied her birth certificate again. "And how did my grandparents get a copy?"

"I'm sure one of the private detectives they hired acquired it for them. Birth certificates can be requested by immediate family members, but I'm not sure how grandparents can request one."

"I bet Grandma Jean wrote the name in. It would make sense that she would know who her daughter was dating."

"Some things we may never know. It's a mystery." Del shook her head from side to side. "I've got more research to do."

"While you do that," Carli said, "I need to print wedding invitations or Lola will have my hide. We have already passed the appropriate date to mail them according to some unknown wedding handbook. Lola wanted to order them, but I can print them myself for much cheaper and they'll look just as nice."

Del had already turned her attention to the laptop, and merely dismissed Carli with a wave of her hand.

Carli turned to leave, mumbling to herself more than expecting Del to answer. She wandered back into the study, turned her computer on, and began searching through invitation templates. Graphics included flowers, bells, doves, or entwined hearts and vines. Nothing seemed to suit her or Lank. She liked simple, and had never been a girly-girl with hair bows and eye shadows. Those kinds of things had never appealed to her.

A box of plain bond letterhead would do just fine with plain envelopes. She could even cut the paper in half and print two invitations on one page. She found two horseshoes with sprigs of greenery on either side. Perfect. And now for the wording.

With both of Lank's parents deceased, her guardians gone, and her birth parents nonexistent, using the wording about requesting your presence at the marriage of their children made her sad. Step outside the box. Why should she follow the rules of established etiquette? At the top of the page she typed, "*We're getting hitched.*" That seemed too country for her taste, so she deleted it. Carli thought about the wedding of a coworker at the real estate agency where she had worked in Georgia. The couple had a website set up at least six months before the date with all the details and she remembered their invitations. Embossed with a ribbon tied at the top, and sparkling papers. It was all very elegant as was the ceremony. That did not suit Carli at all.

"Keep it simple stupid," she muttered.

Carli decided to use names, the date and time, and the place. She spelled out their names, but Carlotta was her great grandmother, not her. No one knew her by that name so she changed it to their first and last only, no middle names. To make it fancy, she spelled out the date and time rather than using numbers. It looked nice. The place was another matter. They had not discussed specifics. It might be the cookhouse or the lawn in front of the cookhouse, or perhaps under the cottonwoods on the creek. She was leaning toward the latter. For the location, she listed The Wild Cow Ranch. Simple and to the point. She typed "*Y'all come*" at the end but deleted that too. Instead, she typed, "*Please join us. Reception to follow.*"

She stacked the paper into the printer drawer and hit fifty copies. While the pages churned out at a snail's pace, Carli began stuffing the envelopes. Just in time. A knock on the door resulted in Del's answer, "It's open."

Lola called out. "It's just me. Is Carli here?"

"Back here," Carli answered.

"Back in her office," said Del.

Lola appeared in the doorway. "Hey there. Just wondering if you've had time to print the invitations."

"Done. And already stuffed," said Carli with some satisfaction, as she held them up over her head.

"I can address them for you," Lola offered. "I'll need your mailing list."

"I don't have any names for you."

"No one? How about your friends in Georgia? Surely your guardians had some family. Coworkers? Didn't you show horses? What about those people? Your past students?"

Carli shook her head. Sad, but true. There had never been anyone close in her life until now.

"Okay then, I need a list from Lank."

"Thanks, Lola," said Carli but she refused to ask what was next on the list. "Del and I are working on the lawsuit."

"I hope that goes well," said Lola. "I cannot believe Billy is still fighting the judge's ruling. We'll get through this. Have faith."

Lola placed a comforting hand on Carli's shoulder.

"I am trying to keep a positive outlook. There is no way to know if he has a strong case against me or not."

"He doesn't," called out Del from the next room. "In my professional opinion."

Carli and Lola both laughed.

"I'd say your future is in good hands." Lola chuckled again.

Chapter 6

Carli

"Did you bring any jeans?" Carli walked into the dining room and studied Del in her usual attorney attire, pantsuit, and blouse in a color to complement her neon hair.

"Why do you ask?"

"Let's go for a ride," Carli suggested.

Del gave a pained look. "What? That's not possible. I only brought work clothes. Plus, I've never even considered getting on the back of a horse. Ever. In my life. Never."

"C'mon, Del. You only live once."

"Carli, I am not riding in my power suit."

Carli grinned. "Then we should run to the western store first. I am the client. And this is an order."

"Hmmpff. Pulling that card, are you? If there's a meal involved while we're out, then fine. But I'm not making any promises that I'll get on the back of a horse."

With much convincing, begging, and pleading on Carli's part, they were soon on their way to Amarillo.

"Shopping or food first?" Carli asked.

"Good grief. Let's get the shopping over with. A late lunch is fine by me," Del grumbled.

By the time they drove to Amarillo, it was late-morning and the Boot Barn was empty of customers. Several employees appeared to offer assistance.

Carli steered Del towards the western shirts, and true to her style, Del picked out a bright purple pearl snap dotted with neon green longhorn steer heads. Next, they looked at jeans, and Del seemed to suddenly be enjoying herself because she decided she needed a leather belt too. Carli was shocked when Del handed her purchases to the girl and wandered towards the boots.

"You're seriously considering a pair of boots?"

"That I am," said Del. "I may as well go all the way."

"I think that's great," said Carli as she followed her into the aisle. "And of course, you'd go for the turquoise with black and silver tops."

"These are really calling to me," said Del. "Who knows? I might secretly be a cowgirl on the inside." Her giant laugh bellowed around the store.

"But are they practical?" Carli asked. "You'll get them scratched and dusty when we go riding. I just want you to be aware."

"I hear you, Carli, but I have to follow my heart when I spend money. I work too hard."

Del paid for her purchases as Carli looked longingly at several blouses. She really needed some new jeans, but decided to keep a tight rein on her money until after the wedding.

"Steak or Italian or seafood? What sounds good

to you?" Carli asked.

Del was admiring her new leather belt and did not answer right away. "Surprise me."

"That I can do."

Carli pulled into a trendy new Cajun seafood bistro, which had not been one of the choices mentioned but she had seen an ad pop up on her phone and decided to give it a try.

"This reminds me of the French Quarter in New Orleans." Del led the way as usual, walking into the main dining area.

The first thing Carli noticed was the bar which spanned one side of the room. A wide variety of wine and liquor bottles made for a colorful and brightly lit backdrop to an impressive carved wooden counter. Carli could hardly take her eyes off the décor that was fashioned under dim lights, rich draperies, dark wood, and unique antiques. A trombone solo played from the speakers overhead.

The hostess led them to a table in the corner. "Welcome to the Drunken Oyster," she said and handed each a menu.

Carli and Del studied the choices. The dishes were unique, the seafood flown in fresh daily. Carli had to smile when she saw steak on the menu. Maybe Lank would come back with her another time.

Del went with the Mahi Mahi and Carli decided to try the risotto and scallops.

"Tell me about your legal career," asked Carli. "I'm glad you came back to Texas to help me with this new lawsuit, by the way. I thought you were only contacted as counsel to find me in Georgia."

"That's correct. They needed a local attorney to assist with locating you and offering legal advice since you resided in Atlanta, but I am now officially your personal attorney. Thanks for hiring me."

"One of the few really good decisions I've made in my life, Del. Thank goodness you're back."

"The firm in Amarillo represents your grand-parents' estate," Del explained, "and the Wild Cow Ranch's interests. I represent you personally."

Carli took a sip of her water. "How did you know you wanted to be a lawyer?"

Del answered with a hearty laugh and then went on to talk for the rest of their meal. Carli was cap-tivated by her interesting stories of law school and then working with one of the largest firms in the Atlanta area.

The meal was over in no time and Carli reached for the check. "My treat. Are you ready to put on your new duds and go for a ride?"

"Duds?" Del laughed. "You are becoming a cow puncher for sure, if that's what you call it."

"Yes, I believe I am." For the first time in her life, Carli understood what the term meant to ranch-ing people and felt a sense of pride at claiming it for herself.

Back at the Wild Cow, Carli and Del changed into jeans. Carli had texted Lank earlier and asked him to bring a horse up for Del to ride. An older mare that she used in her riding school. They'd have to fix the stirrups on the saddle, but other than that the greenhorn attorney should do fine.

Just before they walked out the door, Carli stopped in the entry hall and opened the closet to study an array of cowboy hats that had belonged to her grandfather. She pointed, and Del began to try them on until she found one that fit.

Lank met them in the saddle house and gave a long whistle when Del stepped inside. "Somebody turned Texan."

Del hooked both thumbs in her front pockets and struck a pose. "Adelphia Fenwick, attorney-at-law, at your service." They all laughed. "How am I supposed to get up on that thing?"

"When I was younger, I used to use the fence to climb on my horse," Carli said.

"I've got you covered." Lank presented three steps made of plastic, a mounting block, which he set on the ground next to the horse, Tiny. But this mare was anything but small.

"That's a big horse." Del pushed the hat down on her head.

Carli smiled at Del's appearance. "But she's gentle and slow, and never reacts to anything. You'll love her."

Lank helped Del on her horse and gave basic instructions on steering. Del focused, her forehead lined with deep thought similar to how she looked when concentrating on a legal issue.

Lank asked, "Where y'all headed?"

"Aren't you going with us?" Carli asked.

"No. Got some things to tend to."

Carli stared at him. "I thought we'd take a ride up the creek. It's pretty and easygoing."

Lank smiled. "Enjoy your ride then, cowgirls."

The late fall afternoon had begun to cool, but in the lows of the dry creek bed a few colorful leaves still clung to stately cottonwood trees. The leaves danced and swished as a light breeze filtered through them causing a swoosh noise overhead.

The women did not talk for about half an hour or so. Carli kept an eye on Del, but felt confident in the horse she had put her on. Del was in good hands with Tiny.

Conversations eased into small talk about life in Georgia and how different it was for Carli living in Texas. They talked some about the upcoming hearing. Del would later ask Carli questions as practice on her testimony in case she took the stand.

They came up at a fairly fast clip from the creek bottom to the edge. Carli ducked at the last minute, but Del did not see the chinaberry tree limb. It swiped her, and she lost her balance and leaned to one side, dropping the reins but clinging to the saddle horn with one hand.

"Hang on, Del. I'm on my way." Carli tried to stifle the laugh that bubbled up in her throat. Del's eyes were wide and fearful. She struggled to pull herself up with one hand by the saddle horn. She was sinking towards the ground in slow motion.

Carli hurried back and jumped off just in time to put her hands under Del's shoulder and back and pushed her up. It was no easy task. Del was a good-sized woman.

"Thanks. I'm done," said Del as she tried to swing a leg over the saddle to get down.

"No, ma'am," Carli firmly instructed. "When you fall off, you get back on. And technically, you never fell off. Besides we're over a mile from headquarters. It's a long walk back."

Del frowned. "I have to admit, it is beautiful out here. And I was doing okay until that little bobble."

"We haven't made it to the fishpond yet, and then

we'll ride over the dam and head back. Easy peasy."

"Okay. Fine. Lead on, Ms. Ranch Owner."

Carli laughed. She liked her quirky lawyer. And hoped and prayed she'd be able to help her keep the ranch.

Chapter 7

Taylor

The Miller home sat on a hundred-acre spread outside the city limits of Amarillo. Six bedrooms; they really only needed three, maybe a couple more for guests. Gourmet kitchen, huge entertainment room with all of the latest gadgets, swimming pool and patio area that looked like an oasis in the dusty Texas flatlands. Tin-roofed red barn that used to house at least ten American Quarter Horses. But now, Taylor kept his high-priced investments at someone else's training barn. He didn't have time to spend so many hours with them like he used to, what with his full-time job. And that's how he liked it.

Taylor had made his big money years ago when he and Karissa were in the early years of their marriage. He was anxious to prove himself and had made some important contacts. Landing in the right place at the right time, an older, well-known trainer liked Taylor's drive and mentored him, teaching him all the tricks of the trade.

Taylor brokered and sold a famous stallion he had nicknamed Bud, for close to a million dollars.

The horse business was still talking about that deal. People said he just got lucky. Others said there was something shady and suspicious about the arrangement. Taylor knew, and would swear to this day, that he didn't do anything illegal. He didn't get all of that money, after paying everyone their piece of the pie, but it sure made his bank account look good and would help to pay for the upkeep of his wife and kids. It also encouraged his in-laws to look upon him in a more favorable light, as a successful provider worthy of their little girl.

It was a good thing he had those resources to fall back on since his job as a special agent didn't pay big bucks. He just liked doing it, having his hand in the nitty gritty of the good and bad people of Dixon and the surrounding areas. His wife Karissa's contribution to the marriage didn't hurt either since her family was rolling in dough. Old money. After college she had a trust fund, but she also liked working and had her own decorating business to look after.

She loved her family. And Taylor loved her. It had taken him some years to get to this point—right job, right woman, enough money. Married more than twenty years, they sometimes still acted like newlyweds. He credited his wife for that. Not only was she beautiful, but she was kind, loving, and was the biggest cheerleader not only for their kids, but also for him.

Thoughts of the past swirled in his head and then he felt the warm pressure of his wife on his arm. He turned and they snuggled in their king-sized bed as the sun found its way to the slits at the edges of the drawn curtains. She was warm and he stroked her messed hair.

"I love you, Karissa. You know that, don't you?"

"I love you too, darlin'. Now we had better get out of this bed or we aren't gonna get anything done today. And I do believe we both have jobs, last time I checked." She kissed his stubbly, tanned cheek.

"Mom!" A scream erupted from a neighboring bedroom. "I can't find my pink silk blouse! I'm going to be late for work! Are you guys up? Mom!"

Karissa looked at Taylor and rolled her eyes heavenward. "Lord, help us. The diva is awake."

He continued to stroke her arm as she sat on the side of the bed getting ready to stand. Her tight body was the result of diet and exercise, and good genes, he thought too. "Guess you'll have to pray for patience."

"No, not that," she laughed. "He might give me more trials in order to learn patience."

They both chuckled. He sat up, hugged her slender form, and kissed the back of her neck. In her short, satiny nightgown, he could have touched her forever. Heck with work.

But instead, he rubbed his sleepy eyes and yawned. "I'll get the coffee going, you go help our girl. Do you want me to whip up some breakfast?"

"No, darlin'. I'll be down in a minute to do that."

"What have you got planned for today?" He hopped out of the bed.

"Oh, the usual. Phone calls, maybe a couple of meetings. I've got one client who's a bit of a pill to work with. Only wants the best for her new house."

"Well, anyone who hires you for their decorator is already getting the best." He turned around to kiss her forehead.

"How about you? Cow detective work?"

"Today I've got a couple of theft cases to investigate. And then, sometime this week, Buck's invited me to have lunch out at the Wild Cow Ranch."

A shrill voice echoed from the other bedroom. "Mommmm! Are you going to help me find that blouse? I need it, NOW!"

"Good Lord. You'd think it was the end of the world or something. A pink blouse."

"You'd better get in there before she has a meltdown. I'll go make us some coffee."

After setting up the coffee, he ran back upstairs for a quick shower and threw on jeans and a T-shirt for breakfast. When he passed his son's closed bedroom door, he tapped and said, "Hud, you awake? If you want to eat anything, get up now. I'll make some bacon and eggs. Be downstairs in ten minutes."

Sounds of a grumble, but then a "Yes, sir" came forth.

He's a good kid.

Taylor heard Karissa and Shayla in one of the bedrooms, squabbling. He walked out of Hudson's room and passed Shayla's half-open door, but thought better of poking his head in. They were embroiled in women's stuff and he sure wasn't going to get involved in that. But their entire, loud conversation followed his ears as he headed downstairs to the kitchen.

"Mom, it's wrinkled. It should have gone to the dry cleaners with the other stuff." The girl was close to tears.

"Well, did you put it in the dry-cleaning bag for me to take?"

"I don't know. I just know I needed to wear it today. Now I'm going to be late for work. What am I going to wear? You just don't care if I look nice or not. This job is really important to me."

"Now, Shayla, of course I care about you. Let's just pick out something else. You have a lot of pretty clothes. Don't get upset about one little pink blouse."

"But that's what I had planned on wearing today. Just go downstairs. I'll figure this out by myself. That's what I usually do anyway. You're always too busy. Just leave me alone. I don't need you."

"Fine. I was only trying to help you. Try to remember that and don't be so disrespectful."

Shayla had a job in an Amarillo boutique about forty-five minutes away. She had often mentioned to her parents that she hoped to make contacts in the fashion industry. She was twenty-two, going on forty-two, Taylor thought. He didn't want to admit his kids were spoiled, but with Shayla, it might be too late.

Hudson, at twenty-four, had a good work ethic and had a job at the horse breeding operation that housed his father's remuda of high-dollar winners. Even though he had a penchant for sleeping as much as possible and rapidly eating the Millers out of groceries every few days, Taylor thought he'd do well in business. He saw intelligence in Hudson and a desire to be successful.

What more could Taylor Miller hope for? Everything seemed to be working out. Shayla would come around. He was her blood after all. He didn't understand daughters sometimes but was grateful to have one.

Suddenly Carli Jameson popped in his head. Must be strange for her. She never had a family, not the normal kind anyway. No mother. No father.

She looked so much like Michelle, it gave him chills. He shook his head to clear those thoughts away and started breakfast.

Chapter 8

Carli

Early the next morning, Carli tapped on Lank's trailer door and went inside. She had to grab the door facing to keep from tripping over a pile of boxes.

"Watch your step." Lank hefted a box on his shoulder and added it to a stack near the front door.

Carli navigated carefully. "What are you doing?"

"Cleaning out a few cabinets," he said.

She rubbed her nose and looked around. "What is all this stuff?"

He lifted and added a laundry basket to the stack of what looked like leather reins and lead ropes. "Some tack I repaired that needs to go to the saddle house. Over there is a box of pots and pans my mom gave me that I never used. Old T-shirts from high school. I guess those can go to the rag box in the shop."

"I came over to tell you that Del is here and we have a court date. She really enjoyed her ride. Thanks for saddling Tiny."

"Oh, yeah? Does she think it'll work out?"

"We're due to appear before the judge on Tuesday, the same week as our wedding. Didn't Lola decide on Saturday, November fifteenth? It's my wedding and I'm not even certain of the date although I did get the invitations printed."

"That's cutting it close," said Lank.

Carli nodded her head in agreement. "Wish I didn't have to deal with this craziness all in the same week as everything else." She tried to find somewhere to sit and decided on a step stool that wasn't very comfortable. "And I need to tell you something important before you hear it from someone else."

"What's that?" Lank's hands were full but he stopped to look at her.

"I found my birth certificate with the name of my birth father penciled in."

"Who is it?" he asked.

"Taylor Miller."

"Wow! You're kidding. The head of our Texas Cattle Raisers district? That Taylor Miller?"

"Yes. I think he's the same. He knew my mother."

Lank's eyes widened. "That's amazing. Does he know?"

"I'm not sure. Haven't had time to figure it all out. I don't know what he knows, if anything." Carli stood and moved a box. She wanted to change the subject. "How long have you lived in this trailer?"

"Started working at the Wild Cow when I was in high school. Your grandpa Ward did his best to try and convince me to go to college after graduation, but all I ever wanted to do was ride broncs and punch cows."

"And then you got injured," she said.

"Yeah, that head injury put an end to my rodeo career. All I had left was my job here. But I'm not complaining."

"I'm glad they kept you on." She walked closer. She couldn't resist kissing his lips.

"Mmmmm. I'm glad I'm here too. But stop that. We've got work to do."

She just wanted to stay in his embrace but would try to get her mind off that. "Okay, finish what you were saying. About the trailer." She was able to get one more kiss in, then picked up miscellaneous items—an old frying pan, a toilet brush, a rusty can opener.

Lank looked around the trailer and seemed a little overwhelmed. "Where was I? Oh, yeah. I think Ward knew how upset I was about the rodeo deal, so he hired me on as a full-time ranch hand. It became official."

"Gee, I wish I could have known him," she said.

"He would have loved you and your independent spirit. I know he's looking down on us now. Come back this way, babe. I want to show you something."

"Okay."

Hands on hips, Lank showed her what he had done. "I cleaned out the top two drawers of my dresser for you. I'll keep the bottom two. And in the bathroom, I just need the bottom shelf of the cabinet over the sink. You can have the rest."

"For me?" She was dumbfounded as to what he must be thinking.

"Yeah. I'm making room for your stuff for after we're married." Lank smiled.

"My stuff?" Carli frowned.

"I think we should wait until after we're mar-

ried before you move any of your stuff over here."
He looked very serious, like the man of the house.
Carli couldn't help fantasizing how their life to-
gether would be.

"We should wait?" She heard herself talking like
a robot but couldn't help it.

"I love you, Carli. You're all I think about. But
out of respect for Lola and Buck, and you, the future mother of my children, I don't think we should
move in together until after the wedding."

"Me live here?"

"Yes, after the wedding. That's why I'm making
space for you." He scratched his head.

"Lank, I am not living here. Let's talk about this."

"What? I'm not joking. What are you talking
about?"

"I mean that I am not moving into your trailer."
Carli smoothed the bottom of her shirt and looked
out the window.

"Ward gave me this trailer. This is where I live
and I assume that after we're married, we should
live together."

"Absolutely. But not here." Carli thought she
detected a funny smell but wasn't sure what it was.
Old? Musty?

"What's wrong with my trailer?" Lank asked her.

"It's too little for one thing. I can't fit all of my
stuff into two drawers."

"All right," he said. "You can have three."

Carli wanted to shake him. "And what about my
computer and office files? Where can all that go?"

He looked like a little boy who was trying hard
to please. "I thought of that, Carli. I'm cleaning out
the spare bedroom for your office."

"What about Ward and Jean's house where I'm living now? It's nice. Plenty of space. We can remodel."

Lank's brows pinched together. "That could be a bunkhouse for spring branding or a guest house. We could sure use that, don't you think?"

"I love that house. I don't want to move." Carli's voice took on a higher pitch and she stared at him as though he had two heads. She sure hoped they wouldn't have any future disagreements like this. How could two people so in love think so differently?

It was a standoff as though they had drawn a line in the sand. Who would give in? No way, she told herself.

"Come on, Carli. I know my trailer is smaller, but it'll be cozy. Plus, I'll be here. It'll be our love nest." He grinned that handsome, but mischievous, grin she always loved. But he was aggravating her now.

"Lank. Think about this."

"I have.

"So, there's no common ground on this one, no way to compromise, is there?"

"Not that I can see." He folded his arms across his chest.

"Fine." *What a stubborn male.*

"Super." He took the rusty can opener and tossed it in the trash.

Carli was exasperated. "I guess you can live on one side of Wild Cow headquarters and I'll live on the other. Problem solved!"

Lank leaned against the kitchenette counter and watched her but did not reply. She gave him a heavy sigh and left, slamming the door behind her harder than she had meant to. Obviously, there was more than this one issue they needed to resolve before making a lifetime commitment to each other.

For now, Carli chose to ignore the mother of his children comment. She'd save that for some other time. She never thought of herself as the mothering type, and for someone who harbored as much resentment against her own mother as she did, there was no way she could ever hope to raise healthy children of her own.

But that was a topic of discussion for another day.

Chapter 9

Lola

Lola was trying not to lose her patience with Carli who hadn't really shown much enthusiasm for her own upcoming wedding. And Buck had already advised Lola to discuss things with Carli rather than running off, headstrong, and taking matters into her own hands. But she was so frustrated.

The egg salad Lola was preparing for lunch was getting stirred a bit too strenuously. Her whole body tensed when she heard the door open.

"Hi, Lola. I'm here," Carli called out.

Lola knew her husband meant well but what did men know about weddings and all the arrangements that took place in the background? Lola was determined to make everything memorable for Lank and Carli, something they would cherish for the rest of their lives.

She swallowed her agitation. "Hey. Come in. Lunch is almost ready. How does egg salad and coffee sound?"

This was a wedding after all. So many details. If she didn't stay on top of them, who would? It might end up a terrible disaster. Who wants that for their Special Day? Lola never had a Special Day so she knew how important this was. Everything had to be perfect.

She set two mugs of coffee on the counter.

"Carli, we really have to nail down some details for your wedding. It'll be here before you know it. Let's go over your itinerary, what we've got so far."

Lola handed her a couple of pages hot off the printer she had grabbed from her apartment before coming downstairs.

"Where are the guys?" Carli asked.

"It's just us today. I'll read from the top and you follow along so we both have all the information and know what needs to be done. Number one on the page is your engagement party. That'll be on Saturday night, the week before your wedding. A lot of folks have kindly volunteered for various duties so that's coming together nicely. It'll be fun."

Carli didn't say a word. Her face was blank.

Lola continued on. "You and Lank will need to go to the B&R Beanery to taste all the cake samples that Belinda is preparing for you. I'll let you know when that is, after I hear back from Belinda. I'll try to be there too. Oh, and I think she's also having a guitar player so you can get an idea about music. Isn't that sweet of her?"

"Mmm, hmm," from Carli.

"Technically...according to the wedding check-list book..." Lola looked at Carli over her reading glasses. "Technically, the bride's parents host and pay for a rehearsal dinner. Buck and I would be willing to do that for you and Lank. However, I don't think there's time. We'll just do a quick walk-through the morning of the ceremony, before any guests arrive. How does that sound?"

"Fine," was all Carli offered.

Lola adjusted her bifocals and proceeded with her list. "The ladies of the church are throwing you a bridal shower on Friday. Most of Dixon will be there along with friends and neighbors, and some ladies from my yoga class. It'll be terrific! Are there any friends from Georgia you'd like to invite? How about family? I could contact them for you, if you like."

Carli mumbled, "No. No friends. No family. Same as when we talked about the list for the invitations. I didn't have that many friends back in Georgia. I worked all the time, either with the horses or at the realtor's office."

"What did you say, Carli? I couldn't hear you."

"Nobody. Nada. Zip. Nothing on my list."

"Oh. Okay then. Well, there's still so much to do. A caterer for the wedding reception. I'm using my own tablecloths that were made by my aunts and grandmothers. The venue. I'm assuming you want to be married here at the ranch." Lola paused and looked at Carli.

Carli nodded her head slightly. "The ranch is fine."

"I'm getting the wedding volunteer committee together. They're real excited. The ladies will handle shopping, cooking, and decorating. The men will set up for the party, cook, and handle parking, things like that. Oh, my gosh! I almost forgot flowers! I don't even know what colors you like. I was thinking, since you'll most likely want fall colors... I love orange and yellow mums, burgundy roses, maybe a few sunflowers. What do you think?" A big smile stretched across Lola's face. She was in her element.

But Carli was massaging her temples.

"You feeling okay? Do you have a headache?" Lola was worried about her.

In halting, quiet words, Carli spoke. "This is all really great, Lola. And I appreciate your hard work. I'm just not an expert with any of this. I trust your judgment."

"We haven't talked about the most important thing. Your dress. Do you know what style you'd like? We need to go shopping. The sooner the better, so that there will be time for any alterations."

"I'm not sure when I'll have time for dress shopping, Lola. For everything else, why don't you just go ahead with whatever you think is best? I'll be fine with that. Lank too."

Lola was dumbstruck. "But it's your wedding, Carli. You should have all of your favorite things. This is your day."

"I love everything you've chosen, Lola. Just go with it. I have a lot on my mind...the upcoming hearing, for one. I could possibly lose everything if Billy wins this lawsuit. I have to focus on that. At this moment, I've got to go to town and get a coffee. This headache's not going away. Bye." Carli stood and leaned over to give Lola a hug. "Thanks again for all you're doing. I really appreciate it."

Lola called after her. "Well, maybe you can talk to Belinda about cake flavors while you're there."

Lola watched Carli leave the cookhouse. Worry settled over her as she stared at the blanks in her wedding planner. Carli had not answered one question or given her any details. She wondered if a bride could be any less excited about her own wedding. There was only one explanation. Carli and Lank were having problems. "Dear Lord, help them work out their differences and let love prevail."

Chapter 10

Carli

Carli stood on the covered porch of the Wild Cow Ranch cookhouse willing herself to take a few deep breaths. Her head was about to explode any minute, if anyone asked her another question about the wedding. Dresses. Flowers. Lola was becoming a wedding planning monster. Carli had to get away rather than be unkind to her ranch cook. She could just hop on Beau and ride off into the pasture. Her horse was a good listener. But maybe a better one would be her friend Belinda at the coffee shop. She could really use a jolt of caffeine right now and Belinda's coffee creations always tasted better than her own. She jogged across the ranch compound, grabbed her purse, and headed towards town.

Sure, every girl in the world dreamed about her wedding. Except she wasn't like every girl. She had never been the one that went for frills and glitter, polishes or eye shadows. Her main focus had always been her horses and working with her clients. Maybe that's why she never got along with the other girls in the show ring. Other than a love for horses, they had little in common.

Lola might find it hard to believe, but Carli could not remember ever dreaming about her wedding day. Sure, she wanted to find her soulmate, but dressing up in some white froufrou dress for only a few moments to mutter a few words had never appealed to her.

She made it to town in record time and screeched to a halt in front of the coffee shop. The bell above the door tinkled as she entered the B&R Beanery in town.

Belinda was helping a customer but looked up and called out, "Hey, girl! How's the bride-to-be?"

Carli nearly growled. "Ugh, don't remind me." She waited behind a young man as he finished paying Belinda and collecting his coffee.

"Can't be that bad," her barista friend said. "This is supposed to be the happiest time ever. Planning the big event when you get to say 'I do' to the love of your life." Belinda got a mug ready for Carli. "What can I get for you?"

"The usual," Carli replied.

Belinda started making Carli's latte with all of her favorite ingredients. A bit of chocolate, raspberry syrup, light whip, extra espresso to help maintain energy for her busy life.

"It's just that Lola is turning this thing into an extravaganza. 'The Wedding of the Century', she calls it." Carli's face was blank, tired.

Belinda pulled out a muffin from below the counter and pushed it towards Carli on a plate. "Oh, c'mon. Everyone is so excited about your wedding. In fact, I wanted to talk to you about the cake. Lola contacted me about making it and I'd be honored. I just need to know your favorite flavors. Chocolate? Vanilla? How about hazelnut? Toffee? Lemon? Do you want one big cake with lots of tiers? Or maybe a cupcake display?"

Carli covered her eyes with her hands as she rested her elbows on the table. After a few seconds, she looked up at her friend and just didn't want to extinguish her enthusiasm.

"Belinda, whatever you want to do. I'm sure it will taste great."

"What about Lank? We can't forget him," the barista said. "I could make a groom's cake with horses and cows on top."

The first reply that came to mind was that *she* was the actual ranch owner and not Lank. Maybe *she* wanted horses and cows on her bridal cake too. But she held her tongue. That sounded so snippy. Instead, Carli sipped her latte and wished she could dive into it and forget all this craziness. "Okay. Sure. Whatever you want."

"It's what you and Lank want, not me. I don't get you sometimes, friend. What bride doesn't know what she wants? That's not normal." Belinda's brow twitched and her eyes crinkled. "Is everything okay with you and Lank? Oops, a customer." She moved to wait on the person before the bell stopped tinkling.

"Hey, Belinda," Carli called after her. "I'm going to take my coffee with me. Got some errands to do. Thanks much." She kind of fibbed since she really didn't have any tasks. She had wanted to relax in the coffee shop and not talk about the Big Event but it didn't appear that was going to happen.

"Oh, okay, sure, Carli. Have a good day."

As she headed for the door, Carli waved at her friend and hoped she hadn't hurt her feelings in any way. *That was a little awkward.*

Fumbling for her keys, she was almost to her truck when she heard her name called out. "Carli!"

Oh, geesh.

There stood Lola with two other ladies. Carli didn't know their names, but they looked familiar. She had probably met them at church or yoga.

"Hey, Lola. I thought you were back at the ranch."

"Well, I've got so much to do. Your wedding is nearly here, Carli! But wait'll you see what we got on sale today." Lola nodded to the bags she and the other ladies were carrying. "You remember Celia and Lydia from yoga, don't you?"

"Sure." Carli just smiled and fibbed for the second time today. "Hi, how are you?"

The whole group was wearing ear-to-ear smiles, and Carli felt electricity in the air from their energy. It was obvious shopping had been some sort of a drug for them.

Before Carli could figure out how to politely escape this "sidewalk party", Lola began an account of their exciting finds. "We found the cutest little napkins and plates with a gold ring design. Can you believe our luck? They had plenty at the Dollar General right here in Dixon. I know you'll love them. And we have all the fixin's for party favors—the netting to wrap candies and the satin ribbon to tie the netting closed. We found some big paper wedding bells to use when we decorate the cookhouse, along with streamers."

"You just can't have too many decorations," one of the ladies offered.

They all nodded in agreement, huge smiles consuming their faces.

Carli had already started inching her way towards her truck but Lola and the two ladies moved when Carli moved, as though they were all trapped in some kind of wedding planning bubble.

Lola started in again on her list about food and dishes, flowers, and carpet runners for outside so no one would get their pretty shoes dirty, and fifty things they had found at the stores today, and fifty other things they still needed to get, as well as all the folks who would just love to volunteer to lend a helping hand in preparing the food, the party favors, the decorations, and whatever else was needed to make this once-in-a-lifetime soirée an unforgettable success. The other two ladies chimed in, all three chattering at once.

Gotta get out of here. Not sure if she ever had a real panic attack, Carli thought this was feeling pretty close to what one might be like. She would just have to interrupt and apologize later if anyone got hurt or offended.

"I am so sorry ladies. I really have to run. Told a friend I'd meet her and I'm late. Please forgive me. And thank you for all you're doing."

Another fib. Actually, that was a bold-faced lie. What was happening to her? Later she'd have to have a talk with God about all of this. She was just trying to spare everyone's feelings. What else could she do? Sometimes it was just better to tell a white lie, wasn't it?

Lola's mouth hung open a little and the other ladies stared at Carli as she walked to her truck. Polite as they were, they maintained a remnant of their smiles.

As soon as Carli got in her truck, she started it up and hightailed it out of there before anyone else could bring up the "W" word again.

Driving through Dixon she heard a few car horns. Had she cut someone off? No, it wasn't that. A couple of drivers waved at her. The one closest to her leaned out their window and hollered, "Congrats on your wedding, Carli!"

Oh my gosh, when had she become a celebrity of sorts? She half-smiled to be polite and gave a half-wave. But this was becoming insane.

Maybe she should get on her horse and ride off. Away from people and wedding plans.

Chapter 11

Taylor

Taylor Miller put his heavy-duty truck in park outside the cookhouse at the Wild Cow Ranch. When he stepped out, a flood of memories poured into his head. As a teen he could only dream about owning such a truck. Leather seats, all the bells and whistles imaginable.

His father had been a salesman and all-around worker at the hardware store in Dixon. He made deliveries, fixed equipment, and handled whatever came up. Everyone in town knew Taylor's dad. And his mother who was a schoolteacher. She had "raised" a lot of the town's children. Both parents were strict when it came to their own kids—three boys. Everyone worked hard to make ends meet.

It was bittersweet coming to the Wild Cow after all this time. Taylor, his wife, and kids lived in Amarillo now. He had a new life and pretty much avoided this place. But his old friend had asked him to stop by today. So, he did.

"Hey, J.T.," Buck called to him as Taylor walked up. "Do you still go by that?"

Back in the day everyone called him J.T., short for John Taylor.

Taylor shook Buck's hand and patted his shoulder. "Not so much anymore. Now it's just Taylor."

"Well, come say hey to my lady." Buck held out his arm to lead Lola over.

She was still beautiful, Taylor thought.

"Lola, wow, you look just the same. How long has it been?"

They embraced each other and she said, "Now, Taylor, we're not gonna talk about how many years have gone by. But I'll tell ya, it's been a lot."

All three laughed. There were still good feelings between them, and for that, Taylor was thankful. After everything that had happened with Michelle running away, things could've gone in the opposite direction. People could have blamed him for everything—if they had known all what had transpired between him and Michelle. But no one really knew the truth of it all. At least he didn't think so.

"C'mon in the cookhouse. I've got lunch ready for you guys." Lola grabbed Buck's and Taylor's arms and walked between the two.

"I seem to recall you always had a knack for cooking, Lola."

"My mother taught me. And it always seems to make people happy."

She flashed him a big smile and headed into the kitchen ahead of the men. Buck led Taylor to a table where they pulled up a couple of chairs and sat.

"I'm glad you came, man. Wasn't sure you'd have the time."

"Always have time for you and Lola." He hesitated, then added. "I'm sorry we lost touch over the years though."

Lola placed a hand on Taylor's shoulder. "We understand you have a life in Amarillo. How many children do you have?"

"Two," Taylor said. He hesitated, wondering if he should explain that Hud was from his first marriage but then did it really matter? "A boy and a girl. Hudson and Shayla."

Lola winked. "And a pretty wife, I bet."

"Karissa. Yes, she's an angel. I'm a very lucky man."

Buck leaned back on his chair. "We'd love to meet her someday. Your kids too. Bring them all out here sometime."

"The wedding!" Lola could hardly contain herself. "Of course, you're all invited. Come to Carli's wedding. That would be the perfect time."

The last thing he wanted to do was drag his family to attend a wedding of people they didn't know. Taylor was busy too. They had several complicated investigations going. But he forced himself to ask, "When is it?"

Lola jumped in. "November fifteenth. Before Thanksgiving. You've got to come. You'll probably see some other people you haven't seen in a long time."

"Thanks. I'll ask Karissa. I'm not sure what's on her schedule."

Lola was like a firecracker. "I know Carli would like it if you could come. You met her, right? After that scary rustling incident that took place on the Wild Cow."

"Yes," Taylor said. "We met. There was a lot going then. She was busy."

He almost commented that she looked exactly like her mother, but he stopped himself. Maybe he should ask Buck sometime about what happened to Michelle, and Carli, and the whole thing.

Lola had gone to the kitchen and returned with two plates on a tray along with all the fixin's for the two men to make their own beef fajitas.

"Hope you guys like this," she said. "And I left dessert for you under the cake dish on the counter. I've got to make some phone calls about the wedding. So many of the townsfolk are volunteering for different tasks. I'm trying to coordinate everything. You don't mind, do you, Taylor, if I leave you guys to it?"

"No, of course not," he said. "And thanks for this nice lunch. It was great seeing you, Lola."

She hugged his shoulder a little. "Hope you enjoy. And don't be a stranger. We all have a lot of catching up to do. Please come to the wedding and bring your family."

Taylor thanked her again, and he and Buck dug into building their fajitas.

"She's terrific, Buck. As she's always been."

"Yes, sir. I'm blessed, for sure." He kept a napkin handy for the mess he was creating.

The men stuffed their mouths for a couple minutes without saying a word.

"Thanks for joining me," said Buck. "I wanted to talk to you about a few things. First, can you give me an update on the rustlers? Were you able to locate any of our livestock?"

"No sir. I'm sorry to say they must have gone through a sale barn, or more than likely were sold to another rancher with an altered brand."

"What about the charges? Did they stick?"

"Yes. The case is solid. Those two ex-cons will be going back to prison. I think they may plea bargain the younger man, since it was his uncle and father who were his accomplices. He's cooperating with authorities."

"That's good to know," said Buck. "I really appreciate the update."

Then Taylor brought up the subject that had been on his mind ever since he first saw Carli. Now was as good a time as any.

"Buck, there are some things I'm hoping you can clear up for me."

"I thought you might have questions, Taylor. It was all over your face. Carli looks just like her mother, doesn't she?"

"You always could read me. Never got anything past you." He smiled.

Buck wiped his mouth and said, "Remember that time you and Billy got water balloons and climbed into the hayloft? You blasted everyone who passed underneath. Your fathers grounded you rascals for at least a week. But yours still let you play Friday night in the game. Otherwise, the whole town would've come after him. I knew what you guys were up to."

"Geez, I haven't thought of that in forever. We were hellions, weren't we? But you never ratted us out."

They both laughed in between bites. The conversation slowed as they focused on their plates. Taylor broke the silence.

"I wanted to ask if you could refresh my memory about some things, Buck."

Buck grinned. "Well, I'm a little bit older than you but I'll give it a try."

"Towards the end of my senior year I was turning eighteen. And Michelle Jameson was fifteen going on sixteen. That's when she left the ranch. Did you ever find out where she went?"

"No." Buck looked serious. "And believe me, Jean and Ward spared no expense on private detectives trying to find her."

"She must have married at some point in her life, right? When did she have Carli? I assume Carli is the only heir, or did Michelle have other children?" Taylor asked.

"No other children that we know of. Michelle must have been pregnant when she ran away. She gave the baby up right after she gave birth."

Taylor's fork froze in front of his open mouth. Michelle was pregnant when she ran away that night?

Buck kept talking. "Carli's grandparents searched for Michelle and the baby for years. It was just a short while before Ward died that the detectives were closing in on Carli's location in Atlanta. So, Ward changed his Last Will to leave her the ranch instead of Billy Broderick, but, sadly, Ward got sick and passed away. Carli knew nothing about any of this so I'm sure it was a shock when a lawyer told her in Atlanta what she had inherited. They brought her to Texas for the court hearing and Billy contested her ownership. She came to the Wild Cow right after that."

"Must've been a huge surprise for Carli," Taylor said. "I guess she never knew Ward and Jean."

"No, she didn't. Her foster parents did bring her here when she was about ten years old," Buck explained, "and Ward and Jean saw her then. But Carli barely remembered them. Must've been like a dream for her when the lawyers brought her here after the court hearing."

Taylor rubbed his hands together. "I remember Billy telling me some of that story. He's been upset about the whole thing. Thought he'd get the ranch."

Buck pushed his plate to the side. "Yeah. Ward's Last Will was read in court and the judge declared Carli the sole heir. That really steamed Billy. In fact, he's still ticked off and has filed a new lawsuit. One of Carli's attorneys is here now."

"Another court case?" Taylor asked.

"Yeah. Poor Carli. Right around her wedding, too. Like she doesn't have enough to think about. Hey, do you ever see Billy?"

"Actually, quite a bit. We play golf every couple of weeks or so."

"Do me a favor, and keep this conversation confidential, will ya? I mean, it really is Carli's business."

"Of course. I don't tell Billy everything."

"Good. Thanks, J.T. I mean, Taylor." Buck grinned.

"Speaking of confidential, can I ask you a couple of things?"

"Sure. And what you say is just between you, me, and the Good Lord."

"Thanks, I appreciate that." Taylor hemmed and hawed, his mind in a fog as he tried to make sense of what Buck had told him. And then he said what he had wanted to say all along. "Buck, did you know that Michelle and I were seeing each other back then?"

Buck let some breath out along with a grin. "Yeah, Lola and I always suspected. At times it was pretty obvious. But I think you kids were trying to hide it from your folks."

"Yeah, we were. Michelle wanted it that way. She didn't want anyone to know about us."

"Maybe she thought Ward would be upset." Buck sipped his sweet tea.

"I don't know. All I do know is that one night she rode off with some other guy and I never saw her again. It's always been in the back of my mind. But I had to move on with my life."

"You had no choice, Taylor."

"Maybe I should have looked for her."

"Seems she didn't want to be found. Never wanted any part of this ranch, and I'll never understand it." Buck frowned and shook his head.

"So, I've gotta ask you, Buck. Do you know who Michelle ran off with? Do you think he was Carli's father?"

Buck looked at Taylor and paused as if there was something he wanted to say but didn't. He looked away and took another drink of tea. "There's no way for any of us to know that now."

Taylor's mind was reeling. Buck kept rattling on about cows and weather, but he barely heard. Michelle consumed all of his thoughts.

Chapter 12

Taylor

Taylor Miller watched his old friend's face flicker through a range of emotions—melancholy, caution, friendship. If there was one thing he knew about Buck Wallace, it was that he was an honest, God-fearing man. Taylor felt certain Buck would tell him whatever he could reveal. So, he waited to hear what else he knew, and if he could piece together the sequence of events.

Buck rose from the table and cut them both a slice of cake.

"I don't want to betray Carli in any way or talk about her business," Buck continued. "Or her mother Michelle. But you and I are old friends and you never did me wrong. I can see you're struggling to know the truth. This is a big deal. Life changing."

Taylor nodded his head and his face went white.

"I don't know for sure who Michelle left town with that night. I have my suspicions. And I don't know one hundred percent who Carli's father is. But I have my suspicions about that too."

He set an oversized slice of carrot cake in front

of him. Taylor's mouth watered as he picked up his fork, his attention diverted for a second from the topic at hand.

"You would know better than me as far as when you and Michelle spent private time together before she ran away. And I could be way off base. For all any of us know, she might've had another boyfriend after you. She was such a wild child. But there is one thing I feel pretty darn certain about."

"What's that, Buck?"

"Without a doubt, Carli looks like Michelle's double. I can also see some parts of you in her. Maybe it's the mouth. Or mannerisms she does. Just some things in her personality. They're from you. Lola and I have talked about it before, but never told anyone. Is it possible that you might be Carli's father?"

Taylor took in a big breath, let it sift out slowly, and ran his hand through his hair. He leaned back and relaxed for the first time since this whole thing interrupted his life. But he also was light-headed and jittery.

"Are you okay with it?" Buck asked.

"I'm not sure. It's a shock, ya know. A twenty-eight-year-old daughter I never knew I had? I guess I'm processing it and have a lot of questions. What will my wife say? My kids? What does Carli think? Would she even want me in her life? Does she know I'm her birth father? Am I, without a shadow of doubt, her father?"

Buck moved around in his chair. "Carli is a very private person. She doesn't reveal much. She's asked us a lot of questions about the Jamesons since she came to the Wild Cow. I don't think she knows for sure whether you're her father. Lola might know more than I do. Ya know, girl talk."

Taylor took a gulp of his sweet tea. "She seems to be a nice young woman. What do y'all think of her?"

"Carli? She's the best. Hard worker. Kind. Fast learner. And grateful. Grateful, I think, that everyone has welcomed her to town and that she finally found a home for herself at the Wild Cow. All those years of being on her own. Sad really. She has a family here."

Taylor stared as though transfixed in the past. "She had foster parents, right? Weren't they good to her?"

"More like permanent guardians, and I hear they were just fine to her," Buck said. "They were older. Left her to her own devices much of the time. Then they both passed away the same year, I think. Carli just got used to doing everything on her own. She had to. But it made it hard for her to trust and let people in. She's gotten a lot better now. Well, just look at her. She's marrying Lank, ain't she?" Buck gave a hearty laugh.

"Is Lank a good hand?" Taylor hunched forward.

Buck answered, "Yeah, he is. Another hard worker. He has struggles though, like everybody else. His mother passed about a year ago. He sure misses her."

"That's tough. Sorry to hear that."

"What about you, Taylor? Will you talk to your wife and kids and tell them about Carli?"

"I don't know, Buck. This is a big deal. For everyone. I think we'd better make sure first. A hundred percent sure. Maybe take DNA tests. Although I'm not sure how to go about it."

"You'll both figure it out. Want me to pray for you?"

Taylor looked at his old friend. "You mean now?"

"Sure. No time like the present." Buck grinned.

"All right. Go ahead. My wife is more used to praying than I am. But have at it, if you want to."

Buck bowed his head. Taylor squinted and peeked over at Buck. He wasn't sure whether to fold his hands so just rubbed his sweaty palms on his jeaned thighs.

"Lord, we ask for your wisdom and protection in all of this. Please show both Carli and Taylor the truth about their relationship. And if it turns out that Taylor is her birth father, please bless them both with a relationship for years to come. For the years they missed. And Lord, please be with Taylor as he figures this thing out. Should he talk to his wife and children? If it turns out that he is Carli's father, help his family to be accepting of her as their new daughter, new sister. Be with Lank and all the people this relationship will affect. Out of any kind of confusion that may come along, Lord, let your will be done. Please bless everyone involved, even people on the outside looking in. Thank you, Jesus. Amen."

Taylor cleared his throat and opened his eyes. He wasn't sure why but his chest, his heart, felt warmed. Calm. Peaceful.

"Thanks, Buck. I'm not a big praying man, but that sure means a lot to me."

His phone interrupted with a vibrating buzz and he looked at the screen. Karissa.

"My wife. Gotta take this."

He pressed the green button and held it to his ear as he walked a few feet away. "Hey, darlin'. How's everything?" He listened to Karissa, then answered, "Okay, I'll be home around six. Bye bye."

Buck didn't ask, but Taylor offered the information. "She wants me to go to church with her tonight. Wednesday night Bible study."

"Sounds like God might be tapping you on the shoulder, Taylor."

His friend's big, goofy smile embarrassed Taylor. "Karissa loves church and the Bible. I love Karissa. She's the praying person in our family."

"Well, don't knock it till you've tried it." More grins from Buck. "She sounds like a special lady."

"She is. Very special." Taylor slipped his phone into his shirt pocket.

"How do you think she'll take it when you tell her about Carli?"

"I'm not sure, Buck. It might take some time for her to get used to the idea. You know, I had two failed marriages before Karissa. Add Michelle and a possible baby from that relationship...and it's like three strikes."

Buck touched Taylor's forearm for a second. "Don't think of it that way. We all make mistakes in life. They're in the past. How long did you say you've been married to Karissa?"

"Twenty-four years. Our daughter Shayla is twenty-two."

"And it's been good all those years?"

"Yeah, it has. 'Course we've had our ups and downs, what with my horse business. And her decorating business. And we have Hud from my first marriage. He's a good kid. It was a struggle at first getting custody of Hud when he was a toddler. His mother had a drug problem. Then Shayla was born.

Karissa had two babies at once."

"Well, there ya go," Buck said. "So now you're on a good path. You've been blessed with your wife, your children, good jobs. No need to look way back in the past to 'mistakes' as you call them."

"I guess you're right, Buck. Thanks. I'm just a little apprehensive. About Carli. And what my family will think. I'm worried about rocking the boat."

The two men stood and collected their plates to take to the kitchen sink.

"If you rock the boat, and even fall into the raging waves, remember to grab a hold of Jesus," Buck said with a smile. "He'll pull you up and won't let ya drown."

Taylor put a hand on Buck's shoulder. "Seems I've heard that story before."

Both men grinned and shook hands. "Thanks for joining me for lunch today," Buck said.

Taylor walked across the dining hall to the door and his awaiting truck. He had to get home and talk with his wife. He turned and looked at Buck. "I really appreciate it. Thanks. For everything."

Buck nodded his head and followed Taylor outside. "If I learn anything new, I'll give you a call."

"Give Lola my thanks as well. I just might see you both again at the wedding."

"I sure hope so." Buck stood on the porch as Taylor got into his pickup truck.

Taylor gave one last wave as he drove away. He had a lot to think about. He had a lot to tell Karissa.

Chapter 13

Taylor

"Hey, darlin', I'm home." Taylor Miller had parked his truck on the extended parking pad off the side of his brick home and entered through the garage, into the kitchen. His keys jingled as he placed them in the wooden dish on the counter.

Karissa was lifting burgers out of the oven where they were warming along with golden buns. She leaned towards him and gave him a kiss on the cheek. "Hey, sweetie. Just in time. Bible study starts at seven. Would you grab that plate of sliced tomatoes and lettuce out of the fridge, please? I've got some potato salad also if you want. Beans too. The kids are both out with friends. We'll have our very own little indoor picnic. How's that sound?"

"Perfect, Karissa." He reached around her waist and pulled her close. "Just like you."

"You are a flirt, mister," she said with a wink. "Tell me what you did today."

They sat at the kitchen table next to a picture window that afforded a view of their landscaped backyard. Wide oaks and stately elms surrounded a swimming pool and flagstone patio with a fire pit. In the spring, flower beds bulged with color. Today, the fall view was barren and brown, but he still found peace when he looked out the window.

Sometimes when Taylor was out of sorts thinking of his past, he felt like he was living someone else's life, as though he didn't deserve all of this. But then he remembered how hard he and Karissa had worked for it. They enjoyed entertaining, both for his work and for her numerous organizations and charities.

"The usual. Ranch investigation work. A few burglaries. Lots of paperwork, that's for sure." He gulped a big bite of burger and wondered when, how, and if he should have a conversation with his wife about Carli.

God, if you're listening, I think I'm gonna need your help. Like he told Buck, he wasn't a big praying man, but if ever he could use some guidance and the right words, now was surely the time.

He held a napkin to his mouth and muttered, "Also went to the Wild Cow Ranch. Saw my old friend Buck Wallace."

Karissa asked, "Oh. They had rustling trouble, didn't they?"

"Yeah, they did. Remember I told you all about that? Those two girls, uh, young women, Carli Jameson and Angie Olsen, tracked down the rustlers and with the help of some cowboys, captured them."

"Sounds dangerous."

"It was. Those girls should never have gotten into the thick of things like they did. They could've been hurt." Looking down at his plate, he scraped up the last of the potato salad with his fork. His mind suddenly was a million miles away. Quietly, to himself, he whispered, "Seems like Carli has a mind of her own though. Like her mother."

"Did you know this girl and her mother?"

This wasn't how Taylor wanted things to come out. He might've just blown it.

"Maybe I've never mentioned it before, but I used to work at the Wild Cow. And Buck was just telling me stuff. Mostly about the old days."

Karissa stared at him, those clear blue eyes and face framed with dark brown hair. He loved her so much and would never do anything to jeopardize her trust.

He didn't want to have this talk now. As he looked at her face, he lost his nerve. The topic of his high school love and the child that may be his would have to wait.

Taylor stood. "Look at the time. I'll help you put everything away. We should get going."

She still stared at him for another few seconds. Then got up from the table and put the dinner remains away and dishes in the dishwasher.

Karissa told him, "I'm going to run and brush my teeth. I'll be out in a minute."

"I'll start the truck."

They rode to church in relative silence. Karissa asked another question or two about Taylor's afternoon at the Wild Cow, but Taylor steered her away from that topic when he asked about the kids and what they had going on.

At church the majority of the people greeted Karissa with hugs and laughter about some previous shared experience. They warmly welcomed Taylor who hung a little in the background behind his wife. Here, she was the star. Everyone loved Karissa. She volunteered for many projects, spearheaded some, and seemed to have boundless energy for helping others.

Every Wednesday night different Bible studies took place in various classrooms of the church. Some were for women only, some for men, or youth. The one for Karissa and Taylor was for married couples. Their group had about twelve participants. Taylor didn't always attend. Sometimes work got in the way, or, if he were honest, sometimes he begged off saying how exhausted he was. The times he did join the study, he usually learned something new about the Bible and came out feeling good. He loved being with his wife and he always wanted to make her happy. The one thing that gave his stomach the quivers was when people in the group shared their innermost feelings, sometimes even crying. He wasn't very comfortable with that.

When everyone was settled, the leader said, "Glad to see you all tonight. Hope you've been having a good week so far. We're going to continue our study of Matthew 14:27-33. It's about Jesus walking on the water. We're going to focus on the moments when Peter lost his faith, sunk into the water, but Jesus saved him. I think verse thirty is key, when Peter saw the wind, was afraid, but he cried out, 'Lord, save me!' He was starting to sink in the waves. Would anyone like to start us off and share about a time in their life when they had a similar experience? Not literally, but you know what I mean." They all chuckled.

Taylor's thoughts went to his talk with Buck who had brought up this same Bible story. What a coincidence. He had told Taylor, "If you rock the boat, and even fall into the raging waves, remember to grab a hold of Jesus. He'll pull you up and won't let ya drown."

One of the members of the study opened up. "There was a time in our lives when things looked pretty grim." The man placed a hand on his wife's hand in her lap. "We had a sick child, my business was failing, we couldn't pay our bills. I felt pretty lost, drowning in bad stuff every day. It's like the Good Book says. When I looked to Jesus for help, he was there and things turned around for the better."

The man continued, "It's not like Jesus was Santa Claus or a genie and fixed everything right away. We had to pray and work hard. And what I learned was that even if we had lost everything, and even, heaven forbid, if our child had not gotten better, Jesus gave us a supernatural peace. We knew he'd be with us, no matter what. I've never felt anything like it before."

The leader smiled and said, "Thanks, Larry, for sharing. I think that's exactly what this teaching is all about. Our lives are so much better when we reach out to Jesus to help us through our journey. We can't do it alone. Anyone else want to share?"

Taylor took it all in and he felt it was true. He had a churched upbringing, but he'd also been a lawman for years, trained to be no-nonsense and tough. He'd never be able to share his private feelings with strangers. He smiled at Karissa but was hoping the evening would end soon so they could be on their way home.

After a few others in the group shared their stories, the leader concluded with prayer. He patted Taylor's shoulder on the way out and said, "Good to see you, Taylor. Hope you can come more frequently."

"I'll try. Work keeps me busy, you know."

Karissa smiled, but it looked a little too social to Taylor like she was putting on the happy face that was expected. Was anything bothering her?

They drove home in more half-silence just like the ride there. Taylor had to try to get her back to her "bubbly Karissa" self.

As they parked, Karissa noted, "Shayla's home. Not Hud. Doesn't he work tomorrow?"

"Yeah. But it's only nine-thirty. I'm sure he'll be home soon," Taylor said as they walked into the house from the garage. "I'll grab a quick shower. You gonna check on Shayla? Let me know when I can tell her goodnight."

In the shower Taylor tried to let the anxiety leave his body as the hot water hit his shoulders. But his mind was another thing. Should he tell Karissa more about his visit with Buck today and what they had talked about? The possibility that Carli was his daughter? Would she flip out, be upset? Maybe he shouldn't bring it up at all until he was a hundred percent sure. And what about a DNA test? His law enforcement training told him that was the thing to do. Deal in facts. Not romantic memories. But that would mean talking to Carli, getting the test from her too. The news had rocked him. He couldn't deny it.

He wrapped one towel around his waist and rubbed his hair with another. After a quick blow dry, he opened the bathroom door to let all the steam out.

Karissa was in the bedroom, already dressed in her nightgown. She came over to him with a kiss. "No need for you to check on Shayla. I talked with her a little. She's doing fine, was out with a couple girlfriends. Just tired and ready to turn in soon. Said she needs to wake up early and get to the boutique to open."

Taylor stroked Karissa's slender, tanned arm. She was so pretty. And he was so lucky. This was no time to bring up all that other stuff. About Carli. Maybe God would help him find the perfect time. Now was not it.

"Well, we don't have to wake up early, do we?" A mischievous smirk played across his face. Even after twenty-four years, they could still find the spark.

"Why, John Taylor Miller. You are a rascal, sir. And after a Bible study, too." She was smiling.

"God said to love one another. And also, something about it's not good for man to be alone."

"I do declare, sir. You have been paying attention after all."

Chapter 14

Carli

She was thinking of flowers with much disdain, although she tried to stop.

Carli used to love flowers, but now she could live the rest of her life without seeing another bouquet. She swung the saddle over Beau. Lola had dragged her to three floral shops in Amarillo. It had taken them all morning.

Lank emerged from the saddle house with reins and a saddle blanket. "What's with the frown? What did you and Lola do this morning?"

"Chrysanthemums, hydrangeas, roses, baby's breath; we looked at every flower in the city. And the ribbon. Are you aware of how many colors there are of ribbon? I don't know what color combination I want in a bridal bouquet."

"Tell her white. All brides carry white."

"And you need a boutonniere, mister. What color ribbon do you want with that? Brown, teal, beige? Apparently, it's a big deal. Be prepared. You will be tested later."

Carli and Lank mounted their horses, leaving

the Wild Cow Ranch corral to ride the fence line in the east pasture. She took several deep breaths to still her aggravation. Beau was acting a bit fresh. He picked up on her emotions so quickly.

She wanted to ride as far east to the edge of the ranch, as far as she could. Away from the wedding frenzy called Lola.

Lank rode in silence beside her.

"And dresses for bridesmaids. I like all the colors and I could care less about the style. Which brings me to another question. Who are my bridesmaids? Who are your groomsmen? How many do we want? I guess we should ask some people."

Lank just nodded his head but didn't say anything.

Carli continued. "Remember this pasture in the spring? Those little yellow flowers that covered the rise over there? And those purple flowers. And blue. That's the blue I like." She pointed to the sky. "That Texas sky blue, but there's not a bridesmaid dress on the planet in that color."

"You know that some of those wildflowers you like are actually classified as weeds, right?"

"Doesn't matter. I like the colors of weeds then."

Lank raised an eyebrow at that comment but didn't interrupt.

"I feel bad. I know Lola is super excited to be helping us and I really appreciate her efforts. But I almost feel like we're working on her wedding instead of mine. I don't know how many more things we have to do, but I'm about worn out."

"Have you told her that?"

"Just you. She's so excited about this, and, since they never had a daughter, I can't bring myself to say anything."

"But it's your wedding. Our wedding. It should be whatever you want."

"I've never been one of those girls who dreamed and planned about her wedding day. I was always too busy working to pay my bills. I didn't need a husband to support me. And it should be what you want. It's your wedding too," Carli said.

Lank grew silent, pensively staring straight ahead as they rode side-by-side. Carli waited. Curious about the look on his face and the sadness reflected in his eyes. For a second her heart stopped. Was he having doubts?

She stayed patient for as long as she could. "What do you want, Lank? You've never said."

"Maybe no one's ever asked me." He stared straight ahead.

That was true. Not once had Carli or Lola included Lank in any of their conversations.

"We agreed to tell each other everything. No more secrets. Even if the truth may hurt. We're both adults." She stopped Beau. "Tell me what you're thinking."

Lank reined up and spun his horse around, stopping next to her. He met her gaze. "I wish my mom could be at our wedding." His voice flat, his chin trembled slightly.

The empty stare on his face brought tears to her eyes.

"I never thought about that. Of course, your sister will be there. Lola has your nephews all lined up as ringbearers. I know your father's been gone since you were in high school, but I never thought about your mother not being at our wedding. Her loss is still fresh. I am so sorry." His mother. Her birth father, but Carli didn't mention that. The image of her real father walking her down the aisle never left her thoughts.

Lank cleared his throat. "There's nothing we can do to change it. We'll make it through as long as you're by my side."

That didn't seem fair. They were backed into a corner. Carli tried to still her anger. Neighbors were so happy for her and Lank, but they would have a wedding day neither of them wanted. If she said something, Lola's feelings would be hurt beyond repair. How would that affect their friendship? It would make their working relationship awkward and strange. The Wild Cow Ranch couldn't run without Lola and Buck. She loved Lola. She and Buck had become more than employees. They were family.

The wedding hung over their heads like a dark rain cloud, threatening to drench their marriage.

"We should be able to be honest with family without hurting their feelings. Can't we have an open and honest discussion?"

"In some cases, yes. But in this case no," said Lank. "Lola's got the whole town involved. How can we tell them to stop? We'd be public enemy number one."

"I agree," said Carli. "I don't want there to be bad feelings over what should be one of the happiest days of our life."

Carli urged her horse Beau up a steep rise and then stopped. Lank followed. From that vantage point she looked over the Wild Cow Ranch, land she had inherited from a grandfather she never knew.

"What plans do you have for this place since you're marrying the boss?" she glanced at Lank.

Surprise showed in his eyes at the question. "Never thought about it. Are you hinting at a prenup?"

She laughed. "No silly, but now that you mention it."

"You know I like punchin' cows. Maybe train a few ranch horses too. Stuff like that."

"We're partners in this together. I don't know a thing about running a cattle ranch, but you do. How can we make this better?"

"I have a few ideas," he said.

"Yeah, me too. I'd really like to expand the riding school and get back to giving lessons. I want to include special needs kids and learn everything I can about how to use horses in their therapy. Maybe you can help me with training horses?"

"Riding school horses? I was thinking more like rodeo stock. Bucking broncs. I can't ride them anymore because of the head injury I got in high school, but we could raise some fine stock."

Carli frowned but didn't say anything. She wondered how they would handle riding school horses and broncs. Her complaining took up most of the morning already. That would be a topic for some other time. Lank steered his horse toward the bottom of the shallow valley. Carli followed.

They rode in silence. "Should I talk to Lola?" she finally asked.

"As I look at this view and think about our future, what's a little fifteen-minute ceremony compared to a lifetime?"

"You are wise beyond your years, Lank Torres. I guess I can suffer through it too. Everyone is working so hard. We can't get out of it now."

"I'm afraid you're right. I love you, Carli. You're a good person."

"I love you too."

Carli's phone buzzed with a text. "Speaking of. This is from Lola."

When can you go to Dallas? We need to find you a dress, it read.

Her first instinct was to throw the phone as far as she could, but instead she passed it to Lank with a trembling hand. Lank laughed which made Carli grit her teeth. It wasn't funny.

You will make it through this wedding. You will. She would keep telling herself that, and then pray that she could keep her mouth shut and not do anything to hurt Lola's feelings.

Chapter 15

Taylor

Karissa brushed her damp, raven curls in the bathroom mirror. Navy lightweight sweater and tan pinwale corduroy slacks would work for her day. She had an appointment with a decorating client at eleven, then lunch with a sorority sister to discuss a fundraising project.

Taylor came into the room carrying two coffees on a tray and set it down on a small round table at one end of the room. He even brought her a small yogurt with blueberries in a bowl—a favorite of hers. She met him with a giggle and took a seat. "Thank you, hon. Is it our anniversary?"

He leaned down with a smile and kissed her neck. "No, Karissa. Just wanted to do something nice for you. I'm glad we had some alone time this morning without the kids. We don't always get that. And I kinda wanted to talk to you about something."

"It was nice, darlin'. I'm glad too. So, what do ya have going on today?"

"More of the same. Some meetings—another rustling case. This time just a couple missing cows.

But we still have to check it out. How 'bout you?"

"I've got one client at eleven, then lunch with Margie. We have a project for the women's shelter. Trying to raise funds to get supplies—linens, towels, kids' toys, food. They always need things."

"Let me know if I can do anything to help."

"That's sweet. Thanks, hon. What did you want to talk about?"

He stood and walked to a tall dresser, picked up his watch, and attached it to his wrist. He was wearing starched jeans and a starched white shirt. Tried like anything to be calm and not let his nerves get the best of him. But his heart was beating like a drum.

"This is probably not the time nor place, but I'm got something on my mind and I need your support, Karissa. I thought since we both had time this morning, no kids, and neither of us has to rush out the door to work...that maybe I could bring it up."

"You're kind of worrying me, Taylor. What's going on?"

"Remember I told you about visiting my old friend, Buck Wallace, at the Wild Cow Ranch?"

"Yes."

"And I told you about Carli Jameson and the other young woman following those rustlers, and we worked the case?"

"Yes."

"Well, Carli is getting married. November fifteenth. And we're invited. The kids too."

"That's nice. Is that what you're all jumpy about? Sounds like fun."

"There's more." He was super nervous now and wished he could pull back his words. Why in the world did he even bring this up? God, I'm gonna need your help here.

"Taylor, sit down and have your coffee. Tell me the rest. What's bothering you?"

He did as she said and took a couple of sips.

"When we were working that rustling case at the Wild Cow, I met the new owner."

"Okay..."

"When I met Carli Jameson, she looked exactly...I mean, like a twin...of my first girlfriend, serious girlfriend, back in high school. Michelle Jameson." He tried to read his wife's thoughts. He added to be very clear, "Carli's mother."

Karissa had been listening closely but Taylor could tell she hadn't understood completely what was in his mind.

She said, "I've heard the stories around town somewhat. Everyone knows about the Wild Cow. Ward and Jean. They used to always light up their place at Christmas time, real pillars of the community. It was sad they searched for years for their daughter, Michelle, after she ran away from home. She was your girlfriend?"

"Yes."

"So, what does that have to do with you now? You guys broke up, she ran away, and must've had a baby...Carli...with some guy."

All of a sudden, he saw the realization rise to the surface in her brain, and her face turned stony white.

"Taylor. Is it possible that you might be the father?"

"Karissa, I don't know for sure. I'm just trying to figure it out. It's as much of a shock to me as it is to you. At my recent visit with Buck, we talked about it. He was working at the Wild Cow when I was a teenager. He knew Michelle and I were together back then, but no one else did. Well, maybe the town suspected, but not Michelle's parents. I don't want Billy Broderick or anyone to know about this now until I know for certain."

He reached for her hand, but she pulled it away.

"And what are your plans if you find out you are her father?" Her eyes glistened but she sat up tall, pursed her lips, and acted businesslike with him.

"Karissa, I don't have any plans. I'm kind of in shock."

"You're in shock? How about me? We already have one child by a former relationship of yours."

"Hon, you love Hud like he's your own. Please try to understand."

"I do love Hudson. I'm just thinking of all the ramifications. How do you think your son and daughter will react to this news? How will the whole town react?"

"I don't know."

"You don't have any other trysts out there in your past where children are going to come forward into our life?"

"Karissa, that's not fair. Please. Don't let this 'maybe' news drive a wedge between us. I'm sorry. It was twenty-eight years ago. I was a crazy teenage boy. And the possibility that she is my daughter has me totally blown away. I don't know what to make of it. I'm asking for your support. Can you give me that?"

"I don't know, Taylor. It's a lot to process. Right now, I need to get to work." She jumped up from the table.

All he could say was, "Karissa, please," as he stood.

But she was gone. Picked up her bag, no kiss for him like usual, and out the bedroom door she went.

He sat back down at the little table, head in his hands. *God, what am I gonna do now?*

That morning and into the afternoon, Taylor texted his wife and left voicemails for her. She didn't return any of them.

"Please, Karissa. Call me back. Let's talk. I love you. I know this is a shock. But we can get through anything, right? With each other. With God. You're always telling me that. I've been praying. You know that's not normally my thing. I'm trying. I don't want to lose you. We don't even know if this is true. Michelle ran away all those years ago. She probably had lots of boyfriends after me. We were crazy teenagers. Can we just take this one day at a time? Please, Karissa..."

The voicemail recorder ran out of time and cut him off.

He tried doing his job. Paperwork. Phone calls. Meetings. But he felt like a zombie in a dream. He only had one thing on his mind. His family.

Early afternoon he was at the Dixon post office where he kept a box for some of his horse business and Cattle Raisers mail. Other correspondence he received at home. He didn't check this box often and today it was nearly overflowing. Grasping the contents in his arms, he turned and bumped into someone which caused all of the envelopes to cascade onto the floor.

"Oh, I'm so sorry," the young woman said.

Those hazel-green eyes. Carli Jameson.

Taylor's mouth hung open for a few seconds.

She bent one knee and commenced to picking up his mail. He thought maybe she paused at his name on the envelopes. They had met the one time when he came to her ranch about the rustling incident.

As she rose, she held an envelope in her hand and read, "Taylor Miller." And then, "Oh, I'm sorry. Didn't mean to be nosy."

He took the bundle of mail from her hands. Seemed like they were trembling a little. "It's okay. No worries. Thanks for helping me pick it up. I should've brought a bag for it all."

They stood there facing each other, staring into each other's eyes.

He broke the silence. "We met once before."

"Right. I remember. You're the TCR agent, aren't you?"

"Yes. We came to give you the report on your rustling situation."

"Thanks for your help with that. Well, I guess it was Agent McKinney who did the field work. He was nice...uh, I mean, professional."

"Yes, he's a good agent."

Her eyes darted from him to the door. Definitely nervous, he thought.

She hurriedly said, "Well, I've got to go. Nice to, uh, see you."

He wanted to look at her for a longer time. It was like staring into the face of Michelle. He had to make her stay.

So, he blurted out, "Excuse me, Ms. Jameson."

She turned with wide eyes. "Yes?"

"I saw Buck and Lola recently. They said I should come to your wedding. And bring my family. I didn't want to barge in though without an invite."

"Uh, uh," she stumbled over her words. "Uh, sure, the more, the merrier."

"If you're positive it's okay. November fifteenth. Is that right?"

"Uh, I think so. I mean, yes." She started to walk away, then turned back to look at him. "You're welcome to come. And bring your...uh, family."

"Thank you. I look forward to it. And congratulations by the way."

She vanished out the door.

Looks just like Michelle.

Chapter 16

Taylor

Things were a real mess and he knew it was because of him. *I really blew it. What was I thinking?*

Taylor wished he could rewind his life. Back to when he and his wife had enjoyed sweet, private time together. Kisses, hugs. He sure did love her.

But now she was gone all day. He knew she had appointments and a lunch date with a friend about a fundraiser. Still, she had not answered any of his texts or voicemails. That was not like her. Not his Karissa. His angel. The mother of his children. Oh right, children. Was Carli Jameson one of his children? Why hadn't he waited until he knew for certain? Why bring this up now if it turns out to be a false alarm? What a jerk he was.

Taylor was chastising himself in the kitchen as he unloaded various takeout food he had picked up for the family. Not your normal takeout food. He had texted Karissa to say he was leaving work early and would bring home everyone's favorites, but she didn't answer. She usually planned the meals and he wasn't much of a cook, so he decided to take a chance and bring it all home anyway. If no one showed up, or if they didn't like it, well, they'd figure it out. They always did.

Homemade, healthy pizza for him and Hudson, salads for everyone. Caesar for Karissa and Shayla with a nice piece of salmon on top. They all liked the warehouse style food store where you could find items from around the world. Ten different kinds of nuts if that's what you were looking for. Fifty varieties of olive oils. Or so it seemed. Agave nectar, almond butter, avocado ice cream. For dessert, he chose cocoa-oat truffles—fancy name; they just looked like donut holes to him. Flourless chocolate cake, whatever in the world that was. Taylor thought some of the store's inventory was weird and overpriced. But his family liked it. So that's what he was going to do for them. He always wanted to keep them happy.

Shayla was the first to get home from her job. She surveyed the bags on the counter and said, "Great, Dad! You went to Healthy Foods. Thanks!" A big hug from her meant the world to him.

Hudson was next to arrive. "I could smell the pizza in the garage. I'm starved."

The young man went to open the box and grab a slice when Taylor stopped him. "Let's wait for your mom. She should be here any minute."

That's what he was hoping and praying. She hadn't texted with her ETA like she usually did, but this was close to the time she tried to be home for dinner if she had meetings.

"Why don't you both go change and when you come down, hopefully your mom will be here."

As if God was zeroed in on Taylor's every need,

the sound of Karissa's car in the driveway filled his ears. *Thank you, Lord.*

Coming through the side door, a look of surprise covered her face. "What's all this?"

"I texted you, darlin'. Thought I'd bring dinner for everyone."

"I took out some chicken. I was planning to put it in the air fryer."

"Sorry, I didn't know. Did you get my texts today? I left you voicemails too."

"I silenced my phone. I had meetings. Guess I forgot to turn it back on. I've had a lot on my mind." She stared at him.

"That's okay, darlin'. The kids are upstairs changing out of their work clothes. Why don't we all eat together?"

Before she could answer, Hudson came bounding down the stairs.

"Can we have that pizza now?"

Taylor looked to Karissa for the answer.

She hugged her son and said, "Of course, honey. How was your day?"

Taylor put napkins on the table and spread the food out for everyone to partake. He saw that she looked at the bouquet of flowers he had placed in a crystal vase earlier. Picked those up at the food warehouse too. She didn't say anything. How long was she going to give him the cold shoulder?

Shayla appeared in skinny jeans and a long, gray sweatshirt. "Nice flowers, Mom. Dad did good tonight, didn't he?" When there was no answer, she added, "Or else he's in the doghouse." Both kids chuckled.

"Let's just eat, you bozos," Taylor said. "No one's

in the doghouse."

As they gathered around the table, Taylor gently touched Karissa's hand that placed a napkin on her lap. She didn't pull away. He breathed a small sigh of relief.

The kids, young adults now, talked about their day. Hudson was tanned and developing more muscles from his work with the horses. "I'm starting a new two-year-old. You should see him, Dad. Real flashy. But he's a handful."

Shayla resembled one of the pop culture stars who valued fashion and social media above everything else.

Taylor reminded her, "No phone at the dinner table, Shayla. You know better."

"Oh, Dad. It's just one text. I have to answer it."

"Unless it's a life-or-death emergency, you can wait half an hour to finish your dinner and spend a little time with your family."

A big sigh fluttered out of the girl and she looked perturbed.

All in all, it was a nice family dinner. Except for when Shayla went on and on about some demanding customer she had to wait on at the boutique earlier. Or maybe she thought the lady had been demanding. The customer probably only asked for a different size, Taylor thought. He hoped Shayla wasn't becoming a prima donna at work. Things were so different from when he was growing up. He never could have an attitude around his father or there would've been heck to pay.

Family time was cut short when Hudson said he was going to see his girlfriend and dashed out the door.

Shayla wanted to depart fast too—upstairs to pick out her outfit for the next day. And, no doubt, get on her computer and phone to check how many likes her posts had received during the day even though she was supposed to be working. Karissa was able to extract a little kitchen cleanup help from her daughter, but not much.

"Mom, I just got my nails done. I don't want to ruin them."

"Fine, go on. Your dad and I will finish up."

Karissa put leftovers in plastic containers and Taylor threw away pizza boxes and other trash.

He came up next to her as she was sponging off the counter.

"That was nice. I think everyone liked the food. Did you like the salmon, darlin'?"

Quiet for a few seconds, she finally answered. "Yes, it was really good. Thanks for getting everything. I think the kids liked theirs too."

He smiled and placed his hand on her lower back.

"And the flowers? Do you like them?"

When she didn't answer quickly, he gently tickled her waist.

She squealed a bit, then said, "Yes. Yes, I like them. Thank you."

"You're welcome, darlin'." He kissed her neck. "I missed you today. Thought you were going to stay mad at me."

"Taylor, I'm not mad at you. Just stunned by your news. I don't know what to make of it."

"I'm sorry, Karissa. I probably spoke too soon. It might not even be true. I think I was in shock too. And we never have secrets. We usually talk about things that are bothering us. So, I might have blurted it out before thinking it through."

She hugged him and snuggled in his neck. "I'm sorry too. I don't want us to be upset with each other. We'll pray about this and see how it unfolds. I'm glad you didn't bring it up tonight at dinner to the kids. I was kind of afraid you would. I think we should keep it between us until we know more. Then we'll decide how and when to break it to them. Okay? And you're right. No secrets."

Oh, dang. A lightbulb went off in his head and he thought about the post office. Should he tell Karissa about running into Carli? They both had agreed, no secrets between them.

"Uh, babe?"

She finished cleaning up and tilted her head towards him.

"There is something else...I ran into Carli today at the post office." His stomach quivered. "She invited all of us to her wedding. I said I'd check with your schedule. It's November fifteenth."

He watched a red blotch start in her neck and travel up the side of her face.

Karissa cleared her throat, then said, "You're having conversations with her now?"

"No. Uh. I bumped into her. Or maybe she bumped into me. I dropped all of my mail on the floor. She helped me pick it up. Seems like a nice girl."

"You are un-be-leave-able. I don't want to hear another word. And I do not want to go to her wedding."

She turned abruptly and headed towards the stairs.

"Where are you going? I thought we were having a conversation."

"I'm going upstairs to have a conversation with our daughter. Our *one* daughter."

"Karissa..."

Chapter 17

Lola

It was barely five in the morning, no sign of the sun on the horizon yet, but Lola was packed and ready waiting in her SUV outside Carli's house. After checking her list last night with Buck, more times than she cared to admit, she was positive she hadn't forgotten anything. And of course, they'd have plenty of good, homemade snacks on their drive to Dallas. No question about that.

Lola had it all planned. Get there after lunch, go to her niece Rena's house, get settled quickly, then off to the bridal store as soon as they could to find a dress for Carli. And maybe one for herself. What did she want to wear? She never had the chance at her own wedding. Maybe this time she could wear something real dressy. But the most important mission was to find the right dress for the bride—Carli.

"Finally, girl! C'mon, we gotta get on the road," Lola teased as Carli emerged from her house.

Hair a crazy mess, T-shirt half-tucked in and half out, carrying a silver coffee tumbler, and dragging an overnight bag. "I had to make some coffee,

Lola. I'm not even awake yet," she mumbled.

"Well, just get in and maybe you can take a nap while I drive." Lola stared at Carli's nest of hair. Obviously, a brush had not been a priority this morning.

Carli appeared a little grumpy and probably was not in the mood for talking. That didn't stop Lola who was very excited about the trip. She was on a mission to find the perfect bridal dress.

"We just don't have much time, Carli. Your wedding is fast approaching. Yikes! I don't know about you but I've got tons of things circling my brain. Dress, venue, food, flowers, music, cake, catering. What about bridesmaids? Have you thought of who you'd like to have? Better ask them right away and we'll need to decide on their dresses too. I mean, there is a TON of stuff to do!"

Carli slumped in her seat, hair no better than it was before, sipping on her coffee. "I know, Lola. I didn't get much sleep last night thinking of all of this." Quietly to herself she said, "Maybe we should just elope."

But Lola heard it. "What? No way. Please don't do that. You'll hurt a lot of people. There are townsfolk who are very excited about your wedding and many have volunteered their services."

Carli sipped her coffee and closed her eyes. "Okay," was all she said.

This girl had better not run off to get married.

Lola couldn't understand why Carli wasn't as excited as other young women were about their weddings. As thrilled as Lola had been at that age. But Lola hadn't had the opportunity to plan a big wedding for herself back then. They just were too poor and her parents were against her marrying Buck.

"Carli, you awake?"

"Uh huh..."

"If you don't want to talk about wedding plans, tell me what's going on with Billy Broderick. Your lawyer's been around. Does that mean Billy's reared his ugly head again?"

"Yes. He's appealing the judge's decision when he awarded me sole ownership of the Wild Cow."

"Can he do that? I thought it was a done deal."

"I guess anyone can do anything."

"Billy has always been a stubborn young man. Felt like he never measured up to his father's expectations. And was always trying to prove himself. It just came across as arrogant."

"Did you know him when he was a teenager?"

"Sure. Buck and I came to the Wild Cow when Billy was a kid. He knew your mother too. They went to school together."

It appeared Carli was not slumping in her seat any longer. She looked fully awake and interested.

"Lola, I've got to tell you something." She took another swig of coffee.

Her pained expression told Lola to take it slow. "Carli, you know you can tell me anything. I'm here for you."

"I know, and I appreciate that. It's just kind of hard to talk about. I, myself, haven't figured it all out yet."

"Just say it. Maybe I can help."

Step by step, it came out of Carli's mouth. "I found my birth certificate in my grandparents' boxes. My guardians, the Fitzgeralds, had a copy when I was growing up. But the birth father's name was missing. The one I found in Grandma Jean's papers had the name filled in, in pencil. Taylor Miller. Then, when we had trouble with the rustlers, a special agent came to the ranch with Agent McKinney. His name was Taylor Miller. Said he worked at the Wild Cow when he was a teen. He stared a hole through me like he recognized me or something."

Her eyes were filling with tears. "Did you know Taylor Miller, Lola?"

Not sure where all this would lead, and not wanting to hurt Carli in any way, Lola cleared her throat and paused. But she couldn't lie.

"Yes, Carli, Buck and I knew Taylor. He was friends with Billy and your mother. All three went to school and hung out together. Taylor was a senior, the star quarterback. Michelle was a sophomore. I really liked Taylor, for the most part. He was respectful to me and Buck. He had a rough start with his father who worked the boy from sunup till sundown, and sometimes into the wee hours. Billy Broderick was already working at the Wild Cow. Well, he and his family lived here and were running the ranch. I think Taylor liked his job here and had a little bit more freedom when he got out from under his father."

"With that added freedom, do you think Taylor and my mother got together?"

"Buck and I suspected but couldn't prove it. Michelle had become so wild. I think she got into drinking in high school. She loved to sneak out and party. Sometimes we weren't sure if she was with Taylor or with Billy. She had fun teasing both boys, which only infuriated them. But somehow, after she left, the boys remained friends."

"Why do you think she rebelled so much? Didn't she love her parents?" With a tear forming, Carli asked very quietly, to herself really, "Didn't she love me?"

"Oh, Carli. I'm so sorry for the heartache Michelle caused. Life can be so hard sometimes. God told us it wouldn't be easy. But He's always with us." Lola took one hand off the steering wheel and squeezed Carli's. "Who knows why some teens rebel? Some are angels and some are so strong-willed. And why do some get into drugs and drink? I guess you'd have to be a psychiatrist to answer some of those questions."

Lola continued. "The way I look at it with Michelle is this. Maybe it would help you too. Over the years public opinion has changed a lot about alcoholics. Used to be they were never forgiven for all the heartache they caused. But then medical professionals researched and it was determined that alcoholism is a disease. Those who have it really can't help themselves. It's like any other disease, almost like cancer. Now certainly, they should get help from professionals and many end up kicking their habit. I guess it's the same whether it's alcohol or drugs.

"So, I try to remember, Michelle had a disease. She couldn't help herself. She should have gotten help, but she didn't. Why did she rebel against your grandparents? It could have been any number of things. They were what some might have called 'strait-laced'. They liked hard work and they liked rodeoing. Maybe Michelle got tired of being dragged all over the southwest as a child. Maybe she wanted to party with her friends instead of working hard to win buckles and awards like her parents."

Carli still stared at her lap. "And then she got pregnant with me. And didn't want me."

"Honey, we don't understand Michelle's reasons. She was a teenager, sixteen as I recall. Probably scared. No money, no place to live. Was she influenced by someone? A guy? Was she on drugs or alcohol so wasn't thinking straight? We just don't know. That's why I choose to pray for her, to forgive her."

"I'm trying, Lola." She cleared her throat, then said, "And I'm trying to decide if I want to allow my birth father, Taylor Miller, into my life."

"Do you want to know him?"

"Well, sometimes I wonder if he's a nice man. Do I have any of his traits? And Lola, sometimes I have dreams about him walking me down the aisle."

Chapter 18

Carli

Puffy clouds of beautiful white gowns filled every inch of the exclusive Dallas bridal store, Forever Love. Carli had never seen so many different kinds of material—satin, lace, taffeta, tulle, chiffon, organza. Or such a variety of shapes and designs—mermaid, Cinderella ballgown, trumpet, sheath, tea-length, fit-and-flare, and many more. Different colors, too. Bright white, off white, antique white, nude, mocha, ivory, cream. Nowadays, anything went. Some brides even chose black or any color of the rainbow.

White damask couches and oversized chandeliers made the store cheery and blindingly bright. Cabinets stuffed with dresses lined all four walls of the spacious store, with floor-length mirrors in between. Round, carpeted podiums circled the room.

She gulped in big breaths. *No panic attacks today, please Lord.*

Quietly to Lola, she confided, "I wouldn't know where to start."

Bubbly and full of energy, as she usually was, but

even more so today being in a wedding shop, Lola said, "That's why you've got me. You need to see everything so you can make an informed decision. We'll find your perfect dress, Carli. Don't you worry. Lank might plumb faint away when he sees you floating towards him."

The thought almost made Carli physically ill. She knew this was what most girls dreamt of. Some planned the Big Day from a very young age. They married off their dolls, pretended the proposal, then planned for a house and babies. It's what most little girls thought about. Not Carli.

Is there something wrong with me?

Was it because of her upbringing? Her start in life without a mother?

"Ladies. Have you found anything you like, yet?" Lola's niece Rena slung an arm around her aunt's shoulders.

"Not yet. There's so many to choose from." Carli had gotten to know Rena somewhat when the girl had come to visit Lola and Buck, and was glad now to have someone her age to bounce things off when it came to dress shopping.

Carli watched Lola thumb through the garments and the attendant put her choices in a dressing room. A total of ten bridal gowns hung on the rod and Carli decided to dutifully try each one on. For Lola. To make her happy.

The first dress was extremely modest. High neckline, long sleeves.

"What do you think?" Lola asked. "It's gorgeous. Look at that bead work. Back in the day, I wanted something like this."

"I might get too hot in it." Carli didn't even want

to try it on.

"Okay," Lola said. "Maybe that was more the style when I was a young bride. Let's try another."

Dress number two was at the opposite end of the spectrum, which shocked Carli. The midriff had stiff "bones" like an antique corset and very sheer netting in between. The dip down her back was quite low. As was the plunge in the front showing way too much cleavage.

With a red face, Carli said, "Lola, I don't think this one is appropriate. I could never wear it out in public."

"Show if ya got 'em never seems proper, particularly for a bridal gown," Rena said.

"You're right, Carli. You have such a cute figure, I just wanted you to try it. I've seen this dress in magazines and on television. But it's certainly too revealing. We can still have some fun and you can try on all kinds of dresses. There's no harm in that."

All kinds of dresses? How many more? There was that queasy feeling again.

Rena held out the strapless mermaid style dress. "How about this one? It's pretty."

Many young women had been wearing this style the last few years. But Carli wasn't too sure about it. She didn't really know what she wanted. Just go with it. Try them on, so we can go home, she told herself.

Lola zipped up the back for her. The form-fitting satin hugged Carli's slim figure. She tugged to hold the bodice up. "It's a little big," she said. *Angie would look good in this. She has all the right curves.*

"It can always be taken in," Lola said. "Step out here and let's see it."

Carli looked at herself from all angles in the

mirror as she stood atop a small, carpeted platform.

"I don't know. I feel so exposed."

Lola smiled and followed her back into the dressing room. She unzipped her. "No worries, Carli. Try that poufy one. It's beautiful."

Seemed like Lola said that about every single dress. Beautiful. Gorgeous. Amazing. Lovely. Carli just didn't see what Lola saw.

Rena lifted the heavy Cinderella ballgown down from the hanger. As they helped Carli step into the dress, it nearly swallowed her whole. The white dress had a black sash around the waist, trailing towards the hem, which reminded Carli of a killer whale she had seen on a television documentary. Although the whales were colored in reverse, mostly black with white markings. Suddenly she felt imprisoned like the whales in captivity. Could anyone rescue her? Did anyone care?

Once they got her into the dress, and after she struggled to stay upright, the saleslady handed them giant clips to fasten the back closed. It was about six inches too big for her.

She looked at herself in the mirror and felt like she was the plastic bride on top of a cake. On display. Fake.

"Wow, isn't it gorgeous?" Lola said. "You look like a princess. Remember, Carli, they can alter anything. Don't worry about it being too big."

The room was closing in on her and she prayed she wouldn't be sick all over this mountain of organza and lace. *I'd have to at least pay to have it cleaned.*

She knew Lola and Rena were saying things to each other, probably about how pretty the dress was, but Carli couldn't understand any of their words. Was she drowning? Or lost in a fog? Something was wrong with her hearing. She desperately tried to remember why they were in this strange place, so far from the ranch, trying on frilly dresses. Why? Oh right, for a wedding. Her wedding. To Lank. She loved him. And wanted to be married to him. But this scene that she was trapped in—it was all wrong. She didn't belong here. She couldn't breathe.

She felt herself sway and her head grew fuzzy. She toppled off the platform and the dress swallowed her up. The killer whale had devoured her. Everything went black.

Down, down, down. Like *Alice in Wonderland*. Down the rabbit hole. Where was Lank? Where was Beau? Where was the real Carli?

She looked to her right and saw five girls in mermaid style wedding dresses ready to plunge into a pool of water for a swim. Their dresses turned into fish tails. All were laughing and having a great time. To her left were five other girls in killer whale dresses that filled with air causing them to float upwards like hot air balloons. They were laughing and sipping champagne.

Lola appeared and was wearing a chiffon and lacy wedding dress, veil, and carried a bouquet of flowers. "I'm your fairy godmother, Carli. We *will* find you a dress."

In a cracked mirror, Carli's image was that of a soot-covered Cinderella wearing brown rags. She was scrubbing the floor on her hands and knees. Then the ten brides surrounded her, their laughter reaching higher decibels as it bounced off the walls.

Someone was pushing her shoulder back and forth. "Carli! Carli! Are you okay?" Lola was frantic and sent Rena out of the dressing room to find water and the saleslady who had left before to get more dresses.

Drifting and feeling weightless, Carli heard someone calling her. Was it her mother? Or Mrs. Fitzgerald, her guardian? Were they coming to the wedding? What about her birth father?

She blinked her eyes to come through the fog. Was that petite Lola, her ranch cook and wife of her foreman? Were they at the ranch? And why was she on the floor covered by massive amounts of white material?

"Lola?"

The saleslady and Rena had come into the dressing room.

"Easy, Carli. You must've fainted," Lola said. "We should've had lunch before. I'm sorry. It's almost three o'clock. Here, can you sit up and have a sip of water?"

Rena stepped forward with the water and knelt down to Carli's level.

"Slow, Carli. I'll help you," the niece said.

"Thank you." Carli took a little drink, then pushed herself up to a sitting position. She was enveloped in the white, cloudy material. "Could you help me up, please? I don't want to rip the dress."

They got her to her feet and unzipped the voluminous dress. She breathed easier when they freed her from it, dressed her in a satin robe, and helped her to a seat.

"I'm sorry. I don't know what happened. Did I pass out?"

"You must be hungry. We missed lunch. How do you feel now?" Lola patted her arm.

"I'm a little lightheaded. I think I'd like to leave. Would that be okay?"

"Sure, Carli. Let's go back to Rena's, have an early supper, and later a good night's sleep. We can leave in the morning for the ranch," Lola said.

Carli bent over in her seat and held her head. "I was having the weirdest dream. About whales."

Lola and Rena looked at each other and frowned.

Chapter 19

Carli

"I'm sorry I fainted at the bridal store," Carli said. "I ruined everything."

"Nonsense," Lola consoled her. "It's been an exhausting day. We left the ranch before dawn, drove five hours to Dallas, then jumped into dress shopping, and never stopped for lunch. I guess we took on too much. I apologize if I got carried away. I'm just excited."

Lola's niece, Rena, called both of them over to her small dining table. "It's ready, ladies. I made baked chicken, rice, and broccoli. This should make us feel better. And ice cream and a chick flick later. How 'bout *27 Dresses*?" She giggled.

"Ooh, I don't know. That might give me nightmares," Carli said with a half-grin. "I already dreamt about whales and mermaids when I was out."

All three burst out laughing.

"I guess you don't want to see *Runaway Bride* either." Rena passed the food around the table.

"No," Carli said, "I won't be running anywhere. Unless it's towards Lank."

"Aww, that's so sweet," Rena said. "I hope I find the love of my life one of these days. So far, I've just met a lot of frogs."

"You will, honey," Lola said. "Not to worry. God wants to give both of you the desires of your heart. And when you do meet your husband-to-be, we'll find the perfect dress for you too. What style do you like?"

"Oh, I'm not sure," Rena said. "That strapless mermaid one was really pretty. I'm not sure I have the figure for it though. And I'd have to get a spray tan. I'm so pale. It might not look good against such a bright white dress. Wish I had your skin tone, Aunt Lola. You and my mom's."

More talk about dresses. Wish they'd stop. At this point Carli didn't care if she wore a pair of overalls down the aisle. And then guilt hit her. Everyone was being so nice and helpful, and her attitude was less than stellar. What was wrong with her? Why couldn't she get excited about this wedding? Nothing seemed to fit her personality.

"You're beautiful just the way you are, Rena. God designed each one of us with our own unique look. He never makes mistakes."

Carli loved Lola. She always said the right things. Like a mom. She was spending so much time helping Carli with this wedding. And even though Carli was tired of talking about dresses, she couldn't help herself in continuing the topic, for Lola's sake.

"Lola, you liked that dress with the long sleeves," Carli said. "Is that what you would have wanted for your wedding?"

Rena jumped in. "What *did* you wear for your wedding, Aunt Lola?"

From the forlorn look on Lola's face, Carli was sorry she had mentioned it. But there was no retrieving the words now.

"Buck and I were two young kids with no money. My parents weren't happy about my marrying him. They referred to him as a gringo and thought I could do better. They were poor too so they couldn't help us with a fancy wedding, plus they were against it. We were lucky that Buck had a job at the Wild Cow, and then I was hired too as the cook. So at least we had a place to live with salaries coming in."

Lola's gaze drifted to the window. "I had always dreamt of wearing a beautiful wedding dress, covered in lace, organza, and tulle, lots of ruffles, with a long train that would trail the whole length of the church's aisle. And a long, lace mantilla veil. That was from my Mexican heritage. My grandmother had saved her veil for me in a cedar chest. I used to play over and over in my mind the moment when Buck would lift that veil and kiss me.

"Instead, I wore a white, flouncy, cotton skirt and white, cotton peasant blouse. Buck wore clean, pressed jeans and a starched, white shirt. We went to the courthouse and were married by a judge. The witnesses were strangers we'd never seen before. Just people they rounded up to stand behind us for a few minutes. I think our marriage license cost us two dollars."

"Oh, Aunt Lola, that's sad. I wish you could've had the wedding of your dreams," Rena said.

"God always has a plan and things work out by His will. That's why we're going to pull out all the stops for Carli's Big Day. It'll be the Wedding of the

Century. At least around these parts."

After dinner and ice cream, Rena brought out popcorn and the three curled up on the couch to watch *Mama Mia*.

"Good night, girls. I am so glad that you stayed with me," Rena said as she handed Carli a pillow and blanket.

"We've enjoyed it," Lola said.

"Thanks for everything. It's been fun." Carli agreed. "There is so much to do in Dallas. I'd like to come back sometime."

"You are welcome anytime. There are so many unique restaurants we should try and the discount malls are to die for," said Rena.

Lola slept in the guest room, and that left the couch for Carli. She punched the pillow several times and tried to get comfortable but worry clouded her mind. All those dresses, lace and ribbons, train or no train, bejeweled or plain. And then she had fainted. *Good grief.* They had come all this way and there wasn't one dress that she liked. Not one. What was wrong with her? Poor Lank sure had his work cut out for him in partnering with her for the rest of their lives.

The next morning, after a quick breakfast of hot tea and protein bars, they hugged Rena goodbye and started on the drive back to the ranch. Before they left the Dallas city limits, Lola turned to Carli and said, "There's one more place we should stop, if you feel like it."

The enthusiasm in Lola's voice made her agree although she just wanted to get home and sleep in her own bed. Carli nodded yes, so Lola took the next exit off the freeway and drove to the north side of Dallas. Lola drove through an older neighborhood with tree-lined streets and tidy shopping centers. She parked in front of a small boutique, Marilyn's Bridal Shop.

With a heavy sigh Carli opened the car door and followed Lola inside. It seemed as though she had walked into someone's welcoming living room. The quaint shop's main area had two plush couches covered in a dusty blue and were bookended with marble-topped side tables. There wasn't a wedding dress in sight. Original oil paintings and wall sconces created an intimate atmosphere. The most beautiful chandelier that Carli had ever seen hung overhead and anchored the room.

"How may I serve you, ladies? I'm Marilyn." A matronly woman appeared from the doorway, wearing a mauve-colored business suit, her red hair swept up in a stylish bun.

"We need a dress," said Lola. "Rather, she needs a dress."

"Turn around, dear. Let me look at you. Size four or six, I'd say. Nothing too frilly, is my guess."

Carli smiled. "How did you know?"

"That's my job to know, dear. Please have a seat. Can I offer you a drink? We have coffee, tea, or champagne."

"I'm fine, thanks," said Carli.

"Hot tea would be lovely," said Lola. "Thank you."

"Let me put a few selections in a dressing room for you. I'll be right back."

"Nothing white," said Carli. She crossed her arms and leaned against the counter. She was not going to try on anything frilly ever again.

Lola sat on the couch placing her purse on the

marble coffee table while Carli paced the room. One display case held gloves, another a selection of beaded hats with small veils.

"I have a dressing room available for you now. If you'll come with me, please."

Carli glanced at Lola who shooed her along with a gesture of her hand. She walked through the next room which had wedding dresses hung on all sides, and then into a nice-sized dressing room. There were four dresses hanging across one end and the first one that caught her eye made her call out.

"Lola! Come look at this one." Carli couldn't contain her excitement.

"It's perfect," Lola said as she laid a hand on Carli's shoulder. And it was.

Simple, no frills, no lace, just a smooth sweep of cream crepe with a mermaid silhouette. An off-the-shoulder neckline merged into long sleeves. Cloth covered buttons trailed down the back.

Carli stepped behind the curtain. She could hardly wait to try it on. When she emerged, both Lola and Marilyn gasped. She twirled and the fabric floated around her ankles.

Marilyn stepped forward to tug at a sleeve and had Carli spin one direction and then the next. "No alterations are needed. You look stunning, my dear. Your groom is one lucky man."

Carli felt stunning. A word that had never been used where she was concerned. She could hardly wait for Lank to see her.

"You should try this on, Lola. It's your size too." Carli glanced at Lola and had to take a second look. There were tears in her eyes.

"That is one of the most beautiful dresses I've

ever seen," she said as she wiped moisture from one cheek. "I'm so happy you found it."

With Carli's bank account lighter and her heart much happier, they got back on the road towards home. That last shopping stop took a lot less time than Carli would have ever imagined. Their mood was much improved, and Lola couldn't help singing tunes from last night's movie. Over and over. ABBA had always produced such timeless music.

Thankfully, there was no wedding talk. Carli couldn't hold in her laughter as she listened to Lola burst into song. She actually had a beautiful voice, particularly tinged with the Mexican accent. They had the dress. It would be good to get home.

Chapter 20

Carli

Home. Carli walked across the Wild Cow Ranch compound with her suitcase, purse slung over one shoulder, and several sacks. Shopping in Dallas had been fun, but Lola was exhausting. Where did that woman find all her energy?

Just before Lola had stepped out of the vehicle, she had mentioned that she would check the wedding list and get with Carli to figure out what they needed to do next. Carli wanted to run a hot bath and disappear under the water for a day or two. Instead, she dumped her burdens in the entry hall and hurried over to Lank's trailer house. She had texted him that morning to let him know what time they were leaving. It seemed like an eternity since she'd seen him last.

The savory smell of onions and peppers hit her nose as she stepped inside to see Lank standing in front of his little stove. "Dinner's almost done."

"You cooked for me?"

"Yep." He turned to give her a handsome grin.

Carli could no longer deny herself the physical

need she had for him. She walked up behind Lank and wrapped her arms around his waist, rested her cheek on his back, and inhaled his scent.

"I'm glad you're back," he said.

"Shush. No talking." The vegetables sizzled in the cast iron skillet. She closed her eyes and wished they were married already. To heck with all the stupid details that nobody would remember anyway.

"How was your trip to Dallas?" Lank was never one to relish the silence or be still for very long. She opened her eyes and returned to reality.

"It was busy. Lola kept us on a tight schedule, but she did allow us a side trip to a western store. I got you a few new pearl snaps and I bought a pair of Twisted X's. They're so pretty. Orange and turquoise and black stripes." She couldn't contain her excitement over her new canvas shoes.

"Another pair of shoes? What you've always needed. You've never been that excited about our wedding."

"Ah yes, the wedding." Carli frowned.

Lank removed the vegetables and glanced at her. "Mushrooms?"

"Yes, please."

He added a pat of butter to the pan and two handfuls of mushrooms. They sizzled as he stirred. After they were done, he removed them, and plopped a thick piece of beef into the skillet. Added more butter and olive oil. As it seared, he pulled two plates out of the cabinet overhead.

"Set the table, would you?"

"Sure. What are we drinking?"

"Whatever's in the fridge, I guess."

Carli opened the refrigerator door and saw that

he only had one can of soda so she split it into two glasses.

"What are we eating?"

"Sirloin steak compliments of one of the premiere beef producers in the nation. All natural, hormone-free, grass-raised. You might know of it. A little ole' place called the Wild Cow Ranch," he said with significant lifting of his eyebrows.

"I may have heard of it." She laughed.

After he had seared the steak on both sides, he returned the vegetables to the pan and placed the whole thing in the oven. Looking at his watch, he said," Seven minutes for medium rare. Is that okay with you?"

"Perfect." Carli hadn't eaten much beef in Georgia, but she was acquiring a taste for it now in Texas. Mainly because it was so readily available. That's what their freezer was stocked with, and sometimes she had to think hard about different ideas for dishes. Lola on the other hand could cook a month's worth of meals and never make the same thing twice.

"Grub's on," said Lank as he pulled the iron skillet from the oven. Carli couldn't find a potholder, so she folded a kitchen towel and placed it in the middle of the table. The pan still sizzled when he set it down.

"So, tell me more about Dallas?" Lank poised over the meat with fork and knife, giving her a curious glance.

"It was traffic and people and noise. Typical big city, but I did enjoy being with Lola and her niece, Rena. The more I spend time with Rena, the more I like her."

Lank carefully carved their dinner into two pieces and served her plate with meat and vegetables.

"Lola is so organized. She keeps that wedding planner with her at all times and we have not strayed from the schedule. Everything is in order and coming together. Normally it takes over six months to plan a wedding, so I've been told, but she has less than a month to pull off the most beautiful ceremony the town of Dixon has ever seen." On that last part Carli raised her hands and did air quotes.

She chewed while she studied Lank's handsome face. He concentrated on his food without comment.

"You never did tell me what you want."

"About what?" He gave her a curious glance.

"The wedding. Do you have any input for our wedding?"

He hesitated for longer than she thought was necessary which could only mean that he wasn't sharing what he really thought.

"Lank." She reached across the table and put a hand on his. "Tell me. This is your wedding too."

"No disrespect to you. I love you more than anything, but since my mama can't be at my wedding, I could care less what we do."

"It's hard for me to understand your deep sense of loss since I never knew my real mother. Sure, I miss the Fitzgeralds. They raised me and it would have been important for them to know you, but they're gone. That won't change."

"I just want to get on with our life together. I just want you."

"Maybe we can incorporate some of the traditions from your heritage. Tell me about Mexican weddings. I'm sure you've been to some."

"Yes, several on my mother's side and a few in Mexico City. I just remember a big celebration, and family is everything. After mom died, my sister and I lost touch with that side of the family."

"Tell me more," Carli said.

"Godparents are usually involved."

"Well, let's invite them."

"My aunt and uncle, my mother's brother who I haven't seen in over ten years. They used to send me birthday cards but I'm not even sure where they live. Anyway, it is Mexican tradition that the godparents pay for part of the wedding."

"Really?" Carli had never heard of that before. "What else?"

"Thirteen coins."

"Tell me about it. Keep talking."

"The groom presents his bride with thirteen coins to signify my treasure and all that I own is now partly yours. I am gifting you my wealth."

"Why thirteen?"

"It signifies Jesus and the twelve apostles."

"I really like that one. Let's do that." Carli was excited.

Lank laughed. "Does it have to be pure gold, or can I use the tokens from the arcade?"

"Are you saying time spent at the arcade has more significance?"

"I do have some great memories from the place." Lank chuckled and winked at her.

"If Colton was there too," she said, "I'd rather not hear details. I'm sure it ended with a brawl in the parking lot or something to do with girls. What else?"

"There's the money dance," Lank said. "In exchange for a dance with the bride or groom, guests pin money to their clothes."

"That's nice too."

Lank continued. "The wedding lasso is a long string of rosary beads that is draped around the bride and groom, binding them together for the rest of the ceremony. You know, these types of weddings can last over an hour, but I do remember being inside some of the most beautiful churches I've ever seen. Mexico City is an amazing place."

Carli smiled. "Maybe we can go there and meet your relatives sometime."

"That would be nice. I'd like to show you off to my family."

Carli carried her plate to the sink. "What's for dessert?"

"I definitely have something in mind and you'll like it." He wrapped her in a warm hug and kissed the tip of her nose. "I've really missed you, babe."

"Slow down, cowboy. It's not that long until the wedding."

"I have every intention of treating you with the utmost respect, Carli, mainly because my mother ingrained in me that the future mother of your children deserves no less. Also, out of respect for Buck and Lola. But that's not to say we can't snuggle."

"I'm down for that." The fire in his eyes made her knees tremble as they sank back on his couch. She had always dreamed of a home and now her home was at this man's side.

Chapter 21

Lola

"How did your trip go?" Buck met Lola at the bottom of the stairs, took her bags, and followed her up to their apartment on the second floor of the ranch cookhouse.

"Carli had a panic attack in the bridal gown shop." Lola sank into the leather couch and propped her feet on the table.

"What's wrong with her?"

"Not sure, but you know she's always been a worrier. She has struggled with that her entire life, she said. I guess the wedding details are too much."

"How can we help her?"

"She mentioned they should run off and find a judge."

"If that's what they want to do, they should do it," said Buck.

Lola looked at him with her mouth agape. "No. Every girl dreams of her wedding day. Every girl wants to be a bride. If she eloped, I think she'd regret that decision for the rest of her life." Lola leaned her head back and closed her eyes.

"That's what we did," Buck said quietly. "I think it turned out all right."

She stiffened and studied his face. "I didn't mean that. We did what was right for us at the time. You know I love you."

"And you know that I love you with my every breath. But I have often wondered if you regretted not having that big church wedding." He eased down beside her and stretched his legs on the ottoman.

"I'll admit I think about it sometimes, particularly now that I've been helping Carli."

"No regrets then?"

"None." She leaned her head against his shoulder. "I have to keep Carli on task. If she is too stressed to make the decisions, then I'll just decide for her. We have to keep this moving forward and it will come off without a hitch. You'll see."

"As long as you're not the one with panic attacks too. I hope you know what you're doing," Buck said.

"As I recall, the next thing on my list is an engagement party. The whole town will want to come just because it's Ward's and Jean's long-lost granddaughter. We need a place large enough."

"Who's cooking? I'm not, am I?" Buck looked at her with panic in his eyes. "You didn't volunteer me to grill something, did you?"

"Goodness no. You're not skilled enough to cook for that many people. We'll find a professional, but we don't have much time."

"How about our barn?"

"No. I don't have time to clean up for all those people, besides we're having the wedding out here. That's work enough. But who else has a barn big enough?" Lola stood to retrieve the wedding planner from her bag.

"The county," Buck offered. "We could use the livestock barn where they hold the county fair and livestock shows."

Lola stood and paced to the window and then back. "That would be perfect. Does the county manager owe you a favor?"

"We might work out a deal." He grinned.

"Go to town right now and see him. We don't have much time to plan. I'll get on the phone with caterers and see what I can find. I'll also enlist the call list for the yoga class, and I'll call Belinda at the coffee shop. I probably should call the chamber president too."

Lola held out her hand and helped Buck to his feet, put her hands behind him, and urged him towards the door.

"I'm going," said Buck.

"Call me and let me know what he says."

Buck grabbed his Stetson from the coat tree by the door. "Yes, ma'am."

She kissed him on the cheek.

After the trip to Dallas, Lola's resolve was even more determined. Carli Jameson was going to have the most beautiful wedding this county had ever seen. Lola would make sure of it.

Chapter 22

Carli

"I don't want to go. Men don't have to go to such silly things. It's not fair. Why can't I just say no?"

Lank watched Carli shut the silverware drawer too hard and toss a potholder on the counter like a gung-ho baseball pitcher. He had come over early to join her in a cup of coffee before he got involved in a work project.

"You're cute when you pout. It's the whining I don't think I can take too much more of," he said with a wink.

"I am not whining. It's ridiculous, that's all. Grown women playing stupid games. And me as the center of attention. I don't think I can do it."

"Babe, you just need to change your attitude. Get the focus off of you. Think about the thought-ful ladies who put this all together. Women from church and Lola's yoga class. You know most of them. They love you and are excited about doing this. Let them. Don't rob them of blessing you. It'll bless them in return."

She stared at him and wrinkled her brow, then

smiled. "When did you get all religious, mister?"

"Maybe Buck and Lola have rubbed off on me some." He winked again. "Besides, I have a lot to be thankful for. You said, 'Yes' to becoming my wife. How lucky can a guy get? So come over and give me a kiss before I need to go."

She came to him and let him wrap his arms around her. She could hardly remember what she had been bellyaching about.

"If I'm late," he continued, "my boss'll fire me." He stopped hugging and pushed her to arm's length. "Oh, wait, you're my boss. And if you're gonna be my wife too, well, you can't fire me; now, can you?"

"I'll figure out something if you get too smart alecky. You can bet on that."

Lank planted a strong kiss on her mouth and wrapped her in a vise-like hug. "Now, remember, I don't want my wife-to-be acting like a two-year-old today. You go and enjoy that wedding shower. Make nice with all the ladies and enjoy yourself. That's an order."

"An order, is it? Now who's acting like the boss?" Carli did love him. He was like her compass, always bringing her back to reason. Maybe she was acting childish. But she was *not* going to let them make her play silly games.

"And you're right," she said. "I am acting like a two-year-old, but this shower seems so insignificant when we have the hearing date looming. I feel like I should be sitting next to Del poring over file folders or practicing my testimony."

After giving Lank a final kiss and sending him out into the day, Carli went to her closet. Lola had advised her to wear a dress for the shower. It was scheduled for around noontime, a luncheon, but she had noticed cars and trucks already pulling in at this early hour. She figured they belonged to some of the women who had volunteered to set things up, or put some of their dishes in the oven.

Lola was probably flitting around the cookhouse kitchen in her glory—instructing ladies where to put things, thanking them for coming, and giving so much of themselves. Carli thought of what Lank had said. Don't rob them of a blessing. In other words, the women liked doing all of this for someone they loved, a sendoff of sorts to a young woman at the beginning of her marriage. Carli imagined most of them had been given a wedding shower to start them on their way. And later, a baby shower. Would that be in her future too? She was not going to think about that now.

She spent the next couple of hours piddling from one thing to the next, all the while dreading the wedding shower looming over her thoughts. First, she cleaned and straightened the kitchen. Then a load of laundry. Next, wasted time on social media which she hadn't looked at in a long time. *I haven't been missing anything.* Why did it seem there was always something to worry about? If it wasn't Billy Broderick, it was this silly wedding shower.

Carli looked at the time and realized she might be late for her very own event. Lola would have a fit.

As if Lola could read her mind, Carli's phone buzzed and Lola's sweet, perky face appeared. WHERE ARE YOU? the text displayed.

Oh, geesh.

ON MY WAY, Carli typed into her phone.

She ran to her bedroom where she had placed

a tan dress on her bed. Grandma Jean's turquoise boots were beside it on the floor. A turquoise necklace and earrings would top off the outfit. She would look the part. Smiling bride-to-be. That should please Lola. She just wished her stomach didn't feel so queasy.

As Carli entered the cookhouse, a big cheer and clapping erupted from the crowd. And there was a crowd. All women. Low music was playing. Carli thought it might be, *Here Comes the Bride.* There were decorations everywhere, white streamers, white wedding bells, white cake on the back table, white everything.

"Yay, you're here!" Lola came to her and hugged her shoulders. "We're all so excited. You take the seat of honor." Lola directed Carli to a chair adorned with flowers, paper wedding bells, and more streamers. "We're going to start with some fun games, then gifts and lunch. How's that sound?"

Carli had trouble finding her voice. "Uh, sure, whatever you say, Lola."

"Okay, ladies, let's get this party started." They all whooped and hollered. "We're going to start with our first game, called 'Finish the Bride's Phrase'. You should all have a sheet and pencil at your place. Raise your hand if you don't. And let's take this moment to thank our wonderful volunteers." The whole room made noise clapping their apprecia-tion. "Let them know if you need anything. Now the way this game works is, we'll have Carli fill her sheet out while all of you are completing yours. The lady who comes up with the most answers that are like Carli's will win a great gift. Let's get started!"

Well, now they had her playing games. And what

could she do? She was trapped.

Lola gave her a sheet to fill out and Belinda followed with a basket of pencils.

Carli knew her answers might be unorthodox, but she was not going to give the expected ones.

The secret to marriage is: never giving up on your own dreams.

A match made in: Texas.

True love is: hard to find.

A woman's place is: wherever she wants it to be.

Never go to bed: without caking the cows. Carli laughed at that one. She remembered a time when she forgot this chore.

The honeymoon will be: to be determined. She had no idea.

When in doubt: try something. You have a fifty-fifty chance of being right.

Happy wife: hope so.

Lola decided to read from her own sheet and also held three from the audience. Carli kept her paper but turned it over on the table when she heard some of Lola's and the others' responses.

"This game might've been too easy, ladies. Well, here goes," Lola said. "And if you want to answer along with me, go right ahead."

The secret to marriage is: keep God at the center.

A match made in: heaven.

True love is: a blessing from God.

A woman's place is: with her husband.

Never go to bed: angry.

The honeymoon will be: perfect.

When in doubt: pray.

Happy wife: happy life.

Most of the audience answered with the same

as Lola's.

Carli wrinkled her sheet.

Lola turned to her. "How are we going to pick a winner?"

Carli was silent.

"Well, ladies, we have small gifts for everyone." With a slight frown to Carli, she said, "Let's try another game, shall we? This one is called 'Bride or Groom?' You circle the lips or the mustache on your sheet."

Carli started hers.

Who made the first move? Lank.

Who is the most romantic? Lank.

Who initiated the first kiss? Lank.

Who is the better cook? Lank.

Who is more stubborn? Lank. *Well, okay, me.*

Who is the patient one? Lank.

Lola picked up Carli's sheet before she could crumble this one too. They had a little tug of war, but Lola won. She read through Carli's answers and decided to wrinkle the sheet herself.

"Ladies, maybe these two games were a little lame. So, we have another gift for all of you. The volunteers will pass them out, please." Luckily, Lola and the committee had picked up lots of little gifts from the Dollar Store—note cards, purse-sized sanitizers, pens, markers, candies, hair accessories.

Carli lowered her eyes so as to avoid another look from Lola who now smiled and announced, "We have a special gift for Carli." She handed her a spiral book. "It's a cookbook filled with recipes from all of the ladies to help you with cooking. You might say this was made with love."

Carli's heart warmed. She couldn't believe they

had all gotten together and done this for her. Maybe she should stop being so defiant, so rebellious, and get with the program.

Lola was perfect at directing the "show".

"Ladies, we would like to thank y'all again for coming to celebrate Carli's upcoming wedding. And for your generosity. On that note, if y'all don't mind, we'd like to have Carli open some of your lovely gifts. The volunteers will make sure everyone has enough sweet tea and will also pass around your salads that you can go ahead and start on."

As all heads bowed, Lola's gentle voice floated through the room. "First, let me bless the food. Dear Lord, we thank you so much for your blessings. Thank you for these sweet women from the community who are selflessly giving of themselves to wish Carli and Lank a wonderful beginning to their marriage. Please bless Lank and Carli with many years of health and happiness and may they keep You at the center of their life together. And please bless this food to the nourishment of our bodies, and bless the hands that prepared it. Amen."

Chapter 23

Carli

A few volunteers gathered around Carli and handed her one gift after the other. One lady took notes and kept track of the gift and the giver so that later Carli could write thank you cards to each.

An air fryer. A coffee/latte/espresso machine. Electric knife. A set of bowls with horseshoe and lariat design. She made all the appropriate "oohs and ahhs" sounds, and genuinely was blown away by the kindness and generosity, as Lola had said before, of all of these women. No one in her life had ever done anything like this for her before.

The ladies themselves joined in the "oohs and ahhs" chorus. Some offered their stamp of approval on certain items. "That electric knife will really come in handy at Thanksgiving, carving the turkey. My mama had one, and got me one. They're great," one guest said.

The gifts were truly lovely although Carli wasn't quite sure she would use all of them, plus, where would she stow them? There didn't seem to be room in her grandparents' cramped kitchen which hadn't changed from the 1970s. One day maybe they could remodel. But then Lank had talked about them living in his trailer. *Good grief, he must be kidding.* She'd have to set him straight on that. A thought popped in her head. Maybe they could build their own house.

The gift opening continued as the guests were served finger sandwiches, some with chicken salad, some with beef medallions. There was also a side of potato salad and triangle cut toasts. Ladies were eating and laughing, enjoying themselves.

Carli opened one box containing a toaster and said, "This is great, thank you. I have a crazy toaster with a mind of its own." Everyone laughed.

As she opened a second, third, and fourth box of the same size, all could see a trend developing. Toaster after toaster appeared until there was a row of ten.

Lola came over. "Oh, my. Did one toaster have babies?"

More laughter. But then one lady, obviously a little miffed, said, "The email said she needed a toaster."

"I'm glad only ten of you read that." Lola grinned. "Or else there would have been forty or so toasters. But don't worry, please. It's easy to exchange. And I'm sure that Carli, like me, is so very thankful for your kindness. It's the thought that counts, right?"

The toaster-giving lady smiled. All was forgiven for the email mix-up that didn't confirm the number needed.

As the volunteers were sorting the toasters and other gifts, the door flew open with a bang. A fall breeze ushered in a large woman dressed in clean overalls and shirt, red bandanna around her neck, a long jacket and hat. Toting a large box with a pink bow.

Carli was pleasantly surprised as the woman lumbered closer.

"Miss Vera! I'm so glad you came."

"Wouldn't miss it for the world, Carli girl."

Some of the other women watched a little tentatively, but many seemed to know the new guest, for Vera had quite the reputation in these parts. Carli had first made her acquaintance when Vera's dairy cow, Honey Bun, appeared at Wild Cow Ranch headquarters grazing on the lawn. While trying to locate its owner, Carli found out that Miss Vera was her fence line neighbor.

After their initial meeting, she discovered that Vera's imposing physical presence and mock threatening speech was a complete act. The truth was that Vera was a marshmallow, a big softy for animals and most people, especially her new neighbor from Georgia. That was evident when Vera helped in a search last winter when Carli was lost in a freak snowstorm. Another time she helped her and a neighbor round up a few wayward cows that had broken through a fence. Seems like Vera would give anyone the shirt off her back if they were in need.

She was quirky though, that was for certain. Not only was her yard decorated with skulls and crossbones and threatening No Trespassing signs, but it was also home to a grave marker for her first husband, Archie, the love of her life. Townspeople sometimes remarked about Archie's small stature as compared to Vera's towering figure. But never in front of her.

And there was her bloodhound dog named Snot, whom Carli loved. At their first meeting when Vera claimed the dog would take a bite out of her, Carli knew better. Maybe that's when Vera's respect for the girl grew. She couldn't pull a fast one over her.

Maverick, the young bull that Vera bought from Carli was another funny story. And one time Carli saw a pig coming out of Vera's house. "That's Jimmy Dean," Vera had said. Carli loved this eccentric neighbor, friend now, who had more than once given her advice that Carli had found invaluable.

"Oh, good," Vera said, "you're right in the middle of gift givin'. Here's mine." Vera thrust the box onto Carli's lap.

She fingered the wrapping paper which was decorated with onesies, elephants, and building blocks. Definitely not for a wedding shower. "Oh, uh, babies. Uh, thanks, Vera." Giggles erupted from some of the women.

Vera frowned at them. "You can never plan too soon for the little ones. And Carli, I'm a great babysitter. Kids love me."

Lola intervened. "Well, Vera, first we gotta have the wedding." More giggles.

"Just open the box, Carli. You'll see."

Apprehensive and cautious, Carli slowly lifted the lid off the baby shower-decorated box. Pushing tissue out of the way, she stared at the contents. And wanted to die. She was *not* going to pick that thing up. She was not going to show the other women as she had done with the previous gifts.

But Lola stepped in and grabbed the contents.

"How pretty, Vera." She held up the sheerest, pink nightie with pink fuzziness around the hem and neckline. All of the women sounded with various forms of, "Ooh, la la."

Vera jumped in. "There's another little box, Carli. Open that one too."

Pink heels with a poof of pink fuzz on the top of the toe area. She would never in a million years put those things on. What had gotten into Vera?

Suddenly Vera took center stage. "I gotta tell ya 'bout my Archie. Love of my life. My first husband. He was my prince and I was his princess. He would do anythin' for me. Give me the moon if he could. And my best advice to anyone gettin' married is that huggin' and lovin' keeps things goin'."

The room had grown quiet as all faces turned towards the crazy neighbor in overalls.

"Spice things up, ladies. Don't let things get stale. If you do, that man of yours might just go lookin' elsewhere for his sugar. If you know what I mean." She actually winked at the audience, which prompted lots of giggles.

Carli could feel her face burning bright red.

Good grief. Please make her stop.

Vera took off her hat and jacket and plopped into a seat near Carli.

"Dang!" she said. "I sure am hot. Maybe that's why you're turnin' red, Carli. And I've gotta say—I sure am hungry. Whatcha got to eat, Lola? I can help myself, ya know."

"You just stay put, Vera," Lola said. "We'll bring it to you. You want a little bit of everything? And soon we'll have cake, too."

"Yeah, boy, just keep it comin'. Like I said, I'm

real hungry." Then Vera gave a big laugh. "You wouldn't want to see me hangry."

Carli and all the women couldn't keep from laughing.

Even though this whole affair wasn't Carli's favorite thing to do, and even though one of the ladies just placed a paper plate on Carli's head adorned with ribbons from all the gifts and tied it under her chin like an Easter bonnet, Carli had to admit to herself that she was having some fun. And now that Vera was present, she felt a whole lot more comfortable with a roomful of women.

Lola came over and asked, "Are you doing okay, Carli? Having fun?"

"Yes, I've got to say I am. Thank you, Lola, for everything. I can't tell you how much all of this means to me. I know it was a lot of work for everyone."

"It's our pleasure, sweetie. We just want you to be happy. This is fun for us too. We're a close-knit community, like family really. And if one of us gets married, has a baby, or goes off to heaven, well, the rest of us band together and support one another. You're one of us, Carli. So of course, we'd do all what we can to make you and Lank happy. And just wait till the wedding and reception. That'll be over the top!"

Oh, no.

Just what she was afraid of.

But, she told herself, you've come a long way from Georgia. This is your life now. Embrace it.

Chapter 24

Carli

"Broderick's legal counsel will present you in the worst possible light." Attorney Del Fenwick stood across the dining room table from Carli who sat in the 'hot seat'. They were preparing for the upcoming hearing.

The hot seat being a dining room chair placed several feet from the table. Carli wasn't allowed a notepad or pen, no phone, just her in the middle of the room. A vulnerable spot to say the least, particularly with Del's piercing, emotionless stare. This was serious business and Del was all about getting the facts straight.

"How does making me look bad help him?" Carli yawned and took a sip of coffee. Del had banged on her bedroom door early.

"In my opinion, Mr. Broderick really doesn't have a case. Your grandfather's Will was already probated and you were named heir. The only way he can hope to reverse that is by presenting evidence to the court that you are a fraud. We have to prepare you for any type of question they throw at you. They will try to rattle you."

Carli let out a big sigh. "Honestly, that was so many months ago, almost an entire year. Some days I'm still in shock, inheriting a ranch. I can't believe you found me in Georgia."

"I wish I had located you before your grandfather Ward died," Del said. "It's next to impossible to unseal records when the mother gives up her rights. The Fitzgeralds never legally adopted you. They just maintained custody, so I was finally able to get their name on Ward's behalf. Even then it took me a long time to find you, with the help of the detectives. It would have been wonderful for him to see you, and for you to meet him."

Carli blinked a few times as if to gain focus. "My life has always taken strange turns, but I guess that winding path got me here. Buck and Lola have both mentioned that Jean and Ward spent a lot of money trying to find me."

"They never had *me* on the case."

Carli realized that Del's confidence and arrogance were comforting in a way. It was good to have someone with her abilities on her side.

"And after so long," Del said, "I think they gave up until Jean passed and Ward became determined again. He and Billy didn't see eye to eye, but I'm not sure why."

"I have no doubt."

"I'm glad you showed me that birth certificate you found."

"Do you think it's valid?" Carli asked.

"I do and I did some research on Taylor Miller. Do you want to know what I found?"

"I guess so. Yes."

Carli recalled with full clarity when she had almost knocked the man down at the post office. Surprise had flashed in his eyes, and then his expression softened and was an emotion on his face she could not interpret. On the drive to Dallas with Lola, Carli kept replaying that incident in the post office over and over in her mind. She had wanted to tell Lola about it, but she listened to Lola rattle on and on instead. The moment seemed too personal to share and the expression on his face so intense. Maybe because she looked so much like her mother and grandmother, as everyone kept reminding her? Or was it something more? Still, the thought that he might have known about her and did nothing was a truth she could not bear to realize.

Del queried, "You didn't want to know anything about your mother, but you do about this man?"

"My mother's story is tragic. I realized at an early age that she would never be a part of my life. She made that decision for me. Maybe my birth father never knew about me either. But I have to take the chance that we could become a family. I just have to figure out the best way to approach him."

Del looked over her glasses at Carli. "I did confirm what you told me earlier. He works as a district supervisor for the Texas Cattle Raisers, of which you already know. He lives in Amarillo with Karissa, his third wife, and they have a daughter Shayla. He has an older son from another marriage, Hud."

"Yes, I did meet him when we were having trouble with rustlers. How does knowing more about my birth father help the case?"

"The man who is suing you, Billy Broderick, has listed Taylor Miller as a character witness.

Mr. Miller will be present at the hearing," Del explained. "This all may come to light at that moment. You should prepare yourself."

"I don't understand how Billy still has a claim on the Wild Cow since I was declared the heir."

"Billy has what we call 'standing'," Del said, "because he was listed in your grandma Jean's Will. Billy's mom and Jean were best friends. As you already know, the two families lived and worked together on the ranch. Billy's grandfather practically raised your grandmother before she married Ward. When they had your mother, that knocked Billy out of inheriting. The Brodericks were never owners, just best friends of the owners."

Carli was quiet for a second, then said, "That would explain why Billy had always assumed he would inherit. And then my mother disappears. How convenient."

"Interesting case. I'll say that much."

Carli said, "I just remember how angry he was at the hearing when my grandfather's Will was read. Mr. Broderick did not hide his hatred towards me."

"That hatred has not gone away, no doubt. Your grandfather had the right to change his Will, and he did. He left Billy out and named you as his sole heir. I can only imagine the shock for a man who had been cut off from a place where he had spent his whole life."

"He will never forgive me. Can we reach a compromise?" Carli asked.

"Under the law, no. The only way to overturn Ward's wishes is by a lawsuit. Billy can't claim ownership just because he feels it's unfair or he's been left out."

"This is going to get ugly, isn't it?" Carli asked.

"I'm afraid so. That's why you need to be cool, calm, and prepared for any questions they may throw at you. We are going to practice. Are you ready?"

"May I refill my coffee?"

"No."

Carli smiled at her response, and then realized Del wasn't joking. "No coffee. No breakfast. I can't even imagine how you are in court."

"I'm a junkyard dog in court." Del didn't smile.

"Who's a junkyard dog?" Lank asked as he walked in, the front door slamming with a bang behind him. "Mornin', babe."

He leaned down to kiss Carli's cheek.

"My attorney is the junkyard dog. Thank goodness."

"I guess the lawsuit is fast-approaching," Lank said. "Can I help?"

Del cleared her throat loudly. "I don't take anything for granted when preparing for a case, and I don't assume to know what the other side is going to present. We need to be ready for anything."

"Bring it. I'm ready." Carli sat up straight.

Lank plopped into a chair next to Del, both faces staring at Carli. She felt like squirming, plus she needed food and more coffee. Everything seemed to be adding to her discomfort. Was that by design on Del's part?

Del began firing the questions. "Did you ever meet your grandfather Ward?"

"No. Wait. I may have met him when I was about ten or so. My guardians took me on a vacation across the southwest and we stopped at a ranch in Texas. It wasn't until many years later when I first arrived at the Wild Cow that I recognized the house. I think it's where we stopped."

Del almost snapped. "Don't offer too much information, Carli. Just answer one question at a time."

"Okay. Let me try that again. Yes, I may have met my grandfather Ward when I was ten years old but I'm not sure it was him."

Del volleyed another one. "You don't remember any names or where you were?"

"No."

Lank interjected. "If Carli had met Ward and Jean at one time, why couldn't they find her again?"

"She disappeared with her guardians," Del answered. "The records were sealed."

Carli did not reveal her thoughts out loud, but she always wondered if the Fitzgeralds did not want her to be found. Their behavior in all of this had always left a nagging curiosity in her mind, but she couldn't make any sense of it.

Another question from Del. "Were you aware that your grandfather had died?"

"No. I was not."

"When did you find this birth certificate?" the attorney asked.

"After I had inherited the Wild Cow Ranch and was going through some of my grandparents' things."

"Had you ever seen your birth certificate before?"

Carli answered, "Of course, but it only listed my mother. The birth father space was blank."

"Great. Let's keep going. If you hesitate too long in your answers, it may seem as though you are lying." Del asked a variety of questions about her life in Georgia, where she worked, her equine business, her horse training and riding clients, and her acquaintances. Carli answered as clearly as she could, with no hesitation or bobbles.

"I think you'll do fine. Let's take a break." Del turned her focus back to a stack of papers and her notes. Carli stood to make a fresh pot of coffee and rummage through the fridge. Lank followed her into the kitchen.

"Learning more and more about you. I like it," he said.

"There's not a lot to know. Some of it is still a mystery."

"Doesn't matter. I want to know it all." He wrapped his arms around her and she settled into his warm hug. Sometimes it felt good to know that someone was on her side.

A knock on the door resulted in Lola calling out, "It's me. Can I come in?"

Carli peeled away from Lank, peeked her head around the corner from the kitchen, and smiled. "Of course."

Lola had one foot inside the door, walked towards Carli, and into the kitchen. "Let's go shopping."

Carli's spirit fell. *Not more wedding stuff.*

"I can tell by the look on your face it's not the best idea you've heard this morning, but it's not wedding stuff. I promise."

Carli poured her coffee and raised an eyebrow in doubt at Lola.

"Okay, it is wedding stuff in a way, but I need a new dress to wear."

Carli called out into the dining room. "Del. Why don't you come with us?"

"Am I invited?" Lank asked.

Without hesitation both Carli and Lola answered. "No."

"Thank goodness. Bye, babe." Another peck on the cheek and he disappeared out the back.

"I can't go," Del said.

"You need a break too." Carli tried to persuade her.

"I'm sure we can find a neon orange something to match that shade of your hair. It's going to look fabulous," said Lola.

"I have to drink my coffee first." Carli could tell by the look on Del's face that it wouldn't take much to convince her to get into the car. She had been spending a huge amount of time on the lawsuit, although she had been working on other cases too while she was here.

"Okay, but hurry up." Lola offered, "Lunch is on me. Be ready in thirty."

Chapter 25

Carli

Carli's head was spinning. She did not want to go back to court. That stupid Billy Broderick. Why couldn't he leave her alone and stay out of her life? This was all settled a year ago when he took her to court the first time, or so she thought.

What if he won this time? From what Buck and everyone had told her, Billy wasn't the most honest person around. Del had said that he and the judge were good friends. Would he resort to buying off the judge to get his way? Then where would that leave her? And what about Lank? Buck and Lola? Would they all still have jobs if the Wild Cow became Billy's? Would Carli have to go back to Georgia?

The wedding was important to her but the shopping and details seemed so insignificant when compared to the pending lawsuit. One bang of a judge's gavel could change her life forever. They would all be tossed out on their ears.

It was too overwhelming to think about. Maybe it would do her some good to get out, go shopping with Lola and Del. Wait, what was she saying?

"I'm not going to be good company, Lola. Got too much on my mind about the court case. Can't even think about shopping until we get this hearing behind us."

"Oh, c'mon, Carli. You've got to let it go. It'll work out. I'm praying about it."

I am too. But God doesn't seem to be listening. Her mind was in such a turmoil. Some days she felt like screaming and other days she wanted to curl up in her bed and never leave it. But how could she deny Lola's sincere face, and then she had to mention the praying part. Lola was doing so much to give her and Lank a grand wedding.

Carli and Del piled into Lola's car, which seemed to be getting more use than usual with all the wedding errands lately.

"I need a dress for the wedding," Lola said. "The ladies at church told me about an upscale shop in Amarillo called Mariah's. Carli, maybe you can find something to wear to your engagement party. And Del, we'll find something in your color scheme."

On the drive there, Lola babbled about all the wedding tasks she'd been working on. They didn't have that much time left to go before the grand day.

Carli half-listened. She either stared out the window or looked at her phone, checking email, texting back and forth with Lank.

Then Lola switched topics to the style of dress she was thinking of for herself. Maybe a pastel coral color. Chiffon? Something floaty. Off the shoulders. Would that be appropriate for the season? A fall wedding right before Thanksgiving.

When they pulled into the parking lot of Mariah's, Carli checked out the expensive cars—Lexus,

Mercedes, Range Rover, and others, including a few shiny trucks with fancy, chrome hubcaps. This was Texas after all.

As they entered the boutique, a middle-aged woman greeted them with a "Welcome, ladies" to Lola, but an up and down look to Carli who was dressed in her best, dark jeans. And Del didn't receive a friendly nod either.

Great. I already want to leave. This was not Carli's favorite thing to do, that was for certain.

"May I assist you with anything in particular today?"

Lola smiled. "I need a dress for her wedding. Maybe coral-colored. But I'd like to look at everything to get ideas. We might also need bridesmaids' dresses. Not sure yet."

"And maybe a blouse for me," Carli piped up.

The woman gave her a squinty-eyed stare. "I'm afraid we don't carry casual clothes or blue jeans." She said *jeans* like it was a disease and shook her head as if Carli was a child. Del got closer to the woman and glared.

Before Carli's frown grew to fill the whole room, Lola stepped in. "We could start with fancy dresses for me, please." And then to Carli, "You might see something for the party."

The saleswoman's lips were officially pursed now and Carli gave her the up and down appraisal. *Maybe she has a gastro problem.*

"I'll ask one of our younger associates to assist." Without even saying a word, she nodded her head and a pretty, dark-haired, young woman came over. Carli watched the girl swiftly tuck a cellphone into her jacket pocket, which prompted a laser stare from the older woman.

Then to Lola and Carli, Ms. High and Mighty said, "She knows all the latest trends and will be happy to help you." To the pop star lookalike, she instructed, "Show them designers Madelaine and Francesca. Any questions, find me."

Carli wondered if they had been pawned off on the junior associate, not worthy of the seasoned pro.

Ms. Pop Star smiled and said hello to the group. To Lola, she asked, "Are you the mother of the bride?"

Laughter sparkled between Lola and Carli, and Carli answered, "She may as well be. But technically, no. She's not my mother."

The young woman flipped her long, straight hair to one side, and lifted a pointy, manicured tip. "Follow me, please." She proceeded to gather dresses from different areas. Green satin. Blue brocade. Black and red sequins and taffeta.

Lola's face was blank, but she fingered the gowns and politely said, "Nice."

Carli coughed. Actually, nearly choked.

"These are not right at all. Black and red?" Carli was surprised at her own boldness. "We told your, uh, boss, is she? We told her we were looking for coral-colored chiffon. Do you have anything like that?"

She liked how Del gave her a secretive thumbs up, but also told herself that she needed to settle down and not allow her face to turn beet red. But she just couldn't believe it. Who were these people? She would never come into this kind of store on her own. But now she was determined to make sure they were listening to what Lola wanted in a dress. Or she'd walk out and drag Lola with her.

After her morning of stressing about the court

case and role playing with Del, these prissy sales-women had better take her and Lola seriously. And the way the first woman had glared at her because she was wearing jeans. She and Lola, Del too, were as good as anybody else. Even if they weren't driving some fancy car or sporting fake nails.

The young woman cleared her throat. "I'm sorry. She did not convey that to me. I'll find the color you want. Why don't you have a seat right here near the dressing rooms. I'll be right back."

Lola and Carli made themselves comfortable on a sage-colored couch as Del stood behind them like a sentry.

"This is a pretty color too." Lola stroked the velvety couch material.

"Lola, you want coral. And that's what we're going to get for you."

"Now, don't get upset, Carli. This is a process. Let's try to enjoy ourselves."

Ms. Pop Star returned with half a dozen coral-colored dresses and hung them in one of the rooms for Lola.

"Ooh, pretty. Thank you. I'll try on the first one."

The girl said, "If you need my help, just let me know. What size shoe do you wear? I'll bring some heels for you to wear with the dress. When you're ready you can stand on the podium out here in front of the tri-fold mirror."

"That would be great. Size six shoes, please."

Carli peeked in the large dressing room. "That color looks so good on you, Lola. I'll get the shoes."

She was still on her guard as the girl got closer. Carli held out her hand. "Thanks. I'll give them to her."

Passing the tan, medium heels to Lola, she said, "That's pretty, Lola. Were you thinking fall colors when you came up with coral? Or is that one of your favorites?"

"Both, I guess. I wonder if we should go darker for fall. Like rust?"

Ms. Pop Star stood right outside the dressing room door and looked at Lola in horror. "I can show you fall weddings on my tablet and we can order whatever you want. But there is no such thing as the color rust for a dress. How gross. We call that burnt orange and it would look really nice on you. And you can go light or dark. It's up to you, whatever you like."

Lola came out still wearing the first dress. "I'd love to see other options, but we may not have time for an order to arrive."

Carli chided herself and decided to not call the girl Ms. Pop Star in her mind anymore. She appeared to be trying harder to help them. Even if she did have pointy, long nails.

Lola and the girl sat together and reviewed the photos, with Carli now peering over the couch from behind them. Not exactly her thing, but she decided to be calm.

"I see what you mean. They're showing rust but in all different shades, light to dark. See Carli?" Lola seemed happy looking at the fashions.

The salesgirl gasped.

"Burnt orange, I mean," said Lola, a hint of humor laced her comment.

"Uh huh." Carli looked at the time on her phone but willed herself not to say anything that would ruin Lola's moment.

"You've been very helpful," Lola smiled at the girl next to her on the couch. "What did you say your name was?"

"Oh, sorry, I may have forgotten to introduce myself properly. It's Shayla."

Lola quietly stared. "Did you grow up in this area, Shayla?"

"Oh, yes, my dad grew up in the little town of Dixon. And my mom is from Amarillo. My last name is Miller. Do you see anything that you like?"

That got Carli's attention and her head whipped around. Suddenly Del had reappeared after having wandered off, looking quite interested in everything the young girl had to say.

Lola's voice raised an octave. "Shayla Miller? Oh, my goodness. I know your father. He used to work at the Wild Cow, didn't he? Years ago. It was before you were born, so you may not know about it. We are all from the Wild Cow Ranch near Dixon."

"Yes, he did. He has told me about his cow-punchin' days many times." She laughed.

"Taylor Miller. I was going to say I haven't seen him in years," Lola said, "but actually I saw him a few days ago. He came to visit us at the Wild Cow. It's you I haven't seen in some years, Shayla. Probably since y'all moved to Amarillo. You were just a little girl then. How old are you now?"

"Twenty-two."

"And don't you have a brother?"

"Yes. He's older. Hudson."

Carli thought she might faint or possibly throw up. She was having an out of body experience, like in a dream. She was watching the two of them converse, but she felt invisible. Taylor Miller had visited

Buck and Lola at the Wild Cow? When was that?

Was this her half-sister? Del had mentioned earlier about possible siblings. And now, here she was, facing a young woman who could be family. And there could be a brother. A father. And step-mother.

Lord, help me to hold it together.

Chapter 26

Taylor

"Taylor, it's important to me. I've made an appointment for us. Will you please meet me there? Five o'clock."

Good grief. He would rather not talk about private things with the church pastor. But seemed he had no choice. Karissa had been upset for days about Carli possibly being his daughter. If he told her no and didn't join her for the appointment, that would only make matters worse.

"All right. I'll wrap things up at the office and will meet you at five."

"Thanks, hon."

Taylor liked Pastor Jeff and remembered when the somewhat overweight man had shared with the congregation about working on his diet over the summer. "Fellowship and eating are occupational hazards," he had said.

Karissa was already seated in the pastor's office. They were smiling and sharing something funny when Taylor walked in. He shook Jeff's hand. "Looking good, Pastor. How ya been?"

"Thanks. I've been working at it. Darlene keeps me on the straight and narrow."

"It seems God created Darlene to be a pastor's wife. Everyone loves her," Karissa said. "I am blessed that she's my friend."

"Yes, she is definitely the force that keeps me going. Please," he said to Taylor, "have a seat. Would you like water? Or I may have some old coffee left." He chuckled.

"Water would be great." Taylor accepted the plastic bottle.

"Who wants to start?"

"I gave you a little background, Pastor," Karissa said, "on the phone, but here's a recap."

Taylor shuffled in his chair trying to get comfortable.

"It seems that Taylor may be the birth father of a young woman in Dixon, a prominent ranch owner. He just found out."

"But it's not definite. Just a suspicion," Taylor emphasized.

"How does that make you feel, Karissa?" the pastor asked, and looking to Taylor, said, "I'll ask you the same soon."

Karissa rubbed her hands together as if they were cold. "I guess I'm confused about how I feel. I almost feel like it's a betrayal."

"I was an eighteen-year-old boy." Taylor didn't want to come off as combative. "It happened twenty-eight years ago. I didn't even know about it until a few days ago. It's a shock to me, too. But I have to say it again, nothing's definite."

"Karissa, please continue," the pastor moved them along.

"Our son Hud, whom I love very much, is a product of Taylor's first marriage."

"And there was a second marriage before you, Karissa. Is that right?"

"Yes." Her eyes lowered.

"What are your feelings? Do you hold these past transgressions against Taylor? Maybe I should call them life experiences." The pastor had a gentle, non-threatening way about him.

"That sounds a little harsh. I love Taylor. And I try to forgive and forget things that happened in his past. But now here's something else popping up. Will there be others? And how will it affect our current life? We've been happy with our two kids. It was a struggle at first. Hud came into our home when he was very young. We've had to work hard to reach this point."

Pastor Jeff's voice was even and calm. "Karissa, you know God told us life wouldn't be easy. Seems there's always a new challenge for us. Maybe He wants to see how we'll handle things. We can't have perfect lives, the way we want them to be. And the times when we think they're close to being perfect, don't hold your breath because it's pretty much a guarantee that things won't stay perfect. It's as though surprises are waiting right around the corner."

Karissa was silent for a few seconds and she clenched her hands together. "I guess you're right," she almost whispered.

"Taylor, what about you? What do you think of this new possibility in your lives? Another child. From your past."

Taylor cleared his throat. "Pastor, you know

I work as a special ranger with the Texas Cattle Raisers—cattle rustling and other rural crime. I deal in facts. We might be jumping the gun talking about all of this. Wonder if she's not my child? Seems like we should wait until we have one hundred percent proof."

"You're right, Taylor. But for just a few minutes would you be open to talking in the hypothetical? And instead of facts, could we talk about feelings? What if this young lady is your daughter? How would that make you feel? Do you think it would cause a problem in your family? With your wife and kids."

Taylor moved his head around trying to relieve the stress that was accumulating in his neck.

"It's a shock, for sure," Taylor said, "wondering if maybe this girl is my daughter. And it brings all kinds of memories flooding back. I did care for her mother. A lot. This girl looks exactly like her."

He turned to Karissa. "But that was over thirty years ago. I have my family and I love them very much. Nothing will ever change that."

Karissa's eyes glistened and she took hold of Taylor's hand.

Pastor Jeff asked, "Is there anything else you're feeling, Taylor? What about the girl? Would you like to know about her?"

"Well, I have been thinking about some things. I understand she didn't have a mother or father growing up. Her mother died. She had foster parents but they were older and then passed away. For a lot of years, she was left on her own. That just breaks my heart. I think of our daughter Shayla who's almost the same age. Shayla's been given a lot. But wonder if things were reversed, if she didn't have any parents, any family?"

Karissa still held his hand and her eyes misted. Quietly she said, "And now the girl is getting married."

"Oh. And who's gonna walk her down the aisle?"

"I don't know. I wonder," Taylor said.

"Karissa, did your father walk you down the aisle?"

She reached for a tissue. "Yes, he did. He was a good father, a good man. He worked hard and gave us everything imaginable. Everything money could buy. I miss my daddy."

The pastor asked, "Karissa, do you think you could be comparing things to your upbringing, to your father? Maybe you want the perfect homelife, perfect kids, perfect husband?"

"I guess it's possible. But Taylor is a good man also."

"Yes, he is," the pastor said. "But your daddy didn't have children by two other relationships. Maybe somewhere down deep you're holding your parents' marriage as the gold standard, something to aspire to. I'm just saying it's possible.

"Right now, you both have a lot to think about. This could be a big development in your lives, if it turns out to be true. God tells us more than three hundred times in the Bible not to fear, which could also be equated to worry. So, we don't want to waste time on that. But He also gave us a brain and a heart. To figure things out, to try to make wise choices."

Pastor Jeff continued. "I think the best advice is to remember that you love each other. You love your family. It should be unconditional; the way Jesus loves us. Don't hold past mistakes against each other. None of us are perfect. We're trying, but life can be really hard. All we can do is rely on God to walk with us through the storms. And not only are we to love each other and our family, but we're also to love others. What about this young girl? Could she use your help in some way? That's what we're supposed to do. Help and love others. Even our enemies. That's a pretty tall order, I know.

"Now before I pray for you, I'd like you to do something. Look at each other and say one or two sentences about how you feel about this situation. It doesn't have to be fancy or perfect. Just heartfelt."

Pastor Jeff looked at Karissa to start.

She held Taylor's hands and the misty eyes started again.

"Taylor, I'm sorry. I love you. I will strive not to be upset or judgmental about this young woman. I want to support and help you figure this out. For you, our marriage, and our family."

Then it was Taylor's turn. He wasn't used to this sharing feelings business, but wanted to try. He would block out the pastor's presence and pretend he was alone with Karissa in their bedroom.

"Karissa. I love you too. And I love our kids. I'm sorry this thing came up from my teenage past. I would never want to hurt you in any way. I need your help and hope you'll stand by my side. Together we can deal with anything."

Pastor Jeff said, "Thank you both for that. Let us pray."

They all bowed their heads and the pastor asked God to protect and guide Taylor and Karissa and their family. He also asked for guidance with the

Carli situation. However it turned out, whether or not she really was Taylor's daughter, the pastor prayed that this family would keep God in their midst for His ways were better than their own.

After thanking the pastor—with a hug from Karissa and a handshake from Taylor—the Millers drove home, still holding hands.

Chapter 27

Taylor

Entering their kitchen from the garage, Taylor and Karissa were greeted by Shayla who was filling a bowl of salad.

"Hey. Where you guys been?" she asked.

Karissa said, "We had a meeting. What are you making? I can cook some chicken."

"I'm good."

"Well, I need to make something for Dad and me anyway. How was your day?"

"It was good," Shayla said. "Helped a nice bride. Well, actually, her friend who was really sweet. I only say that because the bride seemed very nervous, weirded out. Plus, they kept asking to see rust-colored dresses. Can you believe that? Who says that?"

"What an odd color for a wedding, but since it's November it might work," said Karissa. "I would have never thought of it."

"Besides, it's called burnt orange or paprika. It seemed like they were there forever trying to decide."

Karissa said, "I know customers can be aggravating sometimes, Shayla, but if it weren't for your customers, you wouldn't have a job. I know that you did your best to be kind."

"I tried." Shayla stuffed her mouth with salad and chewed. "It was sad that the bride-to-be didn't have her mother with her. I just can't imagine planning my wedding without you, Mom."

"I'll be all over your wedding, believe me." Karissa gave her daughter a kiss on the cheek. "But you better make sure he loves you and treats you right."

"Okay, sure, Mom, whatever. Anyway...the bride's friend was like a mother substitute, I guess. It just seemed odd because we always get so many mothers and daughters who come in to look at gowns for themselves and their bridesmaids. Oh, and she said she knew you, Dad."

Taylor hadn't really been listening all the way as he poured himself a beer. He turned around and said, "What? Who knows me?"

"The kinda-sorta mother of the bride that I helped today. Lola from the Wild Cow Ranch. Said she knows you, and that you came to visit there recently."

Karissa dropped the silverware she was placing on the table and looked at Taylor as it made a clang. He had already told her about his visit to the Wild Cow when he had talked with Buck, but to know that Shayla had come face-to-face with Carli, it kind of shook him. And obviously Karissa too.

"Did she say anything to you?" Karissa asked.

"Of course, she did."

"What did she say?"

"What do you mean, Mom? I helped her pick

out a dress."

"Is she a nice young lady?"

Shayla's eyebrows pinched together. "Young? I wouldn't exactly call her young. Ask Dad. He knows her."

Karissa's face went white.

"She worked at the Wild Cow when Dad worked there." Shayla popped a piece of lettuce into her mouth.

Taylor wasn't sure what to say so he stood still and watched his wife. He realized Karissa was thinking of Carli and Shayla must be talking about Lola.

Shayla made a scrunched expression. "Why are y'all acting so weird?"

"We're not acting weird," Karissa said. "I just wanted to know if you helped the bride pick out her dress and was she a nice young woman."

"Noooo," their daughter said. "I wasn't helping the bride. I mean she was there. But I was helping Lola, the older woman. She picked out a burnt orange-colored dress. She wanted coral at first, but then decided to go with the darker shade. She was real nice. I didn't talk much to the bride. She didn't try anything on. She wore jeans and my boss about had a conniption because she thinks we should only appeal to a certain level of clientele. I'm not sure if the bride was that comfortable in our store. They also had another woman with them, real tall, neon-colored hair. My boss had given her and the bride a strange look when they first came in. Remember I told you she can be real stuck up?"

"Shayla, try to remember not to judge people. Maybe your boss was having a bad day," Karissa said.

"Well, she must be having a bad day every day

since that's kind of her normal look," Shayla said.

Taylor tried to suppress a laugh but couldn't quite keep it in.

After quickly cleaning up the kitchen, Shayla and Karissa went to their bedrooms.

Taylor tried to watch the television news but worry seeped into his thoughts as to how Carli would blend with his family. Life was getting complicated.

Later in their bedroom, Karissa said, "Thanks for going tonight, Taylor. It helped me to talk with Pastor Jeff about the situation. I hope it helped you too."

"Yeah, it did, darlin'. I've always liked Jeff. He's a straight shooter. I never want to do anything to hurt you. I hope you know this has been a shock for me too. It blindsided me really. But it'll be easier if we can handle it together."

She pulled a nightie from her dresser and laid it on the bed. Before changing out of her clothes, she walked over and kissed her husband's cheek.

"Of course, hon. We're in this together. For the long haul." She winked, then said, "And don't you forget it, mister," with a chuckle.

Taylor kissed her. "Tomorrow I think I'll call the lawyer and get some advice." He filled Karissa in on Carli's background. "It would be good to get the facts rather than just speculating on our own. What do you think?"

"That's a good idea, hon. Better to know the truth. Keep me posted. And, of course, I'll be praying."

"Thanks for being sweet about this, Karissa. I know it was upsetting at first. Still is."

Karissa gathered her hair up into a clip. "I just don't know how the kids are going to take it. What should we tell them? 'Guess what, kids? Here's your new sister.' Half-sister, that is."

"I don't know, darlin'. Once we get the facts, let's just all sit down and we can explain the story."

"I can just see that." Karissa shook her head. "All those times we've disciplined Shayla, Hud too, about staying out late or hanging with the wrong kids, the troublemakers. Now we're going to tell them you got your girlfriend pregnant when you were a teenager?"

Taylor gave her a sheepish, quiet stare.

"I'm sorry, hon. I don't mean to be harsh," she said. "I'm just imagining what might go through their minds."

"Well, it is what it is, Karissa. We're just gonna have to take it one day at a time."

He took her face into his hands and looked directly into her eyes. "I really appreciate your support. I know this is a difficult situation for us to deal with."

"We'll get through this, Taylor," Karissa said as she hugged him.

Chapter 28

Taylor

Early the next morning Taylor made a call and set up an appointment to see his lawyer James Harrington, an old friend.

Once at the high-rise office building in Amarillo, Taylor checked in with the receptionist who was pretty and blonde, with a bright smile.

"Yes, sir, I'll let him know you're here," she said. "Please have a seat. His assistant can bring you coffee, if you like, back in his office. Will that be okay?"

"That'll be just fine. Thank you."

The reception area was opulently decorated with mirrored walls, oil rubbed bronze accents, wood, tile, brick, and plush leather couches. Behind the receptionist was a gurgling fountain and a bronze statue of a bucking horse suspended over the water.

Taylor had been to this office a few times during the decades of his relationship with the lawyer, but mostly conducted his business over the phone. When he surveyed the décor, Taylor imagined money pouring in through a fire hose from all the clients.

He'd only been on the couch a minute or two

when his friend appeared wearing a Texas-sized smile and an Armani suit.

The two greeted each other with strong hand-shakes and pats on the back, then headed to the attorney's office.

"How're ya doin', buddy? It's been a while. Trackin' down any more rustlers?" the lawyer asked with a big laugh.

Taylor would never forget his friend's contagious laugh—it was the same as when they had been on the high school football team together. Back then "Big Jim" had solid muscles, a kind heart, and a con-stant laugh. Taylor thought the man hadn't changed much, but also knew that Jim could be a dangerous opponent in the courtroom.

"Yeah, those guys have been put away," Taylor said. "Now it's back to the same old grind. Break-ins, equipment theft."

"And how's that beautiful wife of yours?"

"Karissa's good, staying busy. Her decorating business is taking off. Still don't know why she's with me."

Jim let out a whoop, one loud cackle, and nodded.

"How's Bonnie?" Taylor asked.

"Too good for me. Ain't that the way it is? We don't deserve these ladies." More laughter from Jim. Seemed it was his default personality expression.

After the assistant poured coffee from a station at the back of Jim's office, Taylor sank back into a leather chair and crossed one leg over his knee.

Behind his big desk, the lawyer asked, "So what brings you here, Taylor? You've got another kid? Is that what you said on the phone?" Jim laughed, then sipped his coffee.

Taylor gave him a blank look.

"All right, I'll be serious and put on my lawyer-ing hat. Tell me all about it."

Taylor started his story. "Well, come to find out there is the 'possibility' that my teenage girlfriend, Michelle Jameson, had a baby, unbeknownst to me...well, I knew she had a baby after she ran away, but I didn't know that maybe I had fathered it."

"That's a lot of qualifiers, Taylor. Possibility, maybe, unbeknownst. I didn't know you used those five-dollar words. Do you even know what 'unbeknownst' means?" Again with his laughs.

Then it was like a switch went off and James Harrington became the attorney the fancy office declared he was. "Okay, sorry. So, what is it you want to know? Whether you have any claim to the Wild Cow Ranch? I heard that your friend Billy Broderick has filed an appeal in that case. So now you want in on it too?"

"No, nothing like that," Taylor said. "Carli Jameson is an adult and I believe she's the rightful owner of her ranch. I'm not claiming anything. What I want to know is how do I find out if I really am her father? Just to know for certain. If I am, maybe we can have a relationship. If she wants to. I understand she doesn't have any relatives. And I need to know for my family's sake, for my wife and kids."

"Okay, okay," Jim said. "First of all, what does it say on her birth certificate? Are you listed as the father?"

"I don't know. I've never seen it."

The lawyer pressed the speaker phone for his assistant, and told Taylor, "Hold on. We can check county records right now. We've got access."

Into the phone he said, "Nancy, would you look up a birth certificate in the county online database?" To Taylor, he asked, "Where was she born?"

"Buck Wallace told me she was born in St. Anthony's Hospital, Amarillo."

"Is Carli her first name?"

"Yes. What do you mean?" Taylor asked.

"Is that her birth name? Or maybe it's a middle name or nickname? Didn't she just inherit the Wild Cow Ranch. We can search court documents to find her name."

"I don't know her legal name. Yes, she inherited the ranch about a year ago."

The lawyer conveyed the information to his assistant along with Carli's age.

Taylor said in a low voice so as not to interrupt, "Buck also told me that the nuns at the hospital placed her with a foster family who raised her. They never adopted her. They took her to Florida, then Georgia. It may not have actually been in the foster system. I don't know."

"Okay, we'll check that too."

The assistant's voice came over the speaker. "I just emailed the birth certificate to you."

"Thanks, Nancy."

The lawyer opened the file on his computer and read over it.

"Hmm..." He rubbed the bridge of his nose.

Taylor's eyes were wide. "What?"

"Her birth name is Carlotta Jean. Birth mother: Michelle Jean Jameson. Birth father: blank."

"What does that mean?"

"Michelle didn't list you as the father."

"Where does that leave us? What's next?"

The lawyer sat up straight, took another sip of his coffee, and said, "You weren't married to Michelle. However, in family law there are 'Unmarried Fathers' Rights'. An unmarried father must first legally establish his paternity. This requires more than having his name on the birth certificate. A person can establish paternity either through an acknowledgment of paternity, like from the mother, but Michelle is deceased, or a paternity suit."

"I don't want to sue anyone."

"You and Carli could take DNA tests."

Both men stared at each other.

"In the case of infants, there is a statute of limitations. If John Doe was presumed to be the father and you wanted to contest that, you would have four years from the date of the baby's birth to do so. If there is no presumed father, there is no statute of limitations, even when the birth child becomes an adult."

"So?" Taylor held his palms upwards. "What should I do?"

"We could request they unseal the documents," his lawyer friend said, "since the grandparents and mother are deceased."

Taylor stood and they shook hands again. The concern now was, did he really want to pursue the truth? Was it worth his efforts to rock the boat? He still had concerns for Karissa, and although she offered her support, he wondered how she really felt. And how would his kids take the news?

Chapter 29

Carli

Grateful that no one was in the barn, Carli greeted her horse and picked up a rubber curry and brush. "Hey, boy, glad it's just you and me. Let's go for a ride. I gotta get out of here."

As she made circular motions with the curry over Beau's back, he nickered his response. It had been some days since she had ridden him, and he appeared to have missed her. She liked to think that he had.

"I know. I'm sorry. It's this crazy wedding. Actually, my whole crazy life. Dress shopping, birth father, half-siblings, court case."

She shook her head. Talking to a horse.

Once she got him saddled, they took off across headquarters and headed over the hill. Finally, she could take in a big breath and fill her lungs with the sweet, crisp November air. "Glad I wore a jacket." Beau seemed to want to continue their conversation and gave another nicker.

She loved his rhythm and the bond they had shared for years. What other sport or activity was there where you could feel you were a melded unit with the animal? Like a centaur, as though the horse's legs were your legs. Wherever you wanted to go, the horse's body moved with you in the same direction. Your brains were somehow linked too.

Although, Carli was glad that Beau could not have all the crazy human thoughts her brain was juggling at this moment. The wedding was one thing. But the shopping, engagement party, bridal shower. She just wasn't used to all of this. She didn't want to be the center of attention. She'd rather just stay in her room. Or, more to the truth, she'd rather be doing what she was doing now—riding her horse. Free. No people. No decisions.

Oh, and then there was Taylor Miller and all of that drama. Was he really her father? Did he want to know her? He had his own life, his own family. She would probably be an intrusion. And was that his daughter in the dress store? Shayla. Was she Carli's half-sister? It was all too much. And now her head hurt.

She rode on and then heard a sound like heavy tapping, which reached her long before she could figure out which direction the noise came from. Coming into view a large figure bent over next to a fence post. Then more tapping. But louder now. The person was hammering.

Carli recognized her fence line neighbor.

"Oh, hey, Vera. I wasn't sure who you were at first."

"Hey, Carli. Well, of course it's me. Who else would be fixin' the fence between us?"

Her liver-colored bloodhound wagged his whole body in greeting when he watched Carli dismount.

"Hey, Snot. How ya doin'?"

"Now don't go stealin' my dog's affection. Ain't ya got yer own? Prissy name, I seem to recall." After her stern expression, Vera winked.

Carli smiled and said, "Lily Jane. Just seemed to fit her. Besides, Lank had been calling her L.J., but initials seemed too boyish for her."

"So, what brings you over this way, neighbor?"

"I've got to check my fence line too. Just like you. What happened here? Did the cows bust through?" Carli asked.

"I think one of my bulls scratched himself on this fence post and pulled the top wire loose. They're always up to somethin'. You know that. Ranchin' is 24/7. Speakin' of that, where's your hubby-to-be? He busy with chores?"

Carli nodded. "I guess. I didn't see Lank or Buck when I left. They must be working somewhere."

"Well, it's good you can get away at times. Even in marriage you can't be with each other twenty-four hours a day. My husband Archie had his favorite things to do. Like huntin'."

"Did you go with him?"

"Noooo. You know me by now, Carli girl, I'm an animal lover. I'd rather adopt a deer instead of shootin' it."

"Was Archie okay with you doing your own things?"

"Oh, sure," Vera said. "We got ourselves a few goats early on. I made stuff like soaps and creams from their milk and sold them at farmers' markets. You know I'm still doin' that. I also liked leather work. I made little purses and sold those. I guess you could say I was always kind of crafty."

"That's great. I don't think I have a crafty bone

in my body."

"I didn't either when I was your age. A person evolves, grows, changes. Just stay open to learnin'. That's what will give you an interestin' life."

"I dunno. My life is a little too interesting at the moment. It's stressing me out, to be honest."

"I know weddin's can throw people into a tizzy. That's normal. But you'll get through it." Vera put her hammer down on the ground.

"It's way more than that. And I really don't know what to do. Truthfully, that's why I had to get away on Beau. It wasn't to check the fence line. I have so much swirling around in my head, I thought it might explode."

"Well, lay it on me. Think of me as your shrink. I have a lot of life experience and I'm a good listener to boot."

"Where to start? First, there's the wedding planning. Lola is so helpful and sweet, but she's also like a whirling dervish. Asks me tons of questions. Do I like this or that? I've gotta have this or that. It's tradition." Carli made air quotes with her hands. "I'd rather keep things simple."

Vera smiled. "First, I'd say, tell Lola that. That you want things simple. She might put up a fuss, but you've got to be firm. Otherwise, people rope you into doin' things you don't want to do. Second, do you actually know what a whirlin' dervish is?"

"It's a sand or dust devil."

"That it is. But it's also men in Istanbul, Turkey who dance and swirl around. They wear long skirts and tall hats that look like giant thimbles."

"How do you know that?"

"I read stuff. And watch things online. I also like

to do crossword puzzles. Knowin' things helps me fill in the right answers."

Carli could only stare at Vera for a long time. Who knew this about her neighbor?

"Okay. Weddin' stress—check. What else ya got? Lay it on me." Vera grinned.

"My birth father. After all these years, I'm pretty sure I know who he is. But we haven't faced each other and talked about it. He has a family. I think I have a half-sister and half-brother. Will they all accept me or run? I don't want to intrude on their lives. But I would like to know about him. I'd even like him to walk me down the aisle. If he'd be open to that."

"Oh, Carli girl. You're a people pleaser. Always worried about what others will think. A lot of time is wasted ponderin' 'what if this' or 'what if that'. You've gotta face things head on. Meet with that man, tell him who you are, and see what happens. You believe in God, dontcha? I do. The Good Lord will take care of everythin'. If the man don't want-cha in his life, then he's not worth the worry. That's not to say he may not come around some day. People change. They're goin' through their own journey. Okay, birth father—check. Got anythin' else on your plate for old Vera to help ya with?"

Vera reached down to stretch the barbed wire across the gap. Carli jumped off Beau and held the other side for her. Using a piece of baling wire, she attached the broken ends together.

"Yeah, the big one." Carli sighed. "Billy Broderick."

"What's that whipper-snapper up to these days? I don't trust him any farther than I can throw him."

"He's suing me again."

"I thought everythin' was taken care of back when you first moved here. Didn't the judge say you were the rightful heir?"

"Yes, he did. The judge declared that my grandpa's Last Will was valid. I guess Billy's been fuming all this time so now he wants to appeal the decision. Vera, I could lose everything. If Billy ends up winning the ranch, I'm sure he'd fire Buck, Lola, Lank, and kick me out. I'm really worried."

"There's that word again, girly. Worry. You have to throw that out of your vocabulary, out of your life. Doesn't God tell us not to worry? The birds don't worry where they're goin' to get their next meal from, do they? God takes care of them. Can we change anythin' by spendin' hours on worry?"

"No."

"You have a lawyer, dontcha?"

"Yes. Her name's Del. I hope you get to meet her while she's here."

"She's probably pretty smart and has won cases before, right?" Vera asked. "And she won the last time Billy tried to pull one over on you. Right?"

"Yes."

"There ya go. Do not worry. That's what God tells us. So, why're ya doin' it, Carli girl?"

"It's hard not to, Vera. I've always been this way. Sometimes we know in our heads that we shouldn't do something. And then we go ahead and do that exact thing."

"That's in the Bible. Do you know what verse?"

"No. What is it?"

"Romans 7:15. *'I do not understand what I do. For what I want to do I do not do, but what I hate*

I do.' Sometimes it's sin. And we all sin at times. I'm not sayin' what you're doin' by worryin' is sin, Carli. It's just an example of how we want to do what's right, like not worryin', but sometimes we don't achieve it. But we can keep on tryin'."

"It's difficult, Vera. I try to free my mind and stop worrying, but crazy thoughts keep jumping in my brain."

"Now listen to me, girly. You're still young on your life journey. I'm old. I've made a lot of mistakes. And I've learned a lot. You might remember I once told you, I had two more husbands after Archie. Complete flakes. Crooks too. Some people might say, 'Don't take advice from her. She's made mistakes.' They're right—about the mistakes. There were various reasons. I was lonely after Archie died. I was sad, afraid, young. I didn't have good counsel around me and believed what those sleezeballs said. They were tryin' to steal from me. I just wanted to be loved again like Archie had."

Vera's eyes misted over.

"I'm sorry, Vera. I hope they didn't get away with stealing from you."

"Some. But I was wisin' up fast. Both marriages lasted less than a year; the last one only a couple of months. I figured out fast what those guys were after. And it sure wasn't my body."

She let out a hearty laugh and Carli had to join in. What a picture. Carli did not want to go there.

Now good tears were flowing from Vera's eyes. Happy tears.

"Uh, oh my." Vera coughed from all the laughter. "It does the body good to laugh, doesn't it? Now why in the world was I tellin' you about my husbands?

Good grief, I'm gettin' old. I guess that's what they call Senior Moments when we forget stuff."

Snot, the bloodhound came up beside her and licked her hand.

"Oh right, mistakes. Not you, Snot. You're my best boy. But thanks for remindin' me. I was talkin' about mistakes, and how you shouldn't worry if you make them. You shouldn't worry period. Crazy stuff is goin' to happen in life. It's not perfect. We're not perfect. The other thing about worry, Carli, is you can't waste your life spendin' so much time on it."

"I don't do that, Vera."

"Not exactly but you seem to dwell on things." She said with a wink. "But the way you're worryin' about Billy Broderick and the court case, it's pretty similar. Now a little worry, a little anxiety—that's human nature, I guess. But just don't spend too much time on it—losin' sleep, gettin' headaches, windin' yourself up like a whirlin' dervish."

A big laugh erupted from Vera, and Carli shook her head.

"Dontcha someday want to be a professional ranch owner, not a snivelin' little girl? Then buck up. Cowgirl up. You've got your lawyer. Let her do the worryin'. And ya know what, Carli? If it all happens to go south and you lose the ranch, there's always Plan B and C and D. God's got ya in the palm of His hand. He's got a plan for you. Are ya gonna trust Him?"

"I'm trying, Vera. Thank you for talking with me. A lot of it made sense. I guess I need to change my attitude."

"Exactly. And anytime you need to talk, I'm here for ya."

Carli rode her horse through a nearby gate and came to where Vera was working on her side of the fence. She got down from Beau to give her friend a hug. "Okay, not too mushy now." Vera abruptly pushed free.

"There's one more thing," Vera said. "You've gotta learn my mantra. Hakuna matata. Say it!"

"Are you kidding? From *The Lion King*?"

"Say it!"

"Hakuna matata." Carli rolled her eyes.

"It's actually a phrase in Swahili," Vera said, "the East African language, that literally means no trouble or no problems. That's what you need to practice. I want you to chill out. Say it again!"

"Hakuna matata."

"What were those critters anyway? Gerbils? Ferrets?" Vera asked.

"Meerkats. One of them rode on the warthog's back."

"So, you do know the movie. It's one of my favorites. Say it again!"

"Vera. Seriously?"

"Say it!"

"Hakuna matata."

Chapter 30

Carli

Carli walked slowly across her yard after riding Beau, curiously aware of the strange vehicle parked in front of her house. The Ford pickup looked brand new, sparkling and clean with not a scratch. A vehicle that seemed out of place on a dirt drive. Definitely not a working ranch truck, a green metallic with tan accents that went over each wheel well and along the bottom under the doors. The running 'W' symbol for the King Ranch edition did not escape her notice. There wasn't anyone sitting on her front porch. Perhaps whoever it was had wandered across the road to the cookhouse to find Lola or Buck.

She stepped on her porch and noticed the inside wooden door stood slightly ajar, but the outside glass door was shut. She opened it cautiously, a flashback of the time she had found an ex-con sitting in her kitchen who had threatened her over an episode of cattle rustling. Her heart jumped to her throat.

"Is anyone there?" she called out as she stepped inside.

"You haven't changed much in this house." A man stood in the middle of the living room looking at the items on the fireplace mantel. Tall and handsome, with a Silverbelly hat that made him seem more imposing. He turned to face her. His dark brown western suit was cut to fit his frame perfectly, obviously custom-made. Neat haircut, clean shaven face, but dark, emotionless eyes that did not reflect the smile that was on his face.

"I'm Billy Broderick. We've met several times." He removed his hat.

He walked towards her with an outstretched hand. She shook it, although she didn't want to. "Yes. We have met."

Carli hesitated with offering a seat or a beverage; after all, he was already standing in her home. She didn't feel comfortable with threats of asking him to leave either. She was more curious than scared. He turned to look around again, walking towards the dining room where Del's papers and file were spread out over the table. For a second Carli panicked. She hoped he hadn't seen anything that might jeopardize her chances in the hearing. How long had he been wandering through her house before she got home?

"You've left everything exactly the same. I can't believe it." He glanced at the table but didn't seem to be interested in the stacks of papers.

"You said that already."

"I loved coming here. Jean and Ward were so much fun. I must have eaten a million meals with them. Spent every Christmas Day dinner here too."

Carli felt a sting to her heart. She knew Billy had said that on purpose. Del's words came to her. Stay calm. Don't let them get you. Is this what this was? An attempt to rattle her before the hearing. It was working, but she would never let him know it.

"I guess you grew up here, in a way?" Carli asked.

"Yes. Our house was south of Wild Cow's headquarters on acreage my grandfather bought many years ago from old man Jameson, but we've worked this land for several generations. Our two families have always been close."

"That's what I hear."

"I'll cut to the chase. May I call you Carli?"

"Sure."

"May we sit?"

She found it impossible not to return his disarming grin.

"Let's go back in the living room." She steered him out of the dining room away from Del's work. He eased into the leather chair next to the fireplace, unbuttoning his jacket as he rested an alligator hide boot on one knee and placed his hat on the floor upside down. He exuded confidence and arrogance, as though he didn't have a worry in the world.

"You don't care about the Jameson legacy." The smile remained on his extremely handsome face.

"It's true I didn't know about my grandpa Ward, but I do care."

"You didn't know about this ranch either less than a year ago, and now you stand a chance of losing everything once the judge rules in the hearing."

"I won't lose."

"Let's make a deal now. Turn everything back over to me, and I'll see that you're taken care of. Why risk it all?"

"I am the heir, Mr. Broderick. My grandfather wanted me to have this ranch."

"That's where you're wrong." Billy's fake smile was fading. "He never even knew about you. He would never leave the Wild Cow to a complete stranger and that is what you are. The old man was senile. He was tricked and I'm going to prove it. Honestly, I don't know who you are or how they found you. I can tell you one thing for sure, there is not one ounce of Jameson blood in your veins."

"There's not one ounce of Jameson blood in your veins, Mr. Broderick. I am Michelle Jameson's daughter and I am the only living heir."

There was that phony charming smile of his again. "I don't want to toss you out into the cold. Far from it. I want to reach some sort of compromise. We can all walk away from this thing winners."

Carli looked into his cold eyes. "Whatever my past, I have come to love this place and I'm learning more and more about my family. This is where I'm supposed to be. This is my home."

"Tell me what you want. What will make you go away?"

The charm and personality had suddenly been replaced with the face of a man who always got what he wanted. Power and money meant he rarely heard the word no. She had no doubt that fear was a big part of Billy Broderick's negotiations.

"I'm not leaving the Wild Cow," she said.

"Of course, you're not leaving the Wild Cow." Del buzzed into the living room from the kitchen. She must have come in the back door.

"Mr. Broderick, this is my attorney, Adelphia Fenwick." Relief washed over Carli. She stood and met Del in the middle of the room.

Del stopped in front of Billy. "Mr. Broderick, if you have anything to say to my client, have your lawyer contact me."

"Knock, knock. It's just us." Lola and Buck suddenly appeared in the entry hall. They walked into the room and stood behind Carli and Del.

"Billy? What are you doing here?" Buck asked, his voice laced with a tinge of hesitation although he did extend a hand in greeting. Billy ignored the gesture.

"Ms. Jameson and I were just coming to an understanding." Billy reached for his hat and stood.

Carli sensed that the people surrounding her cared deeply for her and that gave her confidence. "We do not have any kind of understanding, Mr. Broderick."

"You know you shouldn't be here, Billy," Buck said. "You'll have your day in court and we'll see you there. It's in the lawyers' hands now."

The charming smile was gone and replaced by dark eyes full of hate as he shot a glance towards Carli. He strode to the door with purpose and left.

"What was he doing here?" Del asked. "Did he take anything?"

"I don't know. He was here when I got back from riding."

"Can you tell if anything is missing?" Buck asked.

They followed Del to the dining room where she rummaged through her stacks. "The box lids are still in place. It doesn't look like he went through those." She opened a file folder and sifted through the documents inside. "Everything looks in order. These are on file with the court. Now I need to know every single word he said to you." Del pointed to a chair and Carli took a seat. Buck and Lola sat down too.

Carli sighed. At least she did not have to talk about wedding details.

Chapter 31

Carli

Bright and early the next morning Carli made an escape to the barn before Del woke.

Carli brushed her horse Beau, cleaned out his hoofs with the pick, and double-checked his shoes.

She turned at the sound of someone opening the saddle house door and saw Lank with reins and a bridle looped over an arm. Their eyes met and her heart turned over in response.

Lank smiled and said, "Buck is calling about more alfalfa bales for the horses. He wants you and I to load up a cow with lumpy jaw."

He whistled, shook the grain bucket, and his horse Phoenix came at a quick trot. While the horse polished off the treat, Lank slipped a bridle over his head. He went back to get the blanket and saddle. Carli followed him and soon had Beau saddled and ready.

While Lank went to hitch up the trailer, Carli led both horses out of the corral, shutting the gates behind her, and stood waiting, holding both reins.

They loaded the horses, Lily Jane hopped into

the back, and they pulled out.

"Where are we going?" asked Carli.

"West pasture. Buck noticed a lumpy jawed cow yesterday when he was putting out salt block. We need to bring her in and take a look."

Carli rolled down her window. It was a beautiful fall day. The pasture grass still had a slight tinge of green, the tops turning brown and swaying in the light breeze. The ever-changing landscape amazed her. Every sunset and sunrise completely different and just as breathtaking as the last. She'd inherited the ranch last fall, so she had lived here almost a year and seen four distinct seasons. Each one different bringing a new set of problems and joys. The work never ceased and the needs of the livestock never took a day off.

One of the things that surprised her about cow and calf operations, was the care and attention involved. Of course, the horses were more than something to ride. They were a partner in the job that had to be done; coworkers, and just as important to the ranch as the seasonal dayworkers they hired. Her herd of Angus cattle were the present and future, and the reason they got up every day. These momma cows did the heavy load of producing beef every year. They lived their best life on the natural prairie grasses, and, the Lord willing, with essential sunshine and rains that made their food supply.

As they bumped across the rough pasture road, Carli gazed at a lone antelope standing stone still and watching them from the top of a small hill. His neck stretched tall and proud. So beautiful. She was equally amazed at the wildlife her ranch supported. Not only grazing animals like deer and antelope but the birdlife—from large, graceful cranes to a covey of quail that scattered from the clumps of plum bushes as they drove past. Lank slowed to let a few skitter across the road, their little legs moving in rapid motion. She liked seeing the variety of wildlife on her outings.

They pulled to a stop at the windmill where a cow stood by herself. The rest of the herd wasn't anywhere to be seen. The cow turned her head and Carli noticed that one side of her face was swollen causing the jaw to be out of line.

"She hasn't been eating. Looks thin to me," said Lank.

Carli agreed. "I hope she's able to drink. Is that why she's hanging around the tank?"

"Probably."

They eased out of the pickup and slowly walked around to the back of the trailer. Lank opened the gate, the horses backed out, but before they were mounted the cow grew suspicious and took off in a slow lumber.

They eased around the cow and turned her back in the other direction, keeping her between them as they pushed her towards the open trailer. A few deep "yipps" from Lank, and the cow jumped up inside. Lank swung off his horse and shut the middle gate in the livestock trailer. They loaded their horses and were on their way.

Carli settled back in the truck. They didn't talk. They didn't have to. Working with Lank was the most natural thing in the world. There was a peace to her spirit when he was at her side. She had never experienced that with anyone before. They didn't need to break the silence with a lot of chattering talk. She reached over and took his hand that lay on the middle console. He squeezed her fingers.

"Miss Jameson," Lank broke the comfortable silence. "Do you realize that we've never been on a date?"

His voice was deep and very male, but with a gentle softness. She hesitated a moment before answering, surprised at the realization that he had only asked her out once before when she first moved to Texas. They had gone to a barbecue at the Rafter O Ranch.

"I remember last time you left with someone else, and now here we are. Is this what you call a whirlwind romance?" she asked.

"Why haven't you ever asked *me* out?" His quick reply generated a laugh from her.

"Are you asking me out now?" Carli tilted her head coyly.

"That I am," he said. "You pick the place. Wherever you want to go."

"I've heard people talk about the Clubhouse on Polk. I'd like to try it."

"Whose house?"

"A restaurant on Polk Street. It's on the thirty-first floor in downtown Amarillo. Belinda says you can see for miles. We have to dress up."

"If I can wear my boots, I'm game."

"Great. I'll call and make reservations and you pick me up around six-thirty."

"I can do that. We should have plenty of time. We need to drive this cow into the chute so we can figure out what's wrong. And then I'm yours for the rest of the evening."

"Thanks, Lank." Carli began running the contents of her closet through her head. She needed something fancy, but a little bit sexy too. This would be the first official celebration of their engagement.

***

Carli searched through the closet several times, gave up, and took a shower. While towel drying her hair, she studied her closet some more. She never had a reason to dress in evening wear, so she had never bought anything. Her dresses were simple, well worn, solid colors. She was so practical and safe. Nothing daring or too bright. Could she be any more boring? She groaned and laid back on her bed.

On a whim she wandered into the bedroom where her grandmother's belongings were still stored. She hadn't the heart to give anything away. In some ways, having her grandparents' things filling every nook and cranny made it feel like they were still a part of her life. She didn't want to get rid of them just yet.

Her fingers flittered across the beaded jackets and embroidered western shirts. Her grandmother's rodeo attire all in bright and cheery colors embellished with sequins and fringe. Nothing dull about Grandma Jean. In the back she found a solid black dress and Carli slipped it over her head. The A-line skirt billowed around her ankles as she twirled. It had a scoop neck with cutouts at the top of each shoulder, the sleeves falling to just below her elbows.

"Grandma has a little black dress. Always appropriate for any situation," she said to Lily Jane who stretched out in the middle of the bed watching with ears pricked.

She boldly searched through her grandmother's jewelry box. Turquoise just didn't seem to fit the occasion. Carefully opening a velvet box, Carli discovered dangling diamond earrings. Small and delicate, they were perfect. A squirt of perfume and just in time.

At the sound of a knock, Carli opened the front door to see her fiancé holding a black felt hat minus the Texas dirt that had once coated it, now all brushed and clean. When he saw her, he bowed at the waist. "Ma'am."

He wore starched jeans, a light green paisley shirt and a dark blue vest. He replaced his lid and stared at her. She did love a cowboy in a black hat. Her heart jolted and her pulse pounded. His nearness was overwhelming her senses.

"And might I add, wow. You are beautiful." Lank said, his gaze riveted on her face, then slowly moved over her body.

"You polished your boots," she pointed to his feet.

"I'm glad. When ya said dress up, you weren't kiddin'."

Lily Jane sat stone still on the front porch, except for the wagging tail. "We'll be back soon," Carli said. "I'm sorry you can't go this time."

Lank hurried to the passenger door and opened it for her, stepping aside with a sweep of his hat that he had removed again and held in his hand.

She hopped inside. They drove in silence but she could hardly tear her gaze from his profile.

Carli cleared her throat. "I guess we're doing this backwards. There's a lot of things we need to talk about before we share a life together."

"You got that right. Isn't there something you

need to tell me?" He stared straight ahead, his eyes on the road, and she noticed the flexed muscle in his jaw.

"Are you angry?" she asked.

"I wish you trusted me." His hands now gripped the steering wheel and he still had not glanced her way.

"What makes you think I don't?"

"Did you have a visitor?"

Carli shrunk in her seat and decided it was best to keep her mouth closed, rather than argue and make up a hurried excuse which he wouldn't believe anyway.

Lank finally glanced in her direction. "Were you ever going to tell me that Billy Broderick was standing in your living room when you got home?"

"Oh that. How did you know?"

"Buck and Lola were besides themselves. You have no idea what he might be capable of. I kept waiting for you to come over and tell me."

"Honestly, I had pushed it out of my mind. It was such a beautiful morning and the barn is my escape. I don't like dwelling on things. You know I worry excessively anyway. I have to really work at pushing things out of my mind."

"I want to know when someone has broken into your house. I want to know everything about you." He sighed and loosened the grip on the steering wheel.

"Are you sure about this? Sometimes I realize you're a complete stranger and then other times I know without a doubt that I can't imagine life without you. We should talk about that too."

"Like what?" he asked and then added. "You're

the one. Knew it the moment we first met when you visited the ranch and I handed you my dirty, grimy hat. You put it on your head and rode off. Stole my hat and my heart that day."

Carli looked at him with a big grin on her face. "Since when did you get to be such a master of romance? That was really sweet of you to say."

"Ask me anything. What do you want to know?"

"Favorite color?"

"Blue, like the Texas sky." Lank pointed out the pickup window.

"Favorite food?"

He didn't have to think about his answer. "Chicken fried steak, of course. Lola makes the best gravy. Now let me ask you some questions."

"Fire away." Carli wondered why they had never had this conversation before, and then realized that they were always so busy dealing with the ranch.

"Favorite color?"

"Green."

"Favorite thing about me?" Lank shot her an irresistible grin.

"Your blue-gray eyes in that handsome face." She gave him an air smooch.

"Perfect answer from my future wife. But I hope some of our kids have your eyes too."

"Kids?"

"I want at least four." His reply was matter-of-fact, the same way he had said blue for his favorite color.

She paused and didn't answer. That was a big order to fill particularly since it was her body that would be involved.

He glanced in her direction. "How many are you thinking?"

She hesitated again, wondering how to answer. If they were going to build a relationship on honesty and respect, the time to start would be now.

"I don't want any kids. I decided a long time ago that I would make a horrible mother."

Chapter 32

Carli

"But, Lank…" she touched his arm. "Belinda has been baking all kinds of samples for us. She needs us to come taste them and let her know which ones we like. Just this one stop. I promise."

She stroked his arm some more and kissed his cheek a few times.

"Now that just ain't fair, Carli." He smiled and took her into his arms. "All right. I'll go."

"Lola's already in town, shopping of course. Belinda invited her too."

"Good," was all he said.

They entered the B&R Beanery and were met by Belinda and Lola who were pushing two tables together and setting up the small cakes, plates, and forks.

"Oh, Lank and Carli! Thanks for coming. You guys look great!" Belinda said.

"We're on our way to Amarillo for dinner," Carli explained.

"This is so exciting. I can't wait for you to taste everything. I've been baking for days."

After everyone greeted and got settled, Belinda continued, "Russell will watch the front and wait on any customers so we can have some privacy. Make yourselves comfortable and let's get to tasting!"

Lola put small paper plates in front of everyone. "No sense in dirtying all of Belinda's dishes." She smiled and got cups of water for all.

Lank removed his cowboy hat and balanced it on one of the top points of his wooden chair. He said nothing.

"Okay," Belinda started. "Each tier can be a different flavor. So, if you don't like something, not to worry. Everyone can be happy with their own tier."

Lank looked at the three women surrounding him. Carli reassuringly patted his forearm. Lola and Belinda grinned from ear to ear.

"Now this is a real favorite with a lot of people— Peanut Butter Cup." Belinda cut small bites and placed them on the plates. "Sweet, salty, and nutty. And you could add peanut butter cups to the top!"

"I do love chocolate," Carli said, licking her fork.

Lank swallowed his bite in one gulp. "Yeah, good stuff."

"Now for those who like a little taste of cognac or brandy, this one has Grand Marnier in it. It's kind of citrusy. What do you think?" Belinda asked.

"Mmmm, good." Lola licked her lips.

Everyone took sips of water in between tasting the cakes.

Belinda pushed another towards them. "This one is called Tropical Coconut Guava. It's coconut sugar and caramel, and guava or passionfruit curd. I think it tastes like graham crackers."

"Curd?" Lank asked. "Doesn't sound very appetizing. Plus, I don't like coconut." He didn't taste it at all.

"It's coagulated milk," Belinda explained. "It's a process, like making cheese."

"Sour milk?" Lank made a retching face.

"Here's one for all you chocolate lovers. 'Sultry Chocolate'. Dark chocolate cake, cabernet, fresh raspberries, and French buttercream. Some people add goat cheese or put that on the side. I didn't."

"The chocolate is yummy," Carli said.

Lola mentioned, "I heard some people on a budget use sheet cakes. If the venue has a cake-cutting fee, a sheet cake is easier and less trouble."

Belinda said, "Ooh, this is my favorite. Bananas Foster. It comes from the French Quarter. Butter cake with caramel and banana filling, plus rum and cinnamon. Yum!" She continued with the next one. "This one is Coffee Cream. Chocolate cake topped with coffee buttercream, coffee meringue buttercream, espresso Kahlua ganache, and hazelnut mousse on top of a chocolate torte."

Lank said, "The guests would sure be buzzing after all that caffeine." He bellowed with a hearty laugh and Carli kind of gave him a look. "What? That's a lot of caffeine," he defended himself.

"Then there's lemon," Belinda kept at it with the cakes. "It's darkened with burnt caramel and softened with cream. Lemon goes with anything."

Pushing another plate forward, she continued. "Here's something traditional with a kick. Spiked Red Velvet. Rich layers of red velvet cake and cream cheese frosting. The kick is in the icing. Laced the cream cheese with amaretto." Belinda smiled.

"This one's for Lola. It's actually her recipe.

Mexican wedding cakes are not multi-tiered. Usually, they have a variety of cake types. Rum-soaked fruitcake or tres leches cake. A fruitcake filled with pineapple, pecans and coconut, and rum. Topped with vanilla whipped cream. It's delicious but a little heavy. Tres leches means three milks or creams. It's sponge or butter cake infused with evaporated milk, condensed milk, and heavy cream."

Lola added, "Mexican weddings usually have a table set up with a gorgeous display of different cakes. Tres leches is my favorite."

Carli made a note of that in her memory. Turning to Belinda she said, "Thanks so much for all of this, Belinda. They are all so delicious, it would be hard to choose."

"Whatever you want, Carli. Just no coconut for me." Lank put his hat back on and crossed his arms.

Belinda jumped in. "I also need to make a groom's cake. It could be shaped like a horseshoe or whatever you want. Which one was your favorite, Lank?"

He said, "I guess the peanut butter cups. But it's up to Carli."

"I have another surprise." Belinda signaled Russell who stood at the front counter watching the cake scene. Luckily there were no customers for him to wait on at the moment.

He waved over a teenage boy carrying a guitar who came towards Carli, Lank, and the ladies.

Belinda introduced him. "This is Steven and he's really good. You'll need wedding music, Carli."

With that, Steven played a melody of tunes, from oldies to new stuff. "The Way You Look Tonight", "Unchained Melody", "Perfect", "I Wanna Dance With Somebody", "Uptown Funk".

He wasn't half bad, but Carli wasn't sure of any of it. The cake. The dress. Flowers. Music. A headache was forming.

When the boy was done, the ladies clapped for him, but Carli was glad when he left. She sat quietly moving her fork around the almost empty plate to push remnant crumbs into a little pile.

Lola jumped in. "That was really nice, Belinda. I'm not sure it would be loud enough if we have a crowd of people. We might need a DJ or a band. Years ago, we went to a wonderful wedding of a friend and they had a mariachi band dressed in their charro outfits. They looked good! It was so much fun. They really got the people dancing and they also played sweet, romantic songs. I'll never forget the bride and groom dancing."

"What does mariachi mean?" Carli asked.

"Musician."

"Oh, duh." The wheels in Carli's head were turning. "Ya know, Lank might really like that because of his Mexican heritage. What do you think, babe?" Carli turned to Lank.

Lank stood and said, "It all sounds nice to me. Whatever you want to do, Carli, is fine. Now I think we should get goin' to the restaurant. Don't want to be late for our reservation." He tipped his hat to the ladies. "Thanks much."

Chapter 33

Carli

After they were back inside Lank's truck and on their way to Amarillo, he resumed their conversation. Looking at Carli in surprise, he said, "Of course, you'd make a great mother. What are you saying?"

Carli said, "It's just something I haven't really aspired to." They rode in silence for the next forty-five minutes to downtown Amarillo.

A parking garage attendant opened the door and offered his hand. She took it and stepped out. Lank came around the truck and they walked on a plush rug to a set of double glass doors with dark tint and gold lettering.

Another smiling attendant opened the door and said, "Welcome to the Clubhouse. Enjoy your evening."

Inside they stepped into the designated elevator for Clubhouse on Polk Street. Instead of stopping at various floors, it went straight to the thirty-first at a speed so fast Carli's stomach rebelled. They emerged into a walnut-paneled space with plush chairs and leafy plants. Oversized chandeliers hung overhead but the lighting was dim. Adding to the atmosphere, soft jazz music floated over their heads. It seemed impossible that they were in the middle of the flat, treeless plains. If not for the cowboy beside her, Carli felt as though she had stepped back into her old life. For a minute she recalled drinks at some trendy bar in Atlanta with her boss and their real estate clients. They had dined on whatever her boss thought would be the most impressive, and she had always worn the same knit black dress that never fit right. Thankful it was all in the past, she squeezed Lank's arm to feel his flesh and bones, his reassuring warmth beside her.

A hostess greeted them at the front desk. The statuesque and stunning Asian girl verified that Carli had reserved a table, but there was a problem.

"I'm sorry sir, jackets are required."

Lank looked at Carli and turned on his heel to leave, but Carli stopped him with a hand on his arm. "He's wearing a vest. Isn't that good enough?"

"We do provide jackets for our guests. Let me get you one."

Lank frowned, but Carli said, "Thank you."

The hostess returned with a dull brown knit sports coat, holding it up for Lank to slip his arms into. She took his cowboy hat. Carli couldn't stop the giggle that escaped her lips. The jacket's shoulder width was too small and the sleeves came to the middle of his forearms. Lank struck a pose and Carli laughed again. The young woman at the podium couldn't suppress her smile either.

"Your table is this way. Enjoy your evening," she said.

Windows surrounded three sides of the dining room with arched cornice boards and filmy drapes. Glass went from floor to ceiling and provided a thirty-first-floor vantage point of the city. Beyond the lights of Amarillo, the flat landscape stretched into darkness on the unbroken horizon. Parts of this area were still untamed, rugged. It grew people who were the same.

A waiter stood ready to pull out the chair for Carli, and he shook out her napkin, placing it on her lap. Another waiter did the same for Lank, who shot the man a suspicious glare. A waitress filled their water glasses immediately.

Another gentleman appeared at their table. "Good evening. I'm Walter and it is my pleasure to be serving you."

Carli glanced at Walter and then took a second notice. Although he was an older gentleman, he looked distinguished dressed in head-to-toe navy making her think he might be a wealthy patron instead of an employee.

"May I bring you something from the bar, miss?"

"Just water for me. Thanks."

"Sir?"

"Sweet tea."

"Very good."

After returning with their drinks, Walter stood ready with pad and pen. "Are we celebrating something special this evening?"

Carli hesitated for just a moment, and then flashed her left hand. "We just got engaged."

Walter leaned closer to admire her ring. "That is wonderful. Our specials for this evening are listed here." He handed them another piece of paper. Carli studied the menu and then the paper.

Instead of reading his menu, Lank removed the lime and lemon perched on the side of his glass and laid the fruit on the table. He drank the sweet tea in several gulps. Walter was quick to scoop the beverage garnish onto a small plate.

"Do they have any bigger glasses?" Lank held up the empty glass.

"This isn't the kind of place that sells forty-four-ounce sodas," Carli said. The expression on Walter's face remained stony and unchanged, but he nodded in agreement.

"But this is too tiny."

The beverage waitress appeared again and filled Lank's glass.

"Thank you and keep it coming." Lank took two swallows and emptied the second.

With an impatient sigh, Walter asked, "May I take your order?" With pen and pad he stood ready.

"Steak, rare," said Lank.

"Ladies first." Walter cleared his throat through pursed lips and turned to Carli.

"I'll have the salmon, asparagus, and salad with vinaigrette." Carli handed him her menu.

"And you, sir?" With a glance down his nose.

"Steak. Run it by me rare with French fries." Lank shut his menu and held it out towards the waiter.

The waiter cleared his throat. "You wish to celebrate your engagement to this beautiful young lady with French fries? I think not, and besides we do not offer fried potatoes, sir. We have a lovely tomato Gazpacho soup or Greek salad with olives and peppers."

"Mashed potatoes and an extra side of gravy

then."

Walter leaned closer to Lank. "No. This isn't the country kitchen." He muttered, winked at Carli, and then added, "Sir."

"It was my turn to pick the place tonight. Otherwise, that's where we'd be eating." Carli tried to make light of Walter's remark and she could tell he was just giving Lank a hard time by the twinkle in his eyes. Lank didn't seem to notice.

"Bring me the soup. And just a salad with ranch but nothing else green. Do you have bread?"

"Very good, sir. And yes, we have bread."

"Bring us a big basket full." After Walter left, he leaned closer to Carli. "I bet they don't have long neck beer here either."

Carli shook her head and laughed remembering a quote she had seen once. "The problem with praying for a cowboy is that you have to deal with that cowboy when you get him."

Lank emptied a third glass of tea, shrugged out of the too-tight jacket with some difficulty, and folded his arms on the table.

"You don't want to be a mother?" He stared at her, waiting with a look of concern on his face.

One thing about Lank she was learning, he didn't mince words. He was always direct and to the point and spoke what was on his mind. She had hoped they wouldn't continue this conversation.

"I had a very complicated childhood. You know that my mother abandoned me as a baby and my foster family was much older and never adopted me. They were kind and good, but I decided at an early age that it was me against the world. That's just my lot in life and I accept it."

"What happened to you as a child doesn't mean you can't be a parent."

"Since I never had the love of my own mother as a child, I figured I'd never be a good mom myself."

The conversation paused as the first course was served.

Lank took a healthy bite of his soup and looked at her in surprise. "This soup is cold."

"It's Gazpacho. It's always served cold."

"It's not bad." He emptied his bowl along with three rolls, and by then their main courses were served.

After taking a few bites, Carli continued. "I like my horses and my life. I like my riding school kids, and as I expand the school, I may not have time for much else. The thought of bringing another life into the world just does not fit."

"You have forgotten one thing."

"What's that?"

"Me," he simply said. "How do I fit? Appears you have everything planned out."

Their whirlwind romance had not given her much time to think about how their lives would blend together. Before she said anything she noticed a scowl on his face. Had her hesitation to answer bothered him in some way? Lank looked around, nervous.

"What is wrong with you?"

"It's too dull and quiet in here. Why are we whispering? Everyone is talking so softly."

"You're making this weird and it isn't."

"Wanna liven things up a bit?"

"No. I do not," she said. "Lank. Don't do anything I'll regret."

He laughed and gave her that half-sided grin that made her knees weak. "What's life if you don't take chances and stir things up a bit?"

He made it through dinner without causing a scene, and then she realized he was teasing her. But the easy banter of before had changed to barely a word muttered. They concentrated on their food.

"In celebration of your engagement, dessert is on the house," Walter said as he placed the treat between them.

The Clubhouse on Polk was known more for their desserts than their main courses, and the strawberry shortcake did not disappoint. Snow white cake layered with whipped cream and strawberries. Carli handed Lank one of the forks and pushed the plate closer to the middle of the table. Conversation died again as they focused on dessert.

After Lank had paid the check, he refused to wear the jacket again.

"We're leaving. I don't need it." He handed it to the hostess and took his hat back from her on their way out. When they reached the parking garage he turned to Carli. "Wanna take a walk?"

"Okay," she said. "I have my jacket in the truck."

The November evening was clear and crisp, but her coat was long enough to reach her ankles and cover her legs. She buttoned it up to her chin, stuffed her hands into the deep pockets, and followed Lank up a ramp into the night.

Chapter 34

Carli

Lank reached into Carli's coat pocket and grabbed her hand. "Tonight was nice. I haven't seen you much lately." He led her one block across a parking lot and then they turned right on Polk Street.

Streetlamps cast pools of light on the sidewalk and headlights from a constant stream of traffic illuminated their way. The night was perfect, not too cold with just the hint of a chill. Enough to get your blood pumping after their meal. The energy of the street exhilarated her. Carli breathed deep. It was good to be alive and even better to have Lank at her side. She was excited about their future.

"That's the old neon sign from the Paramount Theatre." Lank pointed across the street. "It's an office building now, but they refurbished the sign."

Carli admired the white deco style architecture of the two-story building with the giant blade sign that burned bright orange and white. It was impressive.

"Yes, tonight was nice. Since you proposed, it's been a whirlwind of activity. Who knew that planning a wedding could keep one little town so busy and take that many people to make it happen? But I have to say Lola is definitely a godsend. I wouldn't know where to begin without her."

"Actually, you were the one who proposed first."

"Best thing I ever did," she said, hugging his arms tighter and stretching her face closer to give him a peck on the cheek.

"I always knew you had smarts, from the first time we met."

Carli laughed and leaned closer to reward him with another kiss, but this time he turned his head and kissed her back. His lips felt warm against the chill of the night. A car honked at them as it passed. Lank raised an arm in greeting.

"After we're married, I can't see things changing that much," Carli said. "But we have to come together on where to live, don't you think?"

"I've been giving that some thought, and my trailer is small, but it will be cozy. You'll always be within reach." He grinned.

"You got that right," Carli smiled but she still hated the thought of trying to squeeze all her stuff into half of a closet and two dresser drawers. Newlyweds or not, it was going to be a cramped space. She finally felt at home after moving into her grandparents' house. She started out in the guest room but had since cleaned out their master bedroom and the closet, bought a pillow top mattress, which she loved, and painted the bathroom a sunny yellow.

"It will be strange for me living in Jean and Ward's house with their stuff all around," Lank said.

"They have really nice things. I'm not getting rid of it, and we can get our own furniture eventually," said Carli. She was not budging on this. "How about a compromise? We live in my house and then maybe we can build a new one just for us one day. My house could become a guest house or cowboy bunkhouse. What do you think?"

"Want a coffee?" Lank asked as he paused in front of a coffee shop.

Lank completely ignored her suggestion for a compromise, so obviously this topic would have to be revisited later.

"Sure," agreed Carli. They walked in and placed their orders. After they were seated at a corner table, away from the crowd, Lank placed his cowboy hat in the chair next to him and took both of her hands in his.

"Now, tell me about your plans for the riding school."

"I need more horses," Carli said. "Without good mounts I can't sign up more kids, but I need a horse trainer first. You're the perfect guy for the job."

He hesitated for a moment and looked down at the table. "We agreed to speak our minds. Right?"

"Yes, always."

"I'm not really interested in training old, broken-down horses for a riding school. I fully support your efforts, but I'd like to start colts and train them for ranch work and maybe a few bucking broncs. I'm thinking we could really build a reputation with our remuda. Of course, it would take years to perfect the genetics, but I think it would really be a money earner for us in the future."

Carli was surprised that their paths seemed to be heading in different directions, particularly if Lank had other aspirations. They weren't joined at the hip after all.

"There are other things we should decide," she said.

"Yeah, I know. You don't want kids and I do. What about a honeymoon?"

"What about it?"

"Maybe we can find something we can agree on."

"I haven't given it much thought."

"Where would you like to go?"

"Definitely not the beach. I'm not really a sand and sun type of girl."

"The mountains then?"

"Will we have to hike anywhere? I'm not a fan of hiking."

"The lake? I know someone who has a cabin."

"I could do fishing, if I had to. Can we take the horses?"

He grinned. "Carli Jameson. I think you're one of those high maintenance chicks."

"Yes, I am and proud of it," she quipped.

He laughed. "Can't say that life with you will ever be boring. Are you ready to leave?" Lank stood and put on his hat.

Carli's heart leaped. He sure was a handsome cowboy, and that Lank Torres was all hers. Bless the broken road that got her here, because she would have lost a whole lot of money betting on that soulmate from Georgia who broke her heart.

After they had walked to the truck and were on the road again back to the Wild Cow Ranch, Lank grew silent. Carli sensed there was more he wanted to say, so she encouraged him. It was uncanny how she could read him so easily.

"Something else on your mind?" she asked.

"I've been thinking about doing something different," he said.

"Really? Like what?" This was news because she had no idea he might be unhappy in his work at the ranch. She held her breath, giving him time to talk. She did not want to push him. He hesitated for several minutes.

"I'd like to go to rodeo clown school," he finally said.

"What?" Carli couldn't stifle the laugh that bubbled up from her belly. "Are you kidding?"

"No. Actually I'm serious." His voice was tinged with hurt feelings.

"I'm sorry I laughed. I had no idea you were thinking about a career change."

"You know I'll always be a cowpuncher. I told you that, but I really miss rodeoing. If it weren't for that injury, I would have made that my career. There isn't a day that goes by, that I don't think about being in the sport. I miss those guys. I could be a clown and not rattle my brain so much."

"Absolutely. Stepping in front of two thousand pounds of solid muscle would be much safer for your brain. Are you crazy?" She exploded and then wished she could take it back. Not a good way to be supportive of your soon-to-be husband. He didn't want to train horses for her, but he wanted to risk his life in the rodeo arena. What was wrong with him?

They rode in silence. Carli fumed and tried to make sense of it all. Were they really that incompatible? Was she making the biggest mistake of her life?

Lank parked in front of her house. She longed to invite him in, but things were still cool between them. And she knew he had morals to uphold regarding the woman he planned to marry. He told her it had been a promise to his mother.

She turned in the seat and when he looked at her, she knew this was the right thing. There was such a peace about her life now, that she never had in Georgia. The strangest mix of circumstances had led her here, and without a doubt this was where God wanted her to be.

"I love you, Lank. I'm sorry if I overreacted. I will support you in whatever you want to do." She leaned closer and what she had planned to be a short kiss, went on for several minutes. He pulled back and opened his door, hurried around to open hers, and as she slid out of the pickup truck, she slid into his waiting arms. They kissed again.

With his arm slung around her shoulder, he walked her to the door, took the keys from her hand and unlocked it. Her breath caught in her throat. For a minute she thought he might follow her inside.

"At least there's one thing we can agree on."

"Muu-huh." She murmured as his lips claimed hers again.

"It doesn't matter how I'll fit into your life. I'm here now. That's the most important thing."

"What do we do?" she asked.

"We'll figure this out as we go along."

"You're right. Together. That's all that matters." She stood halfway inside the door but with one foot on the porch. Neither of them moved.

"You need to go inside, and I need to go home for a cold shower."

She laughed, gave him another peck on the cheek but stood on the porch to watch him drive across the compound and park in front of his trailer. Her first instinct was to run after him. To make sure he wasn't angry at her for not wanting to live in his trailer house. For laughing about rodeo clown school. For not wanting a honeymoon on the beach. For saying she wouldn't be a good mother, or whatever she had said that might have irked him.

What had she said? They talked about so much tonight. It had been good. But her worrying tendencies always got the better of her. She got ready for bed and finally stretched out in the dark thinking about the evening. No doubt the best date she had been on in forever. And no doubt Lank was the one person she could never live without.

All their differences seemed small as she remembered his kisses. Beginning a lifetime with Lank seemed so much bigger.

Chapter 35

Carli

Carli studied the invitation card with a faux wood background and white lettering. It was different from any invitation she had ever seen.

YEE HAW
You're Invited!
I DO BBQ
Saturday
Honoring
Carli Jameson and Lank Torres
Sale Barn South of Town
(NOT the one across the county line)

She laughed. "Leave it to the good people of Dixon to know exactly where and when the party is without the need for details. There is no date, no time, and no address, but the 'yee haw' is a fun touch."

"That's because everyone who lives here probably worked on the planning or the cooking." As Lank drove into the livestock sale barn parking lot on the west side of town, the newly engaged couple was the last to arrive from all indications. The lot was packed so they parked in the very back and walked towards the entrance. The sounds drifted outside from a guitar, fiddle, and the harsh banging of drums that overpowered the music produced by the other musicians.

Since it was being held in a barn, Carli felt comfortable wearing her boots with a fringe skirt. And since she was the bride after all, she chose a frilly, lacy white blouse. As usual Lank looked ranchy and then some, and she was proud to be at his side, on his arm. The arm of her fiancé to be exact.

As Carli stepped inside, she gasped, her feet frozen in place as her gaze drifted to the ceiling. "I stand corrected. Apparently, most of Dixon was on the decorating committee."

The look on Lank's face began as an open-mouthed shock as he shuffled back for a step, but then his face broke into a wide grin. Carli on the other hand wanted to hide.

The show barn had been transformed into a sparkling fairy land with a western flair, of course. The entire ceiling was strung with hundreds, if not thousands of twinkling white lights. A pennant made with a rainbow of bandanas stretched around the walls.

Individual tables were set up with red and white checkered cloths, and candles in mason jars as centerpieces. To complete the tablescape, a variety of old boots were stuffed with yellow and white daisies and tied with more colorful bandanas. White cloth napkins completed the table setting with more mason jars of iced water.

People stood in clumps, talking, laughing. Some sat in the stands, all heads turned to look at Lank and Carli. A slow applause began and built as they got farther into the room.

Lank grinned, lifted his cowboy hat and took a bow. He nudged her shoulder and pointed to the back wall. Carli's mouth hung open in shock at the sight, words hung in her throat. In large metal letters, *Lank + Carli* burned bright behind the band. Each letter housed several bulbs. A large metal heart suspended below the letters blinked red and white. Numerous strands of lights were draped on either side from ceiling to floor covering the entire wall.

Lank tugged on her hand and she followed him towards the dance floor. He immediately wrapped an arm around her waist and pulled her close.

"Can you two-step?" he asked. "We're gettin' hitched and I don't even know if you can dance."

"Of course, I can dance." She couldn't help but smile at the surprise on his face. "We two-step in Georgia, you know."

Over his shoulder she saw her attorney, Del, in all her new cowgirl finery. She had added a cowboy hat with a turkey feather. Del raised an arm in greeting and Carli waved back.

He twirled her around in a tight spin first and she got lost in the love that sparkled in his eyes. They made it twice around the dance floor. A tap on his shoulder made him stop and the sight of Belinda irritated her, even if she was a dear friend. Lank sighed and they moved apart and turned.

"We have a special table reserved for y'all." Belinda pointed. "On that side."

Lank looked as disappointed as Carli felt with the interruption but smiled and tugged her arm to follow. A separate table had been set for two people with more metal letters, *Mr. & Mrs.* They took their seats. The heap of white daisies, baby's breath, and other varieties of white flowers almost hid them from the rest of the room, and Carli was okay with that. She sipped from the glass of water. She did not like being the center of attention and being the bride in a small town was just begging for the adoration of the entire population. Their intentions were heartfelt and sincere, but Carli had spent most of her life avoiding people. She was somewhat angry at herself for feeling uncomfortable. She pasted a smile on her face and ordered herself to relax and enjoy the moment.

Lola and Buck walked up to stand behind them.

"I am overwhelmed." Carli peeked over the centerpiece scanning the room.

Lola laughed. "You're doing just fine. We haven't had anything this exciting happen in a long time."

Despite her anxiety, the laughter and the smiles warmed Carli's heart. "Has the town ever done anything like this before for a newly-engaged couple?"

"Not that I know of," said Lank.

Buck gave her waist a squeeze. "Finding the granddaughter of Ward and Jean and the heir to the Wild Cow is a big deal."

Carli waved as she saw Angie Olsen, a friend from the neighboring Rafter O ranch. Angie waved back and walked across the dance floor followed by her constant shadow of a cowboy, Colton Creacy, Lank's best friend. She made a beeline for Carli with Colton in tow.

"This is amazing," Angie said as she leaned down to give Carli a hug. Colton and Lank shook hands in greeting, and then Colton tipped his hat towards Carli and winked.

"Can you believe this? I'm shocked," Carli said.

"How is the bride-to-be holding up? Are your overawed?"

"To say the least." Carli leaned closer to Angie and lowered her voice. "What is with this town? Is this normal?"

"It is if you're the long-lost queen of the Wild Cow Ranch. But now it's time to dance," Angie grabbed Carli's hand just as the band struck up the first notes of the recognizable *Amarillo by Morning*. "Come on, you two." She wiggled her finger towards the men.

The four of them made their way through the tables towards the dance floor. As Lank spun her around, Carli was more than stunned that this was all for her.

As they passed, folks offered their congratulations.

One girl asked, "Where's the wedding?"

Carli had no reply because honestly, she couldn't remember. It did not bother her that Lola had taken on the job of wedding planner and Carli was more than happy to let her have it. The many details and questions that Lola had been firing at her melded together in her mind and was now all mush.

The two couples laughed and danced, getting in the middle of a tussle when Colton bumped Lank out of the way and Lank retaliated.

"Can you guys stop!" Angie jerked her hands out of Colton's embrace.

"Barbecue is served. Y'all come and git it!" shouted one of the men wearing a black apron and white shirt. "Pastor, can you bless it?"

After the prayer, another man asked, "Where is

the happy couple? Get at the front of the line and help yourself."

"Saved by dinner. Let's eat," said Angie. "After you. They'll want you to go first." She nudged Carli in the right direction towards a smaller room off to one side under the stadium seats.

To say the cooks had outdone themselves was an understatement. Platters of meat anchored one end of the table. Carli grabbed a plate and silverware. Lank followed.

She worked her way past brisket to a pot of pinto beans, and the roasted herb potatoes were in the shapes of little hearts. Then onto several choices of green salads and skewers of fruit with heart-shaped melons and strawberries. The dessert table stood against another wall decorated with a burlap tablecloth. The choices were too many. Red-velvet cookies with white icing, mini apple pies, and brownie pops, all heart-shaped.

"You can sit with us," Carli said. Angie nodded.

Carli and Lank pushed their chairs closer together while Angie and Colton pulled up two chairs on either side of them. Angie's constant chatter comforted her and kept her mind off the enormity of the event. Admittedly, it was some of the best barbecue Carli had ever tasted. The brownie pop was her favorite, and when Lank went back for seconds she asked him to bring her another.

"I have two questions for you," said Carli.

"Fire away," said Angie.

"Will you be my maid of honor?"

"Of course," Angie's gentle laughter rippled through the air. "I am thrilled you asked. What am I wearing?"

"We'll have to check with Lola about that. And the second question is, where did they find those letters?" Carli nodded her head at the stage. "I guess the livestock barn uses them for all their events?"

Angie swallowed the food in her mouth and looked at Carli with wide eyes. She didn't answer the question.

"May I have your attention please." Belinda and her husband Russell stood on the stage. "I want to thank everyone for their help and for coming here to celebrate Lank and Carli."

A round of applause echoed through the barn.

She looked towards the happy couple. Russell said, "We raise our glasses to Lank and Carli and wish them a lifetime of love."

Carli and Lank stood with glasses raised. She took a sip and then Lank planted a kiss on her lips which garnered more whistles and applause from the crowd.

"And now, the most exciting part." Belinda stood at the microphone again. "Carli and Lank. Y'all come up here."

With Carli in the lead, Lank walked beside her with his arm around her waist. They stepped onto the stage. Belinda rested an arm around Carli's shoulder.

"We have a surprise for you," said Belinda. "I think you can agree that the decorating committee has outdone themselves. It is our honor to present you with a wedding gift. If you'll both turn around, the letters you see on this wall are yours to keep." Belinda gushed with excitement and giggles.

Lank hmpffed and Carli was speechless.

Belinda leaned closer to her ear. "Aren't they

great? You can't have the heart because that belongs to the Chamber for their Valentine's dance, but the metal letters are yours. I can hardly wait to see where you hang them."

Carli mumbled something and Belinda gave her a big hug. Russell hugged her too, and Carli turned. She stood frozen in the middle of the stage looking out over the beaming faces of the Dixon community.

Where in the world would she hang those galvanized, blinking giant metal letters spelling out their names? There wasn't a wall in her house big enough. And she knew without a doubt that the question on every person's lips over the next several months would be, "Where did you hang the letters?"

Chapter 36

Carli

Carli Jameson, soon-to-be Mrs. Torres, stood on the stage of the livestock barn and looked out over a sea of smiling faces filling the arena. From the metal stands on one side, a few more faces beamed and clapped. Behind her blinked giant metal letters spelling out her name. Beside her stood her fiancé of only a few weeks, and on the other side one of her best friends, Belinda, owner of the local coffee shop. Both had linked their arms in hers. Love and friendship cast a warm glow around the I Do BBQ event hosted by the entire town of Dixon.

The only thing on Carli's mind was finding the willpower not to throw up.

She took a few deep breaths, focused on keeping a smile on her face, but the delicious meal sat heavy in her throat. She jumped at the sound of a boisterous laugh and jumped again from a loud clatter in the kitchen.

"I had better go see if anyone needs helps," Belinda said, as she hopped off the stage and headed in the direction of the noise.

Carli couldn't take it any longer. She followed Belinda, but instead of going towards the kitchen she veered and pushed through a side door into the parking lot. She hurried to the back alley and found the dumpster just in case she lost the battle with her stomach.

Bending over she planted hands on her knees and focused on breathing. Squeezing her eyes tightly shut to keep the tears from rolling down her cheeks, she counted with trembling whispers. "One. Two. Three. You're not going crazy. Keep breathing. Four. Five. Six."

"Hey, Babe. Are you all right?" Lank bent over next to her and placed a hand on her back.

"No," she said.

"What's wrong?"

"It's too much. Too many lights. Too much of a crowd. Too much barbecue." She gripped her stomach with closed arms.

"Get it together and come back inside," Lank said with a tinge of impatience.

"Take me home."

"Nope. We're not leaving. We can't skip out on our own engagement party."

"Give me the keys. I'll drive myself." She stood and grabbed for his pocket.

"No." He side-stepped and spun away from her. "You're acting like a spoiled child."

She felt her face flush with anger. She could not go back inside and smile and pretend everything was all right.

"This town has worked hard to put this shindig on and we're not leaving."

"You don't have the right to tell me what to do."

Lank held up his hands in defeat. "You're right. I'm sorry. Can you please come back inside and make it through another hour or so? And then we'll leave."

Carli's anger smoldered but she saw the concern on his face. And as much as she hated to admit it, he was right. It would be more than a little rude to leave now.

"Okay. For a few more minutes."

He held out an elbow. "Soon-to-be Mrs. Torres. May I escort you back inside?"

She had to grin at that handsome face. Just before he opened the door for her, he stopped. "Don't say you have to leave because you're sick."

"Why not?"

"If they think you're not feeling well, more than a few good folks will think you're pregnant and then we'll have to suffer through a surprise baby shower."

Carli couldn't control her burst of laughter.

"Now cowboy up and put a smile on your face." Lank pulled open the door and as Carli stepped inside, she felt much calmer with his hand in hers.

"There they are. Just in time!" A voice echoed through the barn. "It's engagement party BINGO! Get your markers and cards over here."

People worked their way up towards the stage and then found seats at the tables. Belinda appeared in between Carli and Lank.

"We have spots saved for y'all up here." She ushered them towards the stage and once again Carli had to face the crowded room. Lank sat on one side of the podium and she had to sit on the other.

"Are you ready?"

Claps and whistles followed in answer to the question. A white-haired man with a Santa beard stood on the stage between Carli and Lank.

"This is how it works," he said. "I'm going to ask a question about the couple and depending on your answer you can mark your BINGO card or not. We'll find out the correct answer from them."

Lank held up his hand. "Give me a minute." He hurried over to the beverage center and dashed back with a cup which he put by Carli's chair. He leaned towards her ear and whispered. "Soda for your stomach." Then he kissed her on the nose which elicited more yee haws and whistles.

How could she stay mad at him? Her stomach was still clenched in a knot, but maybe she could make it another hour or so.

"The first question is, have Carli and Lank gone on a double date? Mark the square if you think yes."

"Hey, Lyle. What if I don't agree?" someone said.

"If your answer is no, and you don't think the situation applies to Carli and Lank, then do not mark your card."

He then turned to Lank. "Have y'all been on a double date?"

To which Lank answered, "Yes, we have." Carli jerked her head in his direction. Not that she could recall.

The emcee continued, "Have you sung a song really loud?" What followed was a myriad of questions that Lank answered yes to every single one.

Watched a sunrise? Visited a zoo? Took pics in a photo booth? Baked something yummy together? Got matching outfits? Kissed underwater? Went to a concert? Gone on a horseback ride together? Carli did agree that they had done that. Carli is the better cook. Getting married was Lank's idea. Lank was interested first and made the move. Finally, much to Carli's relief, someone at the back yelled "Bingo!" More than several minutes passed as they waited for the cashier from Grumpy Jack's Grocery to make her way to the front and hand her card over to be verified.

"It's a winner," said Lyle. "The prize is two packs of coffee beans from B & R Beanery and a rain gauge from the feed store."

And with that the band took the stage and before Carli could remind Lank she wanted to go home, he had her spinning around the dance floor again.

"I think the questions referred to you and me, not you doing those things with someone else. We've never done any of that together."

"Horseback riding." He answered with a smug look.

"Okay, fine. One thing we've done together."

It suddenly dawned on Carli that she was about to marry a man that she knew nothing about. "You're a total stranger," she said. "I don't even know you and I'm about to marry you. That's crazy."

"Is this crazy?" He looked deep into her eyes and covered her mouth with his lips. The caress of his kiss sent the pit of her stomach into a wild swirl, and not the same feeling that she had had only a few minutes before in the alley. His arms tightened around her, and she sank into their warmth. This man. This moment. Without a doubt in her mind, this was where she was supposed to be. She had waited a lifetime for this. Tears bubbled into her eyes, and she looked at the ceiling to stop them from falling down her face.

"Are you sick again?" Lank froze in place and with his thumb he wiped the dampness from her cheeks. "We can go right now."

"I'm fine," she muttered.

"What's wrong then?"

"I just can't wait to be your wife," she said.

He kissed her again. They spent the next hour lost in their own world dancing under that brilliantly twinkling ceiling until the band played the last number. When the music stopped, Carli did not want to leave Lank's arms. They stood together for a minute and then someone turned on the fluorescent lights and the magical night was over.

"Where are you parked?" asked Russell as he held a giant L.

Lank gave Carli a shrug, a peck on her cheek, and turned toward the door.

"Aren't these great?" Belinda asked as she stood next to Carli holding the C.

Over the next half hour, people worked to straighten up the event space and Carli watched several men carry giant tin letters out to the parking lot.

"I can't thank you enough, Belinda. This was just so beautiful. We really appreciate it." Carli gave her a hug.

"We were glad to do it. Everyone is so happy for you two. Lank's had a tough year and so have you. I'm just glad you found each other."

"Thanks, friend. You are planning to be one of my bridesmaids, aren't you?"

"Wouldn't miss it for the world," said Belinda.

Carli waved and said thanks to a few more people as she walked towards the pickup truck. Just before she climbed in, the little lady who had won the bingo stopped and turned towards her. "Where are you hangin' those letters?"

"I'm not sure yet but thank you."

The woman nodded and began her unhurried walk towards her car.

"We're going to have to drive slow so none of the dang things blow out," Lank said as she snapped on her seat belt.

Carli laughed.

"I'm glad you're feeling better," he said.

"I am. It was just a little panic attack I think," said Carli.

"I know this was stressful, but they mean well."

"It was nice dancing with you," she said. "We should do that more often."

They drove home in silence, Carli lost in the thought of being someone's wife. Anxiety nagged her, but not as strong as before.

She felt confident in the future God had planned for her. For them.

Chapter 37

Carli

"Where have you lived most of your life? Do you remember the last time you saw your mother, Michelle? When did you move to Atlanta?"

Del rapid-fired questions from the back seat to Carli on the drive to the Eastwood County Courthouse, so fast she didn't have time to answer in between so she rode in silence and focused on her breathing. Her pulses pounded. She would not allow anyone to know her frustration.

"Do not give any more information than the question raised. If you weren't there, then you cannot testify as to what happened. You cannot assume you know what was said. Unless you have firsthand knowledge, then your answer is 'I don't know'."

"I think she'll do fine," Lank said as he steered into the county building parking lot. He nodded at Carli and gave her hand a squeeze.

"If she can keep her cool. They will try everything in the book to rattle her, make her doubt every word that comes from her mouth. They will twist your words, but you have to be confident. We need to remain professional and let the legal system work for us," Del said.

Carli clenched her jaw and resolved to not let her emotions gain control, no matter what questions they had for her.

"This is an historic courthouse, by the way. Completed in 1891. If those walls could talk..." said Del. They got out of the pickup truck just as Buck and Lola pulled into a parking spot.

Carli admired the Romanesque Revival architecture of the four-story brick structure complete with several towers and a turret. An arch of white stone emphasized the entrance at the base of the tower.

Inside Carli was stunned at the preservation and attention to detail. Dark red wood banister and stained-glass panels above the doors made her feel like she had stepped back in time. The ghosts of history long ago seemed to seep from the walls. Distinguished lawmakers, leaders of the community, and criminals whose lives were forever changed through a vote of twelve. Innocent until proven guilty. It all happened in the same space where Carli now stood.

The group followed Del into a room with more wood and high ceilings, their footsteps echoing on the tile floor. Antique wooden folding chairs were divided by a narrow center aisle. Carli sat next to Del at the front table, and the others filed into the first row directly behind them.

Carli remembered her grandparents' attorney, Patrick, who had helped her before. Very distinguished yet not typical in appearance, wearing a western cut suit, a bright blue shirt, and a bolo tie that had a chunk of turquoise attached. He rose to greet them and extended his hand to Carli, and then turned to acknowledge her support group. She was thankful they were all there. She heard commotion and the footsteps of others who were finding seats behind her, but she never turned around.

Not long after that, Billy Broderick walked with arrogant purpose up the center aisle followed by four suits, each one looking like a carbon copy of the other. Wearing red ties, clean shaven, short haircuts, and all were around Carli's age. They didn't acknowledge her or her counsel.

"All rise. Circuit Court for the Twelfth Judicial District, Eastwood County, State of Texas, is now in session," the bailiff intoned in a sing-song voice that resounded through the room. "The Honorable E. Winston Flagg presiding."

"Good morning, ladies and gentlemen," Judge Flagg said. "Court is in session, and we are on the record. We are here for the preliminary hearing regarding the contested Last Will and Testament of Ward Kimball. Introduce yourselves for the record."

"Thank you, your honor. Patrick Gilcrest representing Ms. Jameson."

"Good morning, your honor. Also representing Ms. Jameson, Adelphia Fenwick. And seated to my left is Carlotta Jean Jameson."

"Morning Winston. You know who I am," Billy said.

The judge flashed his friend a broad grin and then cleared his throat. "How are you doing, Billy? State your full name for the record, please."

"My name is Billy Broderick, and these here are my attorneys because we aim to prove the girl sitting right there is a fraud." He stood and pointed to

Carli, while one of his attorneys placed a hand on his arm. Billy shook the hand off and kept talking.

"It is our intention to prove that Ward Kimball and his hired den of snakes found this girl, falsely claimed she was Ward's granddaughter, and then stole the ranch right out from under me."

"Thanks, Billy, but your legal counsel needs to present the case. We have a specific order of doing things. You know that," the judge said.

"Yeah, Winston. I understand. Let's get this dog an' pony show rolling. The monkeys have to get back to their cages." Billy hooked a thumb in Carli's direction.

One of Billy's attorneys muffled a chuckle. Carli could feel anger rise from Del who maintained her poise. If Del could keep her cool, then Carli could too. They had to present a unified front of professionalism and calm. The law was on their side. Carli wasn't sure what was going on, but she felt the tension in the room. This wasn't a friendly assembly.

"You may all be seated." Judge Flagg opened a file folder that the bailiff had placed in front of him. He studied the documents for a few minutes. "I do agree that Mr. Broderick has legal standing in this case because he was named as sole heir in Jean Jameson Kimball's Will, wife of Ward. And Ward changed his Will only one month before his death."

"Which appears as crooked as a snake in a cactus patch, Winston."

"Billy. Your attorneys have to speak for you, and while you're in my courtroom you must address me as Judge Winston or Your Honor."

"I know, I know." Billy eased back in his chair, stretched his legs under the table, and crossed both arms over his chest.

One of his suits stood. "Your Honor. We contend that Ward Kimball was not of sound mind and was in fact coerced to go against the wishes of his beloved wife, Jean. He was unduly influenced, Your Honor."

"Objection!" Patrick stood, his voice booming throughout the room. "They were not at the signing of Ward's Will, and I was. Mr. Kimball was perfectly coherent and had all of his faculties."

"You're lying," Billy said. "Who were the witnesses?"

Del let out a hmpff sound.

Patrick ignored the outburst and continued. "He understood his assets and exhibited no signs of dementia. Ward Kimball knew without a shadow of any doubt that his only grandchild had finally been found. He asked me to prepare a new Will for him. That child is sitting in this room. Young woman now."

All eyes turned to look at Carli. She shrank under their scrutiny.

"It lists several names as witnesses," the judge said. "Who are these people?"

Patrick said, "Employees of the hospital where Ward spent his last days. I believe they are all present today, if you'd like to question them, Your Honor."

Billy slung a glance to look behind him. The judge seemed to avoid Patrick's eyes and looked down at the file. "That won't be necessary," he mumbled.

Carli rotated slightly in her chair to see the back row filled with several women. Some wore hospital scrubs and their employee badges.

The courtroom grew silent as the judge flipped

through the documents. "I'd like to visit with Ms. Jameson please. Ask her to take the stand."

Carli didn't miss the smug look that Billy gave her. Fear stuck in her throat and her hands grew clammy.

Del leaned closer. "Just keep your cool. You'll do fine."

Carli nodded to show Del she understood and slowly rose as eyes turned to her again.

Here I go. Back to the hot seat.

Chapter 38

Carli

Carli stood and slowly walked towards the witness stand in the Eastwood County Courthouse. After the bailiff had sworn her in, she sat and looked out to see all eyes focused on her. Lank, Buck, and Lola sat on the front row, concern displayed on their faces. Lola's head was bowed, and her lips were moving, no doubt in prayer. Carli could definitely use some divine intervention about now. Lank nodded at her. Del nodded also and gave her a discreet thumbs up using only one thumb.

Behind them she saw Angie Olsen and Colton Creacy. Belinda and Russell from the coffee shop were there too. Crazy Vera was sitting on the very back row and raised an arm in greeting. Her friends and neighbors were there to support her, and their presence gave her courage.

Billy Broderick did not hide the sneer of contempt on his face while on either side of him his legal counsel remained stone-faced. Judge Flagg turned his chair in her direction and rolled it closer. Carli turned slightly in the witness stand to meet his gaze. Her hands were clammy, so she clasped them together in her lap.

"Good morning, Ms. Jameson. How are you?" He gave her a warm smile. She guessed him to be older than he looked, his blue eyes spoke of power and strength, his black robe reminded her of the seriousness of the situation.

"I'm doing fine, Your Honor."

"That's good. Glad to hear it. Have you ever met your Grandpa Ward, Ms. Jameson?"

"Yes, sir. Once when I was about ten, although I didn't understand who he was at the time." Carli felt her stomach knot. Do not offer any extra information. Just answer the question.

"How much did you know about the Wild Cow Ranch?"

"Nothing, Your Honor. I didn't know the Wild Cow Ranch existed until a year ago when I was notified about my grandfather's Will."

"Do we have any documentation that might link Ms. Jameson to her supposed grandparent?" The judge looked towards Del and Patrick.

"Yes, sir. We have her birth certificate which should be in the official papers provided to the court," said Del.

"I don't have it now. Can you produce that, please?" the judge said.

Del sorted through the documents in her file folder. "It's not here," Del answered in an uncertain tone. Her eyes narrowed and her cheeks turned pink as she sorted through the stack of papers again.

Carli didn't miss the bone-chilling grin of satisfaction that came over Billy's face. He leaned back, at ease and in control. Carli gasped as realization hit her.

Billy must have taken the only copy of her birth certificate when he was in her house before. She had given it to Del who had put it in her portfolio. There was no doubt about it. Billy was a liar and a thief.

"Sorry, Your Honor. I can't seem to find it." Del looked at Patrick and shrugged her shoulders.

"Told you, Winston. They are lying! She's no more kin to Jean and Ward than I am to the King of England." Billy stood. "They tricked poor Ward on his deathbed."

"Sorry I'm late. Winston, how are ya?"

Carli looked up to see Taylor Miller sit down on the first row behind Billy and his attorneys. Billy turned and shook his hand. "Thanks for coming."

The judge raised a hand in greeting and smiled. "Taylor. Good to see you. Are you here to help your old boy, Billy?"

Taylor laughed. "Yes, sir, I am. Thought he might need a character witness."

"Ms. Fenwick. I'm still waiting for that document." Judge Flagg appeared bored and aggravated as he glared at Del.

Del stood and looked from the judge to Billy's side of the courthouse and back again. "With all due respect, Judge Flagg, this is a dog and pony show! You know very well that birth certificate was part of the documents. Your assistant and I talked about the files I provided."

The judge's eyes glinted mean as he rapped his gavel. "Your outburst is totally unacceptable in my court and so is your hair color."

"You are trying our case and not letting the evidence tell the story, sir," she argued. So much for keeping a calm demeanor and not letting them get to us. Guess that strategy just went out the window. Inside Carli was cheering but she kept her face rigid.

"Bailiff. Escort Ms. Fenwick to a holding cell."

A collective gasp sounded in the room as stunned faces looked at the judge. Carli's heart thudded in her chest. She couldn't stop the trembling in her hands. Del stood and followed the bailiff across the front of the court through a side door. Everyone watched without saying a word. Carli looked at Patrick. His face stone, no emotion whatsoever. So, this is how you lose your entire family's holdings in one moment.

"With no birth certificate and no solid evidence that she's who she claims to be, I guess Ward's Will is null and void. It was the intent of the Jameson family all along that I inherit the Wild Cow Ranch. Seems like a cut and dried case to me. Thanks, Winston." Billy stood as if to leave.

"Seems like I got here at the right time," said Taylor. "May I speak, Your Honor?"

"Mr. Miller. You have the floor." The judge nodded his head.

"I actually have a copy of Ms. Jameson's birth certificate as well. May I approach the bench?"

"Yes. Let's see it."

Taylor did not look at Carli as he walked towards Judge Flagg. He handed him a piece of paper which the judge studied for several minutes.

"Are you aware that your name is listed as the birth father?" Judge Flagg asked.

Carli's heart pounded and she felt her throat close.

"Yes, sir, I am aware."

"How did you obtain this copy?"

"I was able to request it from the adoption agency. Since the birth mother is deceased and both guardians are deceased, I requested that the files be unsealed. As I suspected, they discovered Michelle had listed me as birth father in the agency files, but my name was not on the official certificate filed with the county. She left my name off. I have no doubt that I am Carli's father."

After several long moments, Judge Flagg picked up his gavel. "This seems in order. Case dismissed." The judge's gavel cracked in the room.

"This is an outrage and you know it, Winston!" Billy's voice boomed with rage. He came out from behind the table and stood in front of Carli within seconds blocking her way from leaving the witness stand.

Billy leaned closer. "I made you disappear once; I can do it again." He murmured the threat so that only she could hear it.

Realization of what he said made Carli's heart ache and she fought back tears. She would never give him the satisfaction of seeing her cry. "You paid them to keep me away?"

"Yes, the Fitzgeralds were easy to deal with. And I kept all of your mother's secrets too. Jean and Ward never knew where she was." He gave her a smug smile of satisfaction. "And you were never meant to be a part of their lives."

"Billy, you need to step away from the witness. Ms. Jameson, you may step down now," the judge said.

With a snide look Billy pointed a finger in her face. "You're a phony. I've had enough of you." His voice boomed throughout the room, echoing off the walls.

He lunged. Carli took a sharp breath and ducked her head. Taylor Miller suddenly stepped in between them. Lank catapulted over the railing and the table to appear on the other side of Billy.

"It's over, Billy. The birth certificate is legitimate, and you know it." Taylor grabbed both of his shoulders. "The Wild Cow Ranch is not yours."

Billy turned on his friend next, his face red and his lips curled. His hand formed in a fist. Taylor did not back down.

"In fact, what did you know, Billy? Michelle counted you as one of her best and trusted friends. She told you more than she ever told me."

Billy took a step back and diverted his eyes from Taylor's glare.

"You're not telling us everything, are you?"

"What do you know about this, Billy?" Judge Flagg leaned forward in his chair. "Birth certificate is legitimate. You might as well accept that and move on."

Billy darted a glance at Carli and then back to Taylor. "I have nothing else to say."

"What did you know?" Taylor asked. "Jean and Ward worried themselves sick and spent their whole lives searching for the baby Michelle had abandoned."

"Ward always resented me. Why should I help him with anything? I can move on, but she'll still be just as worthless as her no-good mother. Yeah, it was me. I gave her a ride to Amarillo on my motorcycle that night." Billy glared at Carli. "I don't need the Wild Cow Ranch. It's just a useless piece of dirt. I have other properties and can build a lakefront community somewhere else. Good riddance." He almost spit the last part.

"That's the most sensible thing you can do, Billy," Judge Flagg said. "Are we still on for golf on Saturday?"

"Sure. See ya then, Winston." Billy turned and left, his legal suits following behind him in a neat line.

Taylor turned to Carli. "I never knew about you. I'm sorry."

"And I never knew about you until I moved here. This isn't the way I had planned for you to find out. I'm sorry too." She stood and walked down two steps out of the witness box holding out her hand. "We met once before, but hello again. I'm Carli. It's good to finally meet you."

"I'm Taylor, your father. I look forward to getting to know you, Carli." Instead of shaking her hand, he wrapped both arms around her in a warm hug.

"This is Lank," Carli said with a nod of her head. "He's my fiancé. Would you consider walking me down the aisle on Saturday?"

"Wouldn't miss it for the world," said Taylor as he turned to shake Lank's hand. "Congratulations and welcome to the family."

Lank had a hand on her shoulder on one side, and Buck and Lola stood on the other. Before long the rest of her friends had gathered around them all talking at once.

"Back up. Give her some air," said Patrick. He walked closer to Carli and gave her a hug. "I'm glad this worked out. Good luck to you. I've got to get Del out of jail now."

"Should we wait?" asked Carli.

"I can give her a ride back to the ranch."

Lank put his arm around Carli. "I should get you home."

"Yes. It's been an interesting morning. We can talk later," said Taylor.

Carli walked to the parking lot, everyone still talking at once about the long- held secrets Billy had revealed. They said goodbyes and she climbed up into Lank's pickup truck. In the silence the situation suddenly hit her. Everyone she had trusted had betrayed her. Her guardians had kept her hidden from her own grandparents, and that explained how they could afford to keep her in show horses and horseback riding lessons the entire time she was growing up. She really had been alone.

Her insides trembled like she was going to throw up, and she couldn't stop her hands from shaking. Lank turned to look at her.

"What's wrong with you?" he asked.

She couldn't find enough air to answer. Her throat seemed closed. She gasped.

"Carli. What's wrong?" Lank jumped out of the truck and ran around to her side, yanking open the door. "Get out." He pulled on her arm.

"Bend over. Put your head between your knees. You won't fall. I've got you."

Carli did as he told her, closing her eyes and focused on not passing out. "I'm better now."

"This is getting ridiculous. With the hearing, finding your birth father, and the wedding in a few days. There's no reason to have to deal with all of this in such a short time. Something has to give," Lank said.

"What has to give?" Carli stood and looked at

him. "Tell me which part I can make go away, because it's all real. This is my life." She couldn't stop the tears that rolled down her cheeks.

Lank pulled her close into a hug. "I'm sorry."

Carli sniffed and wiped her face. "I just have to make it through Saturday. We'll be married and then we can begin again. I can do this."

"There may be a solution before then." Lank helped her back into the truck and he walked around to the driver's side.

"What do you mean? What are you talking about?" Carli asked.

"Don't worry. Close your eyes and relax. We'll be back at the ranch soon." His jaw clenched and his eyes fixed on the road ahead.

Carli didn't press him for more information. She was exhausted, but tomorrow she'd wake up knowing, without a shadow of a doubt, that Taylor Miller was indeed her birth father.

Chapter 39

Carli

"There's one more little thing we've got left to do," said Lola as Carli poured their coffee.

They were sitting at the kitchen table in Carli's house, and of course Lola had her wedding planner notebook open. At least there were highlights and checkmarks, Carli noticed. Progress was being made.

The wedding was on Saturday, and this was Thursday, and surely everything on Lola's list had been done. Carli wanted to bury her head in her hands and collapse on the table, but she used self-control instead keeping her face emotionless. *Please, God, get me through this week.*

"I'll be honest with you," Carli said. "I never dreamed there was this much preparation and decision required for a wedding. I'm exhausted by it all."

"I know you are, and I'm sorry to have kept pressing so hard these past few weeks. But you know I love you and Lank, and I just want you to have a day that you'll never forget. Getting married is one of the most important days in your life.

It has to be perfect."

"Whatever happens on Saturday, I want you to know that we really do appreciate your efforts. Even if it all doesn't come together..."

A gasp from Lola.

Carli continued, "...as long as Lank is at my side, that's all that matters."

"Well, it *will* come together if I have anything to say about it." And by the clench of her jaw and the look on her face, she meant it. "Now, get dressed. We have an appointment in Dixon for hair and nails. Be ready in fifteen." Lola jumped up from the table with her usual bounce of energy. "I'll be back to pick you up."

After Lola had disappeared out the front door, Carli did in fact collapse with her head in her hands. She would make it through to Saturday. She had to. She felt as though she were sinking into a nightmare of dresses, cake, and details that meant nothing to her.

As Carli got dressed, she thought about what little she knew of Lank. They had had a whirlwind romance, no doubt. How strange that she was marrying a total stranger. The thought created a slight panic, but she suppressed it. There were so many things they needed to talk about, but when would they ever have the time?

Her wedding was in two days and now she was wanting to slow things down? Good grief, she was such a coward. Before she could depress herself any further, Lola honked the horn and Carli ran out the door.

"What color do you want your nails, and do you want anything special done with your hair?" Lola asked before Carli could get her seatbelt secured.

"Have not given it much thought until now. I don't know," said Carli.

Lola sighed and kept driving. They rode in silence to town.

One block from the four-way stop in Dixon, a long and low stucco building sported a bright yellow awning over the door. Black letters on the front window read Curl Up & Dye.

"You're gonna love this place." Lola beamed.

With a heavy heart Carli trudged into the salon behind Lola all the while giving herself a pep talk inside her head. Smile. Be kind. This is important for Lola. She's worked so hard to make Saturday special.

The cheery yellow outside did nothing to prepare Carli for the inside. Rock and roll music blasted her ears. The walls were gray, the chairs were black, and the carpet was a deep purple. The only lights hung above the mirrors. A sign behind the front counter declared, "We do tattoos."

And the smell. What was that ammonia smell? Carli hoped her stomach could handle it.

"Lola, love!" A middle-aged woman dressed in head-to-toe black yelled above the music. "Let me turn that down."

"This is Carli," said Lola as they greeted each other with an air smooch. "Meet Chimmi."

"Ah, the bride. Welcome, welcome."

Carli smiled and allowed the woman to lead her to a chair.

"Good bone structure. Beautiful eyes. I know of the perfect color and a good trim."

"I'm leaving her in your hands."

Carli couldn't hide the shock on her face when she cut a glance towards Lola.

Chimmi laughed. "It's all right. No worries."

A young lady with bright purple hair emerged from behind a black curtain and sat behind the manicure booth.

"I can never decide what color I want," said Lola as she took a seat in front of the nail tech.

Carli turned her attention back to the lady who held the destiny of her hair in her hands, and noticed that behind the excessive makeup, the woman was quite attractive. She had violet eyes rimmed with long eyelashes, and her skin was flawless but almost too pale.

The door chimed and another patron entered. The girl who came from the back looked more normal than her two co-workers and offered a greeting. "Good morning. Ready to wash out that curl?"

"Aspen is our nail tech and Olivia rents booth space from me. Are you opposed to some highlights?" Chimmi asked.

"I suppose not," Carli said, "but I've never had any color on my hair before."

Chimmi began mixing up a concoction combined from several tubes. Using clips, she segmented Carli's hair and began brushing on the thick goop.

"Have you picked out your china pattern?"

Carli looked at her in surprise. "No."

"Gosh darn it, Carli. We were supposed to go by *Bed, Bath and Beyond* weeks ago. It wasn't on my list." Lola shook her head; a frown wrinkled her forehead.

"I think our marriage will survive without a china pattern."

"Every girl must have her own china pattern," said the lady who emerged from the back room with a towel wrapped around her wet hair.

"My mother is giving me hers," said Olivia. "I'm going to add pieces to it as I find them."

Carli recalled a similar conversation with Lank's sister last Christmas. "All good Southern women pick out that special china pattern so they can store the dishes in their special china cabinet. The husband and kids are not allowed to eat on the special china." Carli smiled to herself remembering the conversation.

"My grandmother left me enough dishes. I really don't need any more," said Carli.

"So, what's your something blue?" asked Chimmi.

"And your something new?" piped in Olivia.

"I can't believe that's not on my list either," said Lola. "You better start thinking about it now, Carli. We want this wedding to come off without a hitch and for you and Lank to have all the best in your new life together."

Carli had never heard of the traditions of marriage. She didn't have an answer for them.

"Hang on, I've got the blue covered." Chimmi mixed up a small dollop of goop and working at the back of Carli's head, she covered strands of hair, covered them in foil, and put everything up under a plastic cap.

Carli was horrified but didn't have the nerve to ask or argue. If worse came to worse, she'd just grab her cowboy hat and wear it all day on Saturday.

While the color set, Chimmi rinsed out Lola and gave her a haircut. Carli listened to the chatter about wedding traditions and the different weddings Chimmi had been to. She did hair and make-up for many of her clients during special occasions.

Lola had grown strangely quiet, and didn't offer much to the conversation, Carli noticed.

Finally, the color was set, Carli was rinsed out, and Chimmi finished with a trim and blow-dry.

"Gorgeous," said Lola.

"I know," said Chimmi.

She turned Carli around to face the mirror and she looked back at herself with wide eyes and open mouth. The highlights definitely made her eyes look larger, and Chimmi had trimmed at least an inch off the bottom, layering her bangs long to just above her jawline with more layers that tapered to her elbow in length. Carli couldn't believe the transformation and her hair felt so soft and full. She loved it. She was speechless.

Chimmi's laughter filled the shop. "I knew you'd like it. No charge. My wedding present. All the best on Saturday to you and Lank."

Carli's eyes filled with tears at the kind gesture. The people of Dixon were always surprising her at every turn.

Chapter 40

Carli

Beau stood still in the crossties as Carli showered him off with the hose. She had needed that ride, to get away from all the craziness. Only one more day of it. Tomorrow she'd become Mrs. Lank Torres, for which she was ecstatically happy and excited.

But it also meant she would have to wear that dress, although it was an amazing dress she had to admit, keep up with an oversized bunch of flowers, and smile while on display in front of all those people. If only she could have stayed on Beau, maybe ride to the next county and hide out somewhere. Always a private person, she was used to keeping on her own and staying busy. She would rather spend time with her horses than people.

She had kept Beau out in the pasture for as long as she could since early this morning, and reveled in the quiet of the endless view and blue sky. The sound of Beau's hooves crunching the brown grass with each step calmed her nerves, the frenzy of the past month melted away.

There were cars parked in front of the cookhouse as the decorating committee got ready for tomorrow. She was staying as far away from that place as possible. Also, another group had unloaded the backs of their SUVs at the barn where the reception was being held. She had never seen that much lighting and streamers.

What if she quietly left? She could disappear, but she imagined flashing blue lights and police searching for her. That wouldn't be pretty. A runaway bride would throw the good people of Dixon into an upsetting tizzy. No, she would force herself to go through the motions, wear the clothes, smile the expected smile, and just get through the day.

She let the cold water run over Beau's legs while she prayed quietly. No one was around. Lank had said he needed to pick something up in town.

Lord, what's wrong with me? Why am I not like other brides? Please help me to not be so selfish, and instead be thankful for all the people who have worked so hard to make our wedding special. Help me have a change of attitude.

Right then her horse's lips fluttered in a raspberry motion, along with a drippy sneeze, and sprayed Carli's jeans, T-shirt, and hair with green grass snot and foam.

Oh, yuck. Thanks a lot, Beau. And God, I hope that's not your answer. You know I need you to get me through this. Please.

Her back jean pocket vibrated so she set the hose down while Beau continued to flutter his lips. While she fumbled for the phone with one hand, she dropped the hose, and it sprayed the entire right side of her pants leg. Beau ignored her. He was playing and appeared to enjoy the cool down time.

Carli rubbed her hands on her jeans and held the phone which displayed handsome Lank's face. "Hey, babe. What's going on?" she said.

"Where have you been?" he demanded.

"Riding Beau." She was taken aback at his tone but decided not to start an argument with him.

"I've been calling and texting for over an hour."

"Must have been in a low place with no signal. My phone didn't ring." Sure enough, she looked at recent calls and there was Lank listed about ten times. Just then her text messages buzzed and all the texts from Lank appeared in her feed. "There you are. My signal is strong now. Sorry I missed your call."

"I need you, Carli." His voice forceful and tinged with frustration.

"Well, I need you too, babe."

"I mean, I need you now. At the Creek County courthouse in Sanford."

"What? Why?"

"We discovered a problem with the marriage certificate, the date or our names or something, so I'm at the courthouse trying to get a corrected one. The clerk said you have to be present to sign. I need you to come here now."

"But, Lank, I'm a mess. I just rode Beau and am rinsing him off."

"Carli, it doesn't matter. Come as you are, as quick as you can. Okay?"

"Well, all right. If I just need to come in, sign my name, and be done, I guess it doesn't matter what I'm wearing. I'll be there as soon as possible."

Carli put Beau in a stall rather than turning him out where he would probably roll around in the dirt after his clean shower. And after their big ride, maybe he'd have a snooze. Hopping in her truck, she looked in the rearview mirror at herself and tried not to gasp. She ran her fingers through her hair but that didn't help much. While she drove, she reached for a lip gloss to try to improve her appearance.

***

It took Carli only thirty minutes to get to the downtown square. Glad to find a parking spot in the first row nearest the courthouse, she jumped out and headed through the door. Lank was there waiting for her. She hugged him and he kissed her cheek.

"They're waiting for us in room 2-C," Lank said.

Carli looked around. "Why can't I just sign the paper over there at the main counter?"

Lank stammered, "That's what they told me to do. I'm just following instructions."

Carli's face scrunched, but she followed him towards the stairs and up to the second floor.

They opened a door with a plaque that read Judge William D. Richards. Lank stopped in a reception area where a lady behind the desk smiled a greeting.

"Hey, Carli."

Carli's head snapped around to see Angie Olsen sitting on the sofa next to her boyfriend and Lank's best friend, Colton Creacy.

"What's going on?" Carli asked. "What are you two doing here?" Shock gave her a jolt and she squealed. "Are you getting a marriage license too? Oh my gosh! This is so exciting!"

"No, no." Angie jumped up and then giggled. She glanced at Lank with a funny look on her face but didn't say anything else. Just stared at Carli with a big smile.

Lank wore a silly grin too, but nobody was talking. Something was going on and she needed to know what it was. She placed her hands on her hips and squared up in front of Lank to demand he tell her why they were in a judge's office. Before Carli opened her mouth another voice stopped her.

"Hello, Carli."

Carli had not noticed the young couple standing in one corner. Her eyes widened in surprise and her mouth dropped open. "Nathan Olsen? Is that you? What are you doing here?"

Neighboring rancher and Angie's oldest brother Nathan had become Carli's best friend right after she had arrived in Texas. Still as handsome as ever, he had lost his cowboy flair; instead, he looked exactly like the artist he was. His hair went past his collar, and he wore khaki pants with an untucked shirt, but he still wore cowboy boots. She couldn't take her eyes off the stunningly beautiful woman who stood next to him. Tall, slim, African American with a caramel complexion and corn rows that reached to the middle of her back. Obviously, a model or celebrity. They both came towards Carli, and Nathan gave her a hug.

"What are you doing here?" Carli asked, now completely confused as she looked at the people who stood in a circle around her.

"It's good to see you. Mother had told me about your engagement," Nathan said, "so I called to congratulate Lank last night. It was spur of the moment that we decided to drive up. He invited me...us...to, uhhhh...your special occasion."

Carli didn't miss the fact that Lank was vigorously shaking his head no. She glanced in his direction and then back to Nathan.

"And this is my wife, Indya. We were married a couple of weeks ago,"

"You're married?" Carli and Angie asked in unison.

"You just happened to forget that little detail when you saw your sister?" Angie looked at him with furious intensity.

Nathan and Indya both laughed.

"Hi, Carli," Indya said. "So nice to meet you."

Carli shook her outstretched hand.

"Yes, but no one knows," Nathan said. "It's perfect timing for us to be here to celebrate your news. And then we'll tell my folks ours. We're very happy for you both."

"Santa Fe, New Mexico agrees with you, friend," Carli said.

"Yes, I believe it does. We love it there." He squeezed Indya closer as they beamed at each other.

Carli smiled at her friend. Seeing him so at peace and happy made her happy. *Looks like he found what he was looking for.*

The door to the inner office suddenly opened and a man stepped out. "Do I have people waiting?"

"The judge will see you now," the secretary said with a warm smile.

Chapter 41

Carli

Carli stared back at the circle of people who stared at her, and then she cast a glance at the judge who turned and disappeared into his office.

Lank moved towards her. "I know this might be a lot, Carli. I just wanted to surprise you. We could get married here. Now. What do you think?"

A whole range of emotions passed through Carli's mind at once. She had so many questions, shock at seeing their friends, exhaustion from the past month, and intense love for the man who stood before her.

"You got me a non-wedding ceremony for my wedding?" she asked.

"Yes, I did," came the simple reply after the laughter died down, with a look of apprehension as if she might bite at any moment. "I thought the whole wedding hoopla was getting to be too much for you," Lank said, "that maybe you wanted things to be a whole lot simpler."

"I can't believe you did this," said Carli.

Lank leaned closer to her ear and whispered.

"Those panic attacks really got to me. I was terrified. This shouldn't be stressful. This should be one of the best days of our life."

"How did you get to be so wise?" Carli croaked as emotion stuck in her throat and unshed tears clouded her vision.

The man in the suit and robe spoke. "Miss, if you're ready we can get started."

Looking into Lank's eyes, she melted and then horror struck. "Look at me! I'm such a mess. I was washing Beau and he slobbered all over me."

Indya interrupted. "Carli, if you don't mind, I think I can help. There might be a few things in here that will work." She hefted a large shoulder purse and then put an arm around Carli's shoulder. "Come with me. We'll be back in a moment."

"This is my last appointment for the morning, just as long as I can tee off at two. Take all the time you need, ladies."

The guys nodded and Angie said, "I'm coming too. I'm the maid of honor."

When they were back in the outer office, Indya said, "We're about the same size. It would be easy to switch clothes. Where's the ladies' room?"

The secretary gave the directions and they walked down the hall. Carli was in a daze. She had no idea what was said or where they were going.

"I can't ask you to do that. And what would you wear? My slobbery clothes?" Carli was horrified at the thought.

"It would only be for the ceremony, just a few minutes and then we can switch back. What do you say?" Indya was so beautiful and had such a kind expression.

"I think you should do it," said Angie.

Carli took a deep breath and shrugged her shoulders. "Okay. Why not? But I'm keeping my boots on." She washed her face and hands in the sink, and then dropped her dusty clothes on the tile floor.

Indya stepped out of her elastic-waisted long flouncy skirt. It was festive in a paisley design and many colors. She removed her leather jacket. Passing her peasant style white blouse to Carli to put on, Indya then arranged it off Carli's shoulders a bit.

Carli handed Indya her jeans and T-shirt who put them on followed by her jacket, which pretty much covered up the green horse slobber. She looped Carli's western belt around her waist and linked the buckle.

When Carli was dressed, the three women assessed her looks in the mirror.

"Not bad," said Angie.

"What am I going to tell everyone? What about tomorrow?" Carli couldn't help but ask. As usual her doubtful mind and worry took over everything she did.

"Live for the moment, Carli." Angie took both of her hands. "We'll figure out tomorrow, tomorrow."

Carli nodded her head. *I can do this. Help me, Lord.*

"Wait," Indya said. Dumping her cavernous hippy-styled boho bag onto the floor spread with paper towels. "I've got everything in here. Let me fix your hair."

She clipped Carli's hair back on the sides, then took some of the many bracelets from her wrist and put them on Carli's.

"You have beautiful eyes," said Indya.

"Are you a model?" asked Carli.

"You're a celebrity, aren't you? It would be just like my brother to bring a movie star home," Angie added.

Indya's musical laugh echoed in the bathroom as she dug in her bag. "Well, I have been in a few commercials, and I have modeled."

"I knew it!" said Angie.

"Close your eyes." A few dabs of makeup, a swipe of mascara, and then she handed Carli a lipstick tube.

"Not bad." Indya stood back and surveyed her handiwork.

"I can't thank you enough for doing this. I feel a little more cleaned up. I'm sorry you have to wear my dirty clothes."

"It's not for too long. Let's just get you hitched, girl."

Before they left the restroom, Indya exclaimed, "Hey! I could get music on my phone. Do you want *Here Comes the Bride*?"

"How 'bout 'Bless the Broken Road'?"

"Oh, that's a good one. Okay, Bride, let's do this."

They left the bathroom and turned back towards the judge's office.

"Wait. One more thing," said Angie. She yanked a handful of silk flowers out of an elaborate arrangement that stood on an antique sideboard in the hall.

Carli held the flowers in front of her and struck a pose.

"Gorgeous." Indya smiled with satisfaction. "My work is done."

"So beautiful, friend. Lank is going to flip his

lid," said Angie as she leaned in and gave Carli a quick hug.

As they opened the door, Carli stopped short and felt her heart might explode out of her chest.

Taylor Miller, her birth father.

He and a woman stood up and walked towards her.

"Hi, Carli." He smiled. "This is my wife, Karissa. Lank called us."

Carli had been able to hold back the emotion, but this time she failed. Tears streamed down her cheeks.

Taylor Miller stepped in front of her. "Carli, if you would like, I'd be honored to walk you to your groom."

So many emotions flooded her. She sniffed and managed to say, "That would be really wonderful. Thank you."

"It is truly an honor," Taylor said.

"Thanks for coming to the hearing about the ranch this week. I really appreciate all that you did." Carli looked up at him.

"I never knew about you. You have to believe me," he said.

The secretary handed her a tissue. Indya and Angie slid around them, smiling at Taylor Miller. Karissa followed the girls into the judge's chamber.

Carli heard Indya cue the music on her cell phone.

"Are you ready?" Taylor asked.

"Yes, I am," replied Carli.

Taylor held out his elbow to her. He whispered in her ear, "I'm sorry for all the lost years. But we can make up for them. I wish you much happiness with Lank."

With misty eyes, Carli linked her arm with his. "Thank you for being here. It means the world to me."

He smiled at her, then winked at his wife who stood in one corner. She was smiling too.

Carli and Lank's eyes locked. He looked so handsome, with his black hair reaching just past his collar. He had trimmed his beard too, his blue-gray eyes burning bright directly at her. He wore dark jeans, a white shirt, and black vest. He even had on a tie, a dusty blue.

When they reached the spot where Lank and the judge stood in front of his massive desk, Taylor smiled and said to Lank as he placed Carli's hand in his, "I'm wishing you both all the best. Now take care of my daughter. Remember, I know where to find you."

She turned to face Lank. "You polished your boots again."

"Yes, ma'am, I did."

The judge started the proceedings and asked if they wanted to say any vows to each other.

"Just a few," Lank said. "If that's okay with you, Carli."

"I don't have anything prepared," she said.

"Me neither. I just wanted to speak from my heart." He held both her hands in his. "Here goes. Carli, from the first minute I saw you, I fell in love with you. Couldn't help myself. But of course, you were ornery..."

"What?"

Laughter.

"Well, you know what I mean. Stubborn maybe? We've been through a lot in this past year. But now we're standing here, ready to commit our lives to each other. I love you, Carli. And I always will."

Carli squeezed his hands. Then looked at the people around her and back to Lank. Nathan and Indya. Angie and Colton. Her father, Taylor, and his wife. Tears stung the back of her eyes again when she looked at him. She wished Lola and Buck could be here too.

"Ms. Jameson. Is there anything you would like to say to your groom?"

Carli nodded. Her brain swirled in a tizzy, so she took Lank's advice and decided to speak from the heart. "Lank. I know I was stubborn at first. I had to go on my journey. Not only with you and all the people in this room, but with God also. I had to trust Him. This is where I am supposed to be. He led me here. And I think now he has blessed me with everything I could ever want. A loving husband. A father I always wanted. Friends and community. A family I never had. Thank you, Lank, for being patient with me. I love you now and for always."

The judge said the words he was supposed to say, and they answered with the right words, too. "I do." And then Lank surprised her once again when he brought out two gold bands from his pocket. She was already wearing his grandmother's engagement ring. She took that off so that Lank could secure it with the gold bands on either side of the diamond ring. He slid all three back on to her finger.

In a moment of panic, Carli's head whipped around to look at her friend. With a conspiratorial grin on her face, Angie slowly reached into her pocket and pulled out a black silicone band for Lank. "Your maid of honor has your back, girl."

Angie winked.

In all the frenzy of the past month, Carli had not given any thought to a wedding ring for Lank. Her cheeks burned with embarrassment but Lank only looked at her with adoring eyes as she slipped the ring on his finger.

"I now pronounce you husband and wife. You may kiss your bride." The judge's voice boomed around them, and Carli grabbed Lank around the waist, her heart thudding in her chest. She never wanted to let him go.

"I have one more thing, Your Honor." Lank reached into his pocket and pulled out gold coins. Taking Carli's wrist, he turned her palm up and placed the coins in her hand. "It is the custom from where my family originated to give thirteen coins to the bride. To you I trust my wealth and all that I have is now yours."

"Mr. and Mrs. Lank Torres, everyone," the judge said.

"Taylor, would you say a blessing over this couple?" Karissa nodded to her husband. They all bowed as he asked for special blessings on their life together. It was an endearing and honest prayer, and Carli's eyes filled with tears again. "Amen."

A shrill whistle came from Colton, and then the cell phones came out for hundreds of photos. Carli lost count. Congratulations and hugs surrounded Carli and Lank. All except for Nathan. Carli noticed that he had not taken his eyes off Indya.

"Nathan. You're supposed to hug the bride now," Carli said.

"Can Indya keep your jeans? I never realized how good she looked dressed as a cowgirl." Then his face turned red as if he realized he had muttered his thoughts out loud.

"I have something she can wear, Nathan. Indya needs her dress back," Angie said. "What is wrong with you?" She shoved her brother playfully.

Indya laughed and gave him a kiss on the cheek. "Horse snot doesn't bother me in the least. Who knew?"

The girls retreated to the bathroom again and emerged back in their own clothes.

Arm in arm with Lank, and surrounded by the people Carli loved, they walked towards the parking lot in a group.

"We're taking you all to lunch, our treat," said Taylor. "Name the place." The next fifteen minutes were taken up with listing various names of dining establishments from the fancy to the not so fancy.

"Let's let the new bride decide," offered Karissa.

Carli hesitated a moment. "Since Lank surprised me with the most wonderful non-wedding ever, I think we should treat him to something he might like. How does pizza and beer sound?"

A wide smile covered the face of Lank, and the others answered with cheers.

"I love you, wife," said Lank.

She kissed his warm lips. "I know." Inheriting a ranch in Texas was certainly one of the best feelings in the world, but Carli realized nothing compared to this moment. And yet, worry snuck into her head and nearly ruined everything.

"What are we going to do about tomorrow?"

"I might have a solution," Lank said, "but it's going to take some convincing with Buck, and you'll have a lot of explaining to do with Lola. Think you can handle her?"

"Whatever we can do to make this right. I will try."

"I need to make a few phone calls, and then I'll explain on the way home."

"This was right. This ceremony was perfect," Carli said.

"I know."

The look in his eyes was all she needed to believe that things would work out on the day of her wedding after she had already been married today.

Chapter 42

Taylor

Leaving the restaurant, Taylor opened the passenger door to the truck for Karissa and they headed home.

Karissa stroked Taylor's right hand that was resting on the console. "That was really a sweet wedding all in all. A little unorthodox, but sweet. I can't believe Carli showed up in horse-slobbered clothes."

"I guess Lank surprised her. Told her to come as she was."

"Well, thank God for Nathan's wife who switched clothes with her. What was her name?" Karissa asked.

"India. Like the country. I think," he said.

She looked at his face. "That's right. She stood with me in the back when y'all were up front with the judge. She told me she spells it different, with a 'y'."

Taylor smiled at her. "She's a pretty girl. I hadn't seen Nathan in some years. He comes from a good ranching family."

"Yes, he does. I can't believe Indya put on Carli's dirty clothes. Good grief." Karissa laughed. "She told me she didn't mind since it was only for a few minutes during the ceremony. Seemed like a real nice girl. Said that she's an artist and that she and Nathan met in Santa Fe. They just got married a few weeks ago."

"Yeah, she was a nice girl. After wearing Carli's dirty clothes today, I'm sure everyone will get all dressed up tomorrow for the reception," Taylor said.

"Nice of them to invite us. Gee, I'll have to figure out what I'm going to wear. Speaking of which, if we want the kids to go, I think we should give them some notice. Especially Shayla. You know how she is with her wardrobe and all. I'm sure she'll want to make a fashion statement."

Taylor shook his head and laughed. Yeah, that was his daughter. Kind of a fashionista, he thought. *Is that the right word?* What did he know? That was his wife's department.

Taylor nodded. "Okay, let's tell them tonight."

"I'll make some dinner for the kids in case they haven't eaten. I've got meat loaf in the fridge just about ready. I just want to change and then I'll get their dinner started."

"Okay, darlin'."

As Taylor pulled onto the interstate out of downtown, Karissa asked, "How did you feel walking Carli to her groom?"

"Well...kind of surreal, I think," he said. "I guess I felt honored. But strange in a way."

"I can imagine. It's like now you know she's your daughter, and she knows you're her father. But you don't really know each other at all. You're strangers. I wonder what Shayla will think. I mean, you giving Carli away, so to speak, before her. I hope she won't be jealous."

Taylor looked at his wife. "I never thought of that. Maybe because I still think of Shayla as a little girl, not getting married for a long time. And she's kind of less mature than Carli. Don't you think?"

"Yes, you're right. Shayla's into clothes and fashion. Carli owns a ranch."

"Hope I'm not going to be in trouble with Shayla," Taylor said. "You'll have to help me with this, Karissa."

"I'm thankful that Lank called you and I'm glad you decided to go to the courthouse." Karissa patted his arm again.

"Thanks for going with me." Taylor glanced at his wife. "Your support is important."

Later that evening, after Karissa changed clothes and the meatloaf was done, she and Taylor were ready to sit down with the kids.

Just as Taylor was saying, "Where are the kids?" Shayla came bounding down the stairs in somewhat of a whirlwind.

"I can't believe they kept me so long. I wasn't supposed to close tonight but then that...uh, witch... sprung it on me." She looked at her mother, wide eyed and seemingly glad she didn't cuss, then looked at her plate. "What's this? Meatloaf? Mom! I'll just have some salad."

Taylor glared at his daughter and was about to reprimand her slightly when the phone in his pocket buzzed. Normally, he wouldn't answer it at the table but when he glanced at the screen, he saw it was a text from Hud, so he read it.

"Hud will be here in a minute. Said to start without him."

"Okay." Karissa passed the salad. "Shayla, your dad and I ate a late lunch. You can have our salad. Hud can have meatloaf and the rest."

Taylor wasn't as verbose with praying out loud as his wife, but a long time ago she had asked if he would say the blessing as man of the house. So, he did. And he figured short, but sweet was better than nothing at all. He went ahead and blessed the food tonight.

Soon they heard their son's truck motor and then the side door sprung open, and he came in. Hud didn't always join them for meals. Usually, he ran in and ran out, wolfing down some food while standing at the counter. He'd been talking lately about getting his own place with some buddies, but for right now he was saving his money so would continue living at home.

"Sorry. I was working with that young horse and just couldn't stop right in the middle. Man, I could really use a shower."

In a firm voice Taylor said, "Make it quick, Hud. Two minutes, then get to the table. Okay?" Taylor still thought of his son as a youngster at times and wanted to hold onto the family dinner time.

"Yes, sir."

Hud ran up the stairs and Karissa called after him, "I'll keep your dinner warm, honey."

"Thanks, Mom."

Taylor thought he'd bring up the subject of the Wild Cow Ranch reception to Shayla.

He sipped his sweet tea, then said, "Shayla, we're going to an event tomorrow as a family so don't make any plans."

Karissa watched her daughter, warily it seemed,

waiting for the girl's reaction.

"What event, Dad? I've got plans. I'm going to a movie with friends."

With that, Hud came bounding down the stairs, hair still a little drippy from the quick shower.

"What plans? What movie?" he asked, full of energy.

"Dad said we're going to some family event tomorrow." Shayla exhaled a big sigh.

Karissa stepped in. "Why don't we just listen to what your dad has to say?"

"Shayla, remember when you told us about meeting that bride at your store who came in with Lola from the Wild Cow Ranch?"

"Yeah?"

"Well, we're going to her reception tomorrow."

"What? Why would we do that? We don't know them."

"But I do know Lola. Remember? I used to work at the Wild Cow when I was a teenager."

Hud jumped in. "Yeah, you trained horses like me. Right?"

"Well, yes, among other things. Like mucking the stalls."

Shayla sounded whiny. "I still don't know why we have to go to her reception."

Hud asked, "Can I bring my girlfriend?"

"No, bud. I'd rather this just be family."

"Why?" Hud looked puzzled.

Taylor paused for what seemed like an eternity to him, all the while looking over at Karissa, who nodded as if encouraging him to continue.

"Well, as it turns out...the bride, Carli, is your half-sister. My daughter." Taylor had difficulty getting the words out, but it had to be done.

All at once it seemed that a volcano had erupted. Both kids talked at the same time, almost saying the same things.

"What? What are you talking about?" Shayla said. "Your daughter?"

Hud's eyes were big. "I have another half-sister?"

"Let your father explain," Karissa said softly, always the peacemaker.

Taylor explained, "We just found this out and it's a big surprise to us too. When I was a teenager, a senior in high school, my girlfriend was Michelle Jameson. Her parents owned the Wild Cow Ranch."

Hud stuffed his mouth, then mumbled, "And you knocked her up."

"Son, have some respect. Yes, we made a mistake. We weren't married. But it happened. I didn't know it at the time that she got pregnant. And Michelle ran away."

"That's just crazy," Hud mumbled in between bites. "How'd you find out now?"

"Well, Michelle passed away some years ago. Then, after her parents died, the attorneys found Carli in Georgia and she inherited the ranch. She's the spittin' image of her mother. Michelle never told me she was pregnant. But recently, after some research, I found out that I am Carli's biological father."

With tears bubbling in her eyes, Shayla said, "So why do we have to meet her, go to some reception? Why do we even have to know her? That was a long time ago."

Karissa intervened. "Honey, we know this is hard. It was hard for me, too. Hard for your dad to find out he had a child he never knew about. But if we can all just take a breath, I think God would want us to think about the whole situation. Think about Carli who never had a mother or father, never had any family. She's twenty-eight years old now. Let's try to be decent, kind. She just wants to know the father she never had, the siblings she never had."

"Oh, great," Shayla pouted. "So, I'm supposed to be her best friend now? Sisters?"

Karissa said, "You don't have to be anything, Shayla. Just polite and kind. That's all we're asking."

With the final word, Taylor said, "Let's just take this one day at a time. I want us to go to the reception tomorrow as a family. So, be ready."

Chapter 43

Lola

Lola Wallace brushed the smooth fabric with her fingertips. It hung from the closet door in one of the second-floor bedrooms at the cookhouse. Neatly pressed and ready for the bride, the off-white crepe shimmered in the sunlight streaming through the window. It was early. Long before anyone would be arriving. She paused to admire the simple cut and design. Carli had chosen well.

With both hands she spread the lace mantilla and let it float to the floor. She sank back on the bed and dreamed of another time and place, of a Catholic church with glistening stained-glass windows and the pressure of her grandmother's arm around her shoulders.

With a heavy sigh, she trudged to the kitchen. She was happy for Carli and Lank but planning this wedding had taken a lot out of her. It had brought up so many memories of the past, and that had surprised her.

On a whim, she had invited her sister and Rena to Carli and Lank's wedding. After her niece Rena had put them up for the night in Dallas, it only seemed right. Her mood lifted as she thought about seeing her family again.

She paused at the top of the stairs. There was still much to do for the reception which would be in the barn. The couple would exchange vows in the cookhouse dining room that had been transformed into a chapel with rows of chairs and an arbor in front of the fireplace. The decorating committee of Dixon had outdone themselves. Everything was to perfection and beautiful.

Lola frowned. Carli should already be over here getting dressed, and Angie had assured her she would help with makeup. Where were those girls?

And where had Buck gotten off to? She slept like a rock and had not even heard him get up and leave. He'd better not be starting some ranch job that could wait until tomorrow and then be late for the wedding. That would be just like him to saddle a horse and go after a lame cow or some such thing.

Lola found the tea bags in the pantry and filled several large kettles with water. She could at least get the tea made until it was time for her to get ready. The front door to the cookhouse slammed shut and Lola peeked out of the kitchen to see who had come in. Carli, but she didn't have a wide smile on her face. It was her wedding day, for good grief's sake.

"Why aren't you dressed?" Lola walked out of the kitchen to meet her halfway in the center aisle, looking her up and down. She wore a simple skirt with a beige sweater and Grandma Jean's turquoise boots. "Are you sick?"

"Actually I feel better than I ever have in my life, but I have something to tell you. Maybe you should sit down." Carli pulled out a chair, but Lola shook her head.

"We don't have time for chit chat. Let's get you upstairs." Without waiting for an answer, Lola headed back up the stairs.

"We really need to talk, Lola."

Before Lola could answer, the front door opened again and the cackle of a group of ladies broke the silence. They bulged through the door en masse, carrying sacks, covered dishes, and all talking at once.

"Good morning, ladies!" Lola called out. "We're up here. I'll be down in a few minutes."

Carli gave a quick wave and a smile, and then quickly pushed Lola into the bedroom. She closed the door behind them.

"Get over here and put this on," Lola said.

Carli sat on the bed and shook her head. "I can't do that."

"You're having second thoughts. All brides are nervous on their wedding day. It's only last-minute jitters. They'll go away."

"It's not pre-wedding jitters. Believe me. I'm completely calm and confident that Lank and I have done the right thing. God brought us together and it's working out perfectly."

"I'll help you, mija. Come on." She reached up and removed the dress from the hanger. "What shoes are you wearing? Your grandma Jean's boots?"

"Lola. Listen to me." Carli's voice rose louder, tinged with aggravation.

"Let's get this show on the road, Carli. I don't understand what you're trying to tell me."

"It's done."

"What's done? Wait. You said did. You said, 'We did the right thing.' What did you do, Carli?" Lola studied her face, preparing herself for weeping and a total meltdown. Had Carli and Lank broken up? But all she saw was a big, wide smile and sparkling eyes.

"The hard work, the planning, bringing the entire town of Dixon together. The cookhouse is over the top," Carli said. "I know you did this out of love for me and Lank."

With a gush of air Lola sat back on the bed. Anger rose to the surface, and she glared at Carli. Why was she wasting so much time? Guests would be arriving soon. Everything was proceeding according to plan. This was going to happen.

"We got married yesterday in front of a judge. It was perfect. It was exactly what I wanted, except you and Buck were missing."

Lola's heart dropped like a stone. She couldn't bring herself to even look Carli in the face. "What? You're married?"

"This isn't my dream wedding. This is yours." As she walked closer and put a hand on Lola's shoulder, Carli murmured, "Put on the dress, Lola. You're going to renew your vows and have the wedding you've always wanted."

"That's the dress we picked out for *you*. I'm not wearing it," Lola argued.

Carli removed the dress from the hanger and unzipped it. "This is your dream, and the man of your dreams is waiting."

Lola burst into tears. "Oh, Carli, you're right. This has all been about me and what I wanted so many years ago. I can't believe I never saw that.

Will you ever forgive me?"

"There's nothing to be sorry about. This is an exciting day that we both can share." She held the dress out for Lola to step into.

"I have been so self-centered!"

"You're wearing this dress and you're walking down the aisle." Carli's voice meant business.

"No. That's your dress." Lola was not giving up her stubborn pride so easily.

"Put the dress on, Lola. Your man is waiting. I'll put it on you myself, if you don't behave."

"Buck knows about this? Who else?"

A knock on the door interrupted their standoff.

Isabella, Lola's sister, came bursting into the room. "Lola, *mi hermana*. We are here to see the bride."

Lola wrapped her sister in a warm hug, both women squealing like schoolgirls.

"Rena is here too," said Isabella.

Lola gave her niece a hug, and gave Carli a hug, and then it was all a blur, and she couldn't say what was going on from that moment.

Through tears and laughter Isabella and Rena helped Lola into the dress.

Carli touched her arm. "I'm leaving now, but I'll see you after the ceremony."

"No, ma'am," said Lola. "Not before you put on *my* dress."

Carli laughed. "It's a deal. Where is it?"

"Hanging in my bathroom in our apartment. And there's one more thing. Will you pray with us before you go?"

"Of course." Carli's eyes shone with unshed tears as she leaned in to give Lola a hug.

The four women locked arms and bowed heads, and in broken English Isabella offered thanks for the day, reverted to Spanish to bless the newly-wedded couple, and asked for blessings on her sister and Buck.

Lola couldn't believe this was happening.

Chapter 44

Carli

Saturday, early afternoon
Cookhouse, The Wild Cow Ranch

As Carli descended the stairs from the second floor of the cookhouse, she looked in awe at the transformation. She had not noticed before because her main purpose had been to convince Lola to put on the dress. Mission accomplished. Now she could relax and enjoy the first day as Mrs. Lank Torres.

Shimmering white gauze draped the banister, gathered at each post with bunches of white flowers tied with chocolate brown ribbons. Those must be her colors. White and brown. Different, and she liked it.

Rows of chairs replaced the small tables in the dining hall. A bouquet of flowers covered the entire fireplace mantel carrying the theme of white in addition to colors of the fall with mums in burnt orange, yellow, and for contrast, a deep burgundy. Brown ribbon was woven throughout. Centered on a cowhide in front of the fireplace stood a grape vine arbor with greenery and more white flowers, but not too overdone. Sometimes less is more, as the focal point was more the branches as they twisted together from the arch. All tasteful and country simple. Carli loved it.

Her cheeks grew warm remembering the decorating her groom had done the night before. Lank had filled his trailer with candles and bouquets of white roses, so how could she not agree to spend at least the first night as husband and wife there. Now she had to convince him to move his stuff across the compound into her house. Not an easy task. She realized that her husband was a strong-willed, Texas cowboy.

Carli stopped midway on the stairs to admire the transformation of the dining hall when the door opened and Buck appeared, a look of panic on his face.

"The minister fell and might have a broken hip. His wife just called. They're on their way to the emergency room. What'll we do?"

"I'm sure we can figure out something." Carli hurried down the stairs to meet him. Buck grabbed her arm and dragged her outside.

"It's bad luck for the couple to see each other. Where's Lola?"

"She's putting on her dress."

"How'd that go?" asked Buck, wide-eyed with concern.

Carli laughed at the expression on his face. "It went as well as expected. You have a strong-willed little lady right there."

"Don't I know it," he said and gave her a wink. "Wouldn't want her any other way."

Just then her fence-line neighbor Crazy Vera pulled to a stop in front of the hitching post. She hopped out and her bloodhound Snot jumped to the ground behind her.

"Vera," Buck called out. "Do you know of a minister who might be willing to conduct a ceremony on very short notice?"

"Actually, I do," she said. "Know one very well as a matter-of-fact and I know they would be glad to do it."

"Thank goodness," said Carli. "You might have just rescued this entire day from disaster."

"What's his name so I can give him a call?" Buck asked.

"You're lookin' at 'im." Vera stuck her arms out and curtsied.

Carli smiled. "You're a minister? That's terrific."

"It's not somethin' I tell everyone, but I've preached on occasion, done a few weddin's, and a few funerals."

"Great, you're hired." Buck grabbed her arm and pulled her inside. "Come with me."

Confusion fell across Vera's face as she looked at Carli and then Buck. "There's been a slight change. I'll fill you in on what's going on and what I want to do," he explained.

He had Vera inside before she could ask any more questions.

It was then Carli remembered Lola's new dress, so she spun on her heels and went back upstairs to the apartment where she found the dress they'd bought in Amarillo, hanging on the back of the bathroom door. Carli changed clothes right quick and had to admit the dress fit her well. She felt beautiful. And not even a part of her was sad about the gorgeous wedding gown that Lola now wore. No regrets. Carli hurried back downstairs lighter in step and in heart. It was going to be a good day.

She made a pass through the kitchen, which was full of ladies stirring this and mixing that. Two stood at the sink washing dishes. *Might as well get this over with.* Carli plunged into the lion's den.

"Good morning, ladies."

"Carli, why aren't you dressed?"

"Having second thoughts? We all went through it."

"It'll be okay. You'll see."

They all gathered around her like a cluster of hens, clucking and patting her arm.

"I'm not getting married today," she said. "There's something you should know."

As if someone hit a switch the clucking stopped. All eyes turned towards her, some tinged with concern and even unshed tears.

"I'm already married," she announced holding up her left hand. "See."

The clucking resumed at a higher pitch and intensity, followed by hugs and a few tears. She then slipped out the back door to find her husband, exhilaration making her heart flutter at thinking of the word "husband" and Lank as one and the same. She found him opening the wire gate to the pasture next to her house, as Colton directed a car through. They'd have to maneuver traffic into some type of organized parking on the grass. He looked busy, so she decided not to distract him. However, as far as the guests were concerned it might seem strange that the groom and best man were parking cars.

They would have to explain later.

Carli wandered back upstairs on the iron steps located on the outside of the cookhouse and sat on the balcony. From there she had a good view of the hustle and bustle of Wild Cow Ranch headquarters as cars began to arrive. She noticed several ladies buzzing back and forth on a golf cart between the kitchen entrance and the barn where the reception would be held.

Belinda and Russell pulled up in their B & R Beanery SUV. They carried covered trays and ice chests into the barn, going back and forth. Carli watched them work and thought about the life she wanted with Lank. Whatever they chose to do, she wanted it to be together. She wanted them to work as a team, yet they should be able to pursue their own interests as well. She sighed. If he wanted to be a rodeo clown, which was the stupidest idea in the world, then she should support him and not pressure him to train horses for the kids. The riding school was not his passion, it was hers. Maybe there could be a way they could combine both their endeavors and support each other's choices.

A steady stream of cars was now lined up from both directions, waiting to turn into the grassy parking area. A few saw her on the balcony, and she returned their waves.

She looked at her watch. It was almost time. Time for her wedding to begin that was not her wedding any longer. Typical for how her life usually went, but this time she was thankful for the strange turn of events.

Chapter 45

Carli

Carli hung back out of sight as she watched guests arriving for the wedding ceremony at the Wild Cow Ranch. She motioned towards Lank who was helping Colton and a few other men direct cars. It's time he came in. They had talked about how to break the news of their vows before the judge, and then decided to not make an announcement. It might take the focus away from Buck and Lola. They could all explain it later.

Lank and Colton walked towards her.

"You guys need to get ready. Colton, aren't you best man, or did Buck make a change?"

"I've been demoted," Colton said. "Lank is best man."

"Sorry, babe. I can't sit by you," Lank said to her. "I told Buck I'd stand up for him."

"That is perfectly okay. I'm going to stay out of sight at the back because we've stirred things up enough. The minister fell and cancelled. Vera is going to officiate."

"Crazy Vera?" Colton exclaimed.

"Boy, the surprises keep on coming," observed Lank.

"You can say that again." Carli stepped closer to Lank and brushed off his brown pearl snap and leather vest. "Where'd you get that shirt?"

"This is what Lola told us to wear."

"You guys look very nice. Why don't you go dust off a bit after standing in that pasture with cars driving all around? I'll see you inside."

"Good deal." Lank leaned forward and gave her a quick peck on the lips. "See you in a minute."

Colton followed Lank to his trailer and just as they disappeared inside Angie walked across the gravel drive.

"I love that dress," she said.

"It was Lola's that she picked out, but I really like it too."

"Any regrets?" asked Angie.

"None whatsoever. This way I can hang at the back of crowd, without anyone noticing me. Exactly the place I like to be. I don't like being the center of attention."

Angie put an arm around her friend. "I'll sit with you. I've been fired as maid of honor."

"And I've been fired as the bride. We make a great pair, don't we?" Carli said. Laughter bubbled up and Angie joined in.

They waited until everyone was inside and then slipped in through the kitchen and found seats at the very back of the room. Del scooted in quickly and sat down next to Carli. It was a full house.

"Wow," said Angie. "This looks amazing."

Carli nodded in agreement. From the back of the room, she noticed their friends and neighbors.

The Olsens sat with Nathan and Indya. Russell had corralled their kids. Belinda was probably setting up something or stirring something. That woman never stopped. She couldn't see Taylor or Karissa, and Carli admitted that she was a little nervous about meeting her half-brother and half-sister. She wondered what they would think of her.

Crazy Vera walked up the center aisle in a deep purple robe, carrying a white Bible, looking more like a priest than minister. She had slicked back her long gray hair into a tidy bun and applied a bit of makeup. Carli hadn't realized what a pretty woman she was. She turned around to stand behind a podium and face the front. That was when Carli noticed the long brown feather dangling from one ear. Typical rebel.

Vera nodded and raised her hands. Everybody stood just as the music started. From the side, Buck walked to stand by Vera followed by Lank and Colton.

Lola's niece Rena descended the stairs first, followed by Isabella. They walked slowly towards the fireplace and stopped to stand on the other side of Vera. Their dresses were mismatched but it worked. Rena looked beautiful in a light rose and Isabella wore a darker shade of burgundy. They carried fall bouquets that reflected the same colors as the mantel arrangement and again with deep chocolate brown ribbons that fluttered and twirled as they walked.

Instead of the traditional "Here Comes the Bride", a Spanish song played. "That's '*Te Amaré*'," Del leaned over and whispered in Carli's ear. "It means 'I will love you'."

Lola stopped at the top of the stairs. She was stunning. Of course, the dress fit perfectly. The off-white shimmer of the crepe looked beautiful against Lola's dark skin and dark hair. Her eyes sparkled like diamonds as she stared at Buck. He in turn never took his eyes off her as she began to descend the stairs.

A collective gasp went through the crowd. Carli heard various whispers, "It's Lola. Where's Carli? That's Lola." But all quieted as Lola got to the foot of the stairs. She walked slowly up the center aisle by herself, never once averting her glance away from Buck. The smiles on their face were as if they were the only two people in the room. Carli sighed. If only she and Lank were that lucky. To be with the love of your life for so many years and still be just as in love as you were at the beginning. More so even.

Lola stopped and they both turned to face Vera.

"I hold the secret to a happy marriage in my hand," Vera said. She reached down behind the podium and pulled out a box of breakfast cereal which she held over her head. "Lucky Charms!"

The crowd tittered and howled. Vera waited for them to settle down before continuing.

"C for commitment to each other. H for holiness; keep God involved in your marriage. A is for affection; keep it spicy. R is for respect. M is for mercy. Forgive each other just as God forgave us. Lastly, S is for service. Help each other, be kind to each other. I think Buck and Lola are the perfect examples of a Charms marriage. By the way they are lookin' at each other, you can see that it's true."

More laughs, and heads nodding in agreement.

"In Ephesians 3:20-21, Paul wrote, '*Now glory be to God, who by his mighty power at work within us is able to do far more than we would ever dare to ask or even dream of—infinitely beyond our highest prayers, desires, thoughts, or hopes.*'

"If He is workin' within us," Vera continued, "can you imagine what He can do with two people? A couple totally devoted to each other with God at the center, workin' as a team can accomplish much. Please stand. Buck has asked to lead us in prayer."

The sounds of chairs scraping the cement floor and the bustle of noise as the crowd got to their feet. Buck's deep voice sounded over bowed heads.

"Heavenly Father, I just want to take a moment and thank You for all the blessings you give to us. They're all around us if we all just take a look. In the sky, the land, the animals, and the people. For me, I thank you for my health. I've had a few scares, but you always bail me out. I thank you for my work and the Wild Cow Ranch. For Carli Jameson coming here and becoming our boss. Lord, you had to be in that one, 'cuz none of us could've dreamt it up on our own."

Chuckles fluttered throughout the crowd. And Buck continued, "Mostly, Lord, I thank you for my beautiful wife, Lola. What she sees in me is a dang mystery, but don't tell her that or she might get other ideas. I need to keep her as all mine. She's as good as gold, not only to me, but to every single person she comes in contact with. Thank you for Lola, Lord."

He wiped a little tear from his eye, and then went on. "Just a couple more things, Lord, then I'll be done. Sorry for taking up your time, and sorry for saying 'dang' earlier. I want to pray a special blessing over Lank and Carli. It may not have been a church wedding yesterday for them, but I'm sure it was beautiful. Lord, please bless them mightily. Marriage is not just a piece of paper. It's a covenant between them and you, Lord. Let them always keep You at the center of their marriage. And I ask you to bless them with many years of good health and happiness and service to You."

Buck smiled at Lank, and Carli teared up in the back of the room. "And lastly, Lord, but certainly not least, we thank you and ask your blessings upon all the good people gathered here today to share in our happiness. We are more than a community. We are one big family and we come together during happy times and sad. Lord, please stay with us, guide us, and protect us. In Jesus's name, we pray."

And everyone said, "Amen."

Vera said, "Thank you, Buck. On behalf of the couples here today, we've had some changes that you may have noted. Lank and Carli were married by a judge yesterday at the courthouse. Buck and Lola decided to renew their vows today. Any further questions, I'll let you take it to the couples themselves to explain. Reception is following at the barn. Please stay and eat and drink, and I believe Lola's sister has arranged for some surprise entertainment. Isn't that right, Isabella?"

"Si, I have brought my cousins and their maria-chi band!"

Lola motioned to Carli to come up front, so she worked her way through the crowd to stand by Lank. He grabbed her hand. From that point she hugged and kissed lots of people and showed her ring more times than she could count. And all four of them answered an endless stream of questions. The crowd began thinning out. She turned to Lola.

"You look amazing," she said.

"It was perfect," said Lola as tears bubbled up in her eyes.

"Yes, it was." Carli wrapped her arms around Lola, and they hugged. She then turned to Vera. "Beautiful service, Vera."

"Thank ya, thank ya. It was short and sweet. Now we dance to the mariachi."

Laughter erupted from the couples as Buck grabbed Lola's hand. "Best idea I've heard all day."

"I should probably check on the kitchen and get a handle on clean up."

"No!" They all shouted in unison.

"We've got all week to do that after everyone leaves," said Carli.

"And I'm coming over to help," interrupted Angie.

"Go have fun, and that's an order because I'm the boss," said Carli. She gave Lola a hard stare.

Carli watched them all walk towards the door as quiet descended on the once-crowded dining hall. Lank tugged on her hand. "Aren't you coming?"

Just then Belinda came rushing out of the kitchen. "Lank. Would you mind helping me carry more ice over to the barn?"

"Sure thing," he answered.

"I'll see you in a minute," Carli said as she leaned closer to give him a kiss.

"Love ya, babe," he whispered.

Chapter 46

Carli

The quiet and peace of the now empty Wild Cow Ranch cookhouse brought a calm to her spirit. Carli stood still and absorbed the serenity for a minute to catch her breath and prepare for the noise and frenzy of the reception.

Even though it had not worked out exactly as everyone had imagined, both ceremonies had turned out beautifully. She had no complaints. Turning with a sigh, she walked through the kitchen and out the back door making her way to the sounds of a mariachi band. Her boots crunched on the gravel. She'd never two-stepped to a lively Mexican band before. This could be interesting.

Outside in the dry grass a wooden welcome sign stood on an easel. Under Carli and Lank's names, someone had scratched out today's date and added yesterday's. At the top of the sign, Buck and Lola's names were written in black marker with today's date and a big heart around the word "Forever".

The barn doors were flung back as wide as they could go, and as she stepped inside the view took her breath away.

More white gauze fabric looped from the rafters. Suspended in the very center was a huge, round circle covered in white flowers. Pendant lights in clear glass jars hung all around. Tables and chairs anchored the edges of the room with bright white cloths and more flickering tea lights and candles. Her barn had been transformed into a fairy land and she felt like a princess entering a foreign kingdom.

"What do you think?" Angie walked up to stand next to her, both remaining silent as they looked over the crowd. Some danced, some ate, some visited.

Carli's throat closed with unshed tears, and she could not answer. After a few more minutes, she finally managed, "I can't believe all this."

"Talk later. I see Colton, and he still owes me a dance." Angie hurried away making a beeline for Colton who stood on the far side of the barn, talking to Lank and a group of guys.

Carli wandered over towards the food, her stomach reminding her she had forgotten about breakfast and lunch. Platters were piled high with an assortment of fruit and vegetables with dip. The garden salad was impressive and made Carli's mouth water. Metal servers with Bunsen burners kept a wide variety of food warm, from juicy rib eye steaks and mashed potatoes to grilled chicken breasts, almond green beans, and sweet, buttery corn. The entire tablescape was lighted with various sized bottle and jars filled with strands of white seed lights. A black chalkboard read, *Party 'Til the Cows Come Home*.

Wandering past the main course table, she came to a small table with a tower of Oreo cookies built on a cake plate. There were other treats for the kids too. Small plastic cups with bits of cake, whipped cream, and strawberries. On the other side of the tower, large plastic bowls held servings of spaghetti and sauce with a sprinkling of cheese on top.

An archway of balloons and flowers drew her attention to the far end of the room where a photo booth had been set up. Under the arch stood an antique velvet couch in the funky color of deep magenta. A sign read, *Strike a Pose*. The back-drop was a sheer curtain with a coppery-colored "LOVE" balloon at the top. *How did these women think of this?*

"How do you like the couch?" Her friend Belinda suddenly appeared at her side.

"I have never seen that color on furniture be-fore," Carli said.

"Moved it out of my daughter's room. We looked forever for that color and finally took my grand-ma's old sofa to an upholsterer. I have to admit it turned out great."

Carli nodded. "Yes, it did. Is this normal for the kind of weddings that happen around here? This is just over the top. I can't even imagine the work that went into this."

"Maybe not this elaborate, but not everyone who lives in Dixon has a barn this size," said Belinda. "It's been a blessing and a joy how everyone has come together for this special day. What a twist of events, and Lola in that dress."

"I agree. She was so beautiful," said Carli.

"This will be the talk of the town for months on end." Belinda giggled. "I need to refill tea pitchers. Love you, friend, and congratulations." She gave

Carli a quick hug and was gone again.

Lank appeared at her side. "Come on. I've requested a special number from the band." He pulled her into the middle of the room and other guests cleared the floor.

"Is this our first dance?" asked Carli.

Lank pulled her close and looked down at her with humor and a mix of mischief which made Carli suspicious. She turned to look at the musicians.

The band tuned on their guitars a minute and one of them picked up a fiddle. And then they struck a chord and began to play *Cotton-Eyed Joe*. Carli busted out laughing and Lank's face spread into a wide grin.

"Let's go," he said. He spun her around to his side and they line-danced the steps for one round, and then the floor swarmed with others who joined in. Colton grabbed Carli's arm and Angie appeared on the other side of Lank. Who knew a mariachi band could perform such a fine rendition?

By the time the song ended, Carli was breathless and bent over in a fit of giggles from something Angie had said. She was thirsty so she wandered over to the beverage table.

By the time she drank a glass of tea, Carli had lost sight of Lank again, but she did spy a table set apart from the rest with their names on it. She filled a plate and sat down, watching the crowd as she ate. The one person she didn't see was the one person she wanted to see the most and the only one she was hesitant about approaching.

She scanned the crowd for Taylor Miller, her birth father.

Chapter 47

Taylor

The Miller family left late to the Wild Cow Ranch. The discussion at home about the new half-sister, Carli Jameson, had delayed them, and was heating up again. As Taylor pulled through the gate to find a parking place, he noticed the crowd moving from the cookhouse towards the barn. Driving up and down the haphazard rows of vehicles parked in the roped off lanes of the pasture, he tried to maintain his cool as he searched for a spot.

"This whole thing is so weird," Shayla started. "So, Carli was the girl who came to my boutique with Lola and that other woman, right? The one with the neon-colored hair. And turns out Carli is my half-sister?"

Taylor said, "Looks that way."

"I don't understand why we have to go to her wedding. Or whoever's wedding it is today. Since you said you went to hers at the courthouse yesterday," Shayla said.

Karissa said, "Looks like the whole town is here."

Shayla kept up her rant. "Sounds mixed up to

me. Why do we have to become friends with her? We don't even know her."

Hud chimed in. "I don't understand why I couldn't bring my girlfriend. This is messed up."

Karissa said, "We wanted it to be just family. This is the first time you'll be meeting your half-sister."

Hud smirked. "After we all say 'Hey,' then what do we do? Sit around and stare at each other?"

Taylor chided him. "Don't be rude, Son. We're hoping you and your sister can be polite and that we all can enjoy this event."

"Which sister? My first half-sister? Or my second half-sister?" Hudson grinned. Shayla wrinkled her nose at him.

"Hudson." Taylor's voice was stern. "You know you'd better not have a smart tone when you're talking to me."

"Please. Let's everyone just be nice," Karissa pleaded.

"Whatever," was the girl's response.

Taylor was about to say something, but Karissa touched his arm gently and gave him a look that told him not to even go there with their daughter. It would be an uphill battle.

Taylor finally found a spot to park the truck and they all entered the crowded barn. "It's so pretty," Karissa said, "with those twinkling lights. There's Carli," she said to Taylor. Various guests were giving their congratulations. Lank was nearby at the drink table. "This is a good time. Why don't you introduce everyone?"

Taylor's stomach flipped a bit. He thought Carli looked beautiful and he felt a surge of courage to do this. With one arm around Karissa and the other directing his kids to come forward, he said, "Carli, I want to introduce you to my family."

She turned towards the group with wide eyes, but a warm smile, and extended her hand to Karissa. "I met you yesterday. You look beautiful. Thank you for coming today. And yesterday too."

Taylor leaned in to give her a hug and touched his cheek to hers. "Sorry we missed the ceremony."

"Actually, it was a renewal of vows for Lola and Buck since we said our vows at the courthouse. Lola was really surprised. I think she loved it."

With a little nudge at their backs, Taylor said, "This is my son, Hudson, or Hud. And this is Shayla."

"His daughter," Shayla said. Her expression conveyed she'd rather be somewhere other than where she was at the moment.

A few awkward glances were exchanged until Carli said with a sweet smile, "I'm really happy to meet all of you. I know this might be a shock. It was for me too."

Hud halfway moved in for a hug, stopped, and said, "Uh, you look pretty, Sis," which prompted Taylor to shove him a little. "What?" Hud whined. "Just tryin' to be friendly. We're family, right?"

"Well, don't act like a jerk," Shayla said. Her mom frowned at her.

"We met at your store," Carli said to Shayla who smirked. Carli took hold of her reluctant hand and said, "I know this is weird, Shayla, but I hope we can be friends someday."

The girl did not smile.

"And I hope y'all will visit me at the Wild Cow whenever you can." Carli looked at the whole Miller family. Her new, extended family.

Lank soon returned with two drinks and said hello to everyone. He shook Taylor's hand, then Hud's, and said to the young man, "Hey, I hear you're working at the *Four Ds Ranch*. Pretty soon you'll be as good as your daddy was, back in the day."

The three men laughed.

In the center of the room Buck and Lola were dancing as the crowd watched and smiled, witnesses to true love.

As the music neared the end, Karissa squeezed Taylor's arm and whispered. "You should dance with Carli. Father/daughter."

"Really? Do you think so?"

"Of course. She might've dreamt about this moment for a long time."

"Do you think Shayla will mind?" Taylor asked.

Karissa said, "I'll talk with her. Ask her for the next dance."

He gripped her waist and pulled her close. "And what about my wife? When do I get to dance with her?"

"The very next one after your daughters."

"Daughters. That sounds a little strange. I love you, my beautiful wife. You know that?"

"I do know. And I love you, my handsome husband."

The next song started up and as Lank was about to lead Carli to the dancefloor, Taylor approached and held out his hand. "May I have this dance, Carli? You don't mind, do you, Lank?"

"No, sir."

Before Carli could answer, the announcer said something about the Father/Daughter dance.

"I guess that's us," she said. Her eyes grew big,

and she placed one hand on Taylor's shoulder.

She's trembling. Poor thing.

"Are you okay? I don't bite, you know," he said.

"I just never thought this day would ever be real. Mostly I thought I'd never know my birth father. It's all a little surreal."

Taylor said, "That's how I felt when I stepped forward in the judge's chambers. It was strange to think that you're my daughter, and I'm your father, but we're really strangers." He squeezed her hand and smiled. "I hope we can get to know each other and become friends."

Carli smiled. "I'd like that."

He guided her around the dance floor, and she giggled at some of the things he said. At the end of the song, he returned her to Lank.

"Thank you, Carli. And thanks, Lank. Sorry I took her away for a few minutes."

"That's okay, Mr. Miller. Uh, Taylor. I guess I'm gonna have to share her with her new family from now on."

They all smiled, then Taylor said, "I had better ask my *other* daughter to dance and my wife before they disown me. Suddenly I have a lot of women to keep up with."

Lank patted him on the back and said, "And that ain't all bad, I've come to learn." The two men shared a hearty laugh.

Taylor walked over to Shayla whose arms were crossed. She was next to her mother who was whispering words to her as Shayla rolled her eyes.

Karissa smiled at Taylor who extended his hand to his daughter. "You look beautiful, sweetheart. May I have this dance?"

She grumbled. "You've already been dancing with your *new* daughter."

"Please don't be that way, sweetheart." He looked down at her stiletto heels, grinned, and said, "You sure you can dance in those things?"

"Yes, Dad, I can dance in them. They go with my dress." Her mouth was taut, and she seemed to be on the verge of yelling at him, so Taylor knew he had to tread lightly with this powder keg.

He pressed his hand against her back and said, "Honey, it was the right thing for me to do at her wedding. Someday I'll be dancing with you at your wedding. But right now, I want to dance with the daughter I've been with her entire life since she was a baby."

He took her hand and squeezed tightly, leading her to the dancing area.

"Oh, Dad," Shayla said. "Don't get all mushy."

He smiled at Karissa as he took his daughter away to dance.

"You know, Shayla, it's true. I was there when you were born. A little pink wailing thing. Your mom and I picked out your name together. You're part of our flesh and blood and I love you more than you could imagine."

She looked up at him and gave a little smile.

"I know this whole thing is strange. It came out of the blue and surprised all of us. But now it's here and I hope we can make the best of it. None of us know Carli, but she seems like a nice person. I hope we can all try to be patient and kind. And just remember, she never had a real mother or father, no sisters or brothers, no family really. Maybe we could give her a break. Okay?"

Shayla still felt a little stiff to him. He tickled her side.

"Okay, Dad." She wiggled a little and another half-smile leaked out of her stone face.

"Shayla, I want you to know...you've been my one and only daughter for twenty-two years. I love you with all my heart. Nothing is going to change that. But I also want to make room in my heart for Carli. She's part of me too. Will that be okay with you?"

She relaxed a little in his firm hold. "Yes, Dad."

The song ended and Taylor led Shayla back to where Karissa stood with Hud.

He reached for his wife and said, "I believe the next dance is ours."

As they glided together to the music, Karissa said, "So, how was it? Two daughters."

Taylor let out a big sigh. "I think I have my work cut out for me. Especially with daughter number one." He chuckled.

"You looked good with both of them. It'll just take time. For all of us."

"How are you doing with it all?" he asked.

"I'm coming around, I think. Carli's a nice girl. It was sweet to see her and Lank yesterday at the courthouse. And you standing up with her before the judge. Then today seeing all of this—sorry we missed Buck and Lola's ceremony."

"Yeah, seems like we've all been through a lot in a short time," he said.

"Like you said, hon, one day at a time. And as long as we stick together, we'll be able to get through it."

He held her close. "Life's a journey and some-times throws a curve ball at us."

Karissa looked up into his eyes. "That's for sure. I think God wants to see how we'll handle the surprises."

"Have I told you lately that I love you, Karissa?"

"Hmmm, just this morning, I think."

"Well, that's not enough. I'm gonna have to up my game."

"Sounds good to me, Taylor. I love you too."

Chapter 48

Carli

Lank stood at Carli's side kissing her neck and whispering, "You look beautiful, Carli. Is this everything you wanted?"

Carli took a few moments to answer as the dance with her birth father still lingered in her mind. She worked hard to keep her emotions in check. In her wildest dreams, she never imagined that she would find herself in Texas, dancing with the man who gave her life. There's no explaining God's plan.

"Yes. Everyone has been so nice. I can't believe all the townspeople who helped to decorate the barn. It looks like a dream with all these lights."

"Makes you look like a princess."

"And you're my favorite cowboy, Lank." She kissed his lips.

"Hey, knock it off, you two. What do ya think, you're married or somethin'?" Nathan Olsen appeared before them, his voice full of spunk, his face full of smile.

"Thanks, man, for being here. We really appreciate it," Lank said.

The two punched each other's arms and shuffled around. They'd been friends for years.

"Had to make sure it was legal yesterday, your wedding. I'm here to eat up all your food and dance with your beautiful bride." Nathan pushed Lank's shoulder.

Lank laughed.

"Carli, would you do me the honor?" Nathan asked and extended his hand.

Carli looked at Lank and then at Indya, Nathan's wife, who smiled.

Lank said. "I'll take your lovely wife for a spin around the dance floor." To Indya he held out his hand. And to Carli he said, "Okay with you, babe?"

"Yes, yes, go." Carli grinned. "Be careful, Indya, he might step on your toes. C'mon, Nathan, show me what you've learned while you've been making it big in the art scene of Santa Fe."

When Carli had first moved to Texas, Nathan Olsen had become one of her best friends. Eldest son of a ranching family with a long heritage, they were neighbors, and he took a liking to her right away, and always offered his help. As time went on, she realized he wanted to make their relationship permanent, but her heart just wasn't in it in that way. Nathan ended up leaving town and they hadn't seen each other in some time.

Dancing with him now, she remembered what it was like to be in his arms. He was tall, strong, and kind. She could've had a life with him, but she knew it wasn't right.

"We're both married now," Carli said. "Can you believe it?"

Nathan held her and smiled. "I know. I figured

all along you'd end up with Lank. To be honest, I was angry at times. But I guess you figured that out. Now, I want you to know, I sincerely wish you both all the best."

"Thanks, Nate." She was about the only person who ever called him that. "And Indya. She is beautiful. Tell me how you met."

Nathan's face seemed to change like Carli had never seen before. Kind of wistful or dreamy like. "Well, moved to Santa Fe, as you know. My dad had a fit, wanted me to take over the ranch. But I pursued my art instead. You remember all that, right?"

"Yes, of course," Carli said. "Who was that older guy who mentored you?"

"Brad Travers. Remember you went with me once to visit him at his home near Amarillo?"

"Right. He was such a nice man. And I liked his wife. I think she had Alzheimer's, didn't she?" Carli asked.

"Yeah, that was sad. But they're still doing fine. Brad introduced me to a lot of people in Santa Fe. One of the galleries exhibits his sculptures."

"Did he introduce you to Indya?"

Nathan shook his head. "No, we met at an art workshop. She's an artist too."

"Wow, that's pretty neat. What kind of art does she do?"

"Painting," Nathan said. "She's really good too. A lot of people think so, not just me."

Carli moved her hand on his shoulder. He was such a nice guy. But she knew deep down that she'd rather be in Lank's arms. And she was so happy that she and Lank were now married.

"I'd love to see some of her paintings sometime,"

she said. "You remember how I love art and went to a museum with you?"

"Yes, Carli. I remember everything."

"Nathan, I want to tell you..."

"You don't have to say anything, Carli."

"But I want to, Nate. I just want to say that I miss your friendship and I was sorry when you left town. I'm also so glad you followed your dream, your heart. It just wasn't my dream. My dream was here."

"With Lank."

"Yes, Nate, with Lank. Took me almost a year to figure that out."

Nathan twirled her around and said, "It's all good, Carli. I understand now. And I am so happy with Indya. It was meant to be this way. Hey, I've got some other news."

"Indya's pregnant!"

"We've only been married a few weeks, Carli. No, what I was going to say is, we might be moving back here. It's not for sure, but we've been talking. We could always go back and forth to Santa Fe, like Brad does. But I miss my family and would like Indya to be more involved with them."

"That's great, Nate! Then Lank and I can see you both. That would be fun. And, by the way, did you have a big wedding? Did your family come to Santa Fe? We didn't get an invite." She fake-pouted, lip stuck out.

Nathan got a little quiet. "Not exactly. We were married in Santa Fe but it was really small, private. Just the two of us and a few friends, at sunset, on a ranch in the hills. It was beautiful. Brad Travers knew the people who owned the ranch."

Carli asked, "Have your parents met Indya?"

"Yes. They're happy for me, but mom cried. Missing the wedding of her oldest boy and all. They'll come around and they love Indya as much as I do. Typical of the Olsen family, Mom and Dad are throwing us a party to make the announcement official. You and Lank will be there, I hope. I guess I'd better retrieve my wife from your bumbling cowpuncher. Thanks very much for the dance, Carli. Remember, I wish you and Lank all the best."

With that, Nathan kissed her cheek and returned her to Lank, and then led his wife away. To face the music.

Chapter 49

Carli

Things were winding down for the night. Carli stifled a yawn. What a day.

"If the two couples would come to the floor. We have one more song to play in their honor."

Lank walked through the crowd, grabbed Carli's hand, and as they made it to the center of the dance floor, Buck and Lola joined them. Buck shrugged his shoulders with a questioning look on his face. Lola grinned and winked at Carli.

The band began playing, and Carli recognized the opening strains immediately. "Your cousins know "Amarillo by Morning"?" asked Carli.

Lola laughed. "They sure do, only because I kept hounding them until they learned it."

As Carli and Lank danced, they moved through the crowd ending up at the very back of the dance floor; she looked over and found herself facing Lank's sister, Kelly. She stopped dancing and leaned closer.

"I haven't had the chance to tell you that I am sorry it worked out you weren't at your brother's wedding. We are glad that you are all here tonight," Carli said to both Kelly and her husband Matt.

Kelly smiled and gave her a warm hug. She motioned them off the dance floor where they all gathered at the barn entrance farther away from the stage.

"That's better," said Kelly. "I've been wanting to talk to both of you all evening, but you've always had a crowd around you."

"You aren't mad at us?" asked Lank.

"Of course, not. You did what was best for you and your life together. It has nothing to do with me, although I would have loved seeing my only brother say his vows. But we've got tonight."

"We're happy for y'all," said Matt. "Welcome to the family." They all leaned in and Carli found herself in the middle of a family hug.

They laughed and broke apart. Carli fought the tears that stung her eyes.

"I understand how difficult it would have been for Lank without mother there. She loved weddings. Lord knows she dragged us to a ton of them."

Lank nodded in agreement as a tinge of sadness clouded his eyes. "We love y'all."

"We love y'all too. Now go be happy. Everything turned out beautifully." Kelly smiled and patted Lank on the shoulder.

"Kelly," her husband said. "Your son just knocked down the Oreo cake."

"Oh, no," she turned and disappeared inside, Matt trailing behind.

"Hold on, you've got something in your hair." Lank reached around behind Carli.

"Ouch." Carli jerked his hand away.

"You have some kind of blue streamer, and I can't get it off."

"That's my something blue," she said. "The hairdresser dyed a few strands for luck."

"Whatever makes you happy." Lank wrapped his arms around Carli and they swayed to the last strains of the music. It has been perfect. Just what she wanted.

Lola came strolling by with a package of plastic cups in one hand and the trail of her skirt in another, still wearing that gorgeous wedding dress.

"The ceremony was beautiful, Lola. I hope you got the wedding of your dreams," Carli said.

"I'll never forget what you did for me," Lola said, just before Buck appeared and twirled her away to the dance floor.

"Buck, let me go," she said as she held tight to the package.

"You girls can talk later." Buck ignored Lola's protests.

Carli leaned her head against Lank's shoulder. This was the calmest she had been in a month. They moved farther inside and he two-stepped her around the cement floor. She looked at the faces who had become so precious to her. The town of Dixon had really come together to make everything so perfect. The cookhouse, the barn, the shower. It had all been so much.

Suddenly her feet stopped moving and tears tumbled down her cheeks. She couldn't stop and she couldn't explain why she was crying.

Lank grabbed her by both shoulders. "Carli, are you having a panic attack?"

She shook her head no.

"What's wrong? Tell me." Lank squeezed her shoulders.

"I have acted...so...horribly. You're crazy for marrying me." More sobs overtook her, and she couldn't stop.

"You're not horrible. What is wrong with you?" he raised his voice.

The music had stopped, and the band was putting away their instruments. People were picking up decorations, sweeping trash, stacking chairs and tables.

"What'd you do to her, Lank?" asked Colton as he slung an arm around his friend's shoulders.

Angie patted her back. "Carli. Why are you crying?"

"What's going on here?" Del squeezed in between the small group.

"I have been complaining for an entire month." Carli wiped her face with both hands. "While everyone was working so hard to make this day special, I dreaded every second of it. I didn't want to go shopping. I whined about the bridal shower and opening presents. People brought me gifts and that's the way I acted. If no one ever speaks to me again, that is the very least I deserve."

"You weren't that bad," said Angie. "And since you're already upset, there's one more thing you should know."

Carli looked at Angie with a questioning glance. Hesitating a second, Angie avoided her friend's face, then looked back at Carli with a sheepish stare.

"Just tell me," said Carli.

"Your wedding invitations had a typo. They said 'Carl and Lame'."

"Are you serious? Why didn't anyone say anything?" Carli took note of the giggle that Angie was unable to suppress.

"What good would it have done?" asked Angie. "They were already mailed, and everyone knew you two. Just another story you can tell your grandkids."

Lank let out a deep belly laugh.

"And you!" Carli turned towards him. "We couldn't agree on anything, we know nothing about each other, and I doubted everything we were doing. But sometimes I felt so sure. You never wavered. You never doubted me or my love. You must hate me. The whole town must hate me."

Lola and Buck appeared on either side of her. "Carli. It's all right. It was just nervous bride emotions."

"I am so sorry for the time I wasted worrying and grumbling. I should have put my trust in God and had the faith that everything would work out."

"That's right," said Lola. "You can't go wrong with that kind of thinking. Find joy in everything you do. That's what life is all about."

"We love you, Carli. Your grandparents would be so very proud." Buck put his arm around her shoulders and gave her a hug.

"Love ya, girl," said Angie as she leaned in for a hug.

Del nodded in agreement and pulled a tissue from her pocket to blow her nose.

As the tears began to subside, Carli wiped her face again. "I've got to tell everyone thank you."

With that she turned and headed towards the first man she came to as he broke down a table.

"Thank you," she said, and then proceeded to work her way around the room stopping at each person and giving them a hug.

"I'll meet you at the entrance when you're done," Lank called out after her.

The rest of the small circle of supporters laughed, but Carli didn't mind.

"The buggy's here!" someone announced. "Time for a romantic ride."

Carli turned to see a carriage parked just outside the barn door. Her cheeks hurt from smiling so much and she had shaken every hand in the place.

Carli and Lank motioned to Buck and Lola, but they shook their heads.

"Shall we?" asked Lank as he held out his hand.

They walked closer and saw Crazy Vera at the reins. "Climb on up. You kids can handle it."

Lank climbed into the driver's seat and took the reins from Vera as she got down. Carli climbed up after him. Vera handed Carli a canvas jacket, and she snuggled up against Lank, linking her arm in his.

The air had a chill that made her nose tingle, and the setting sun left a faint glow in the west. Dark would overtake them before they got back, but Vera's draft horse would be able to see the road.

"I'm glad you're at my side, Carl." Lank laughed.

"I'm proud to be your wife, Lame," she said. "And I've decided where we're living."

"Oh, yeah?" He smooched and Vera's horse Pinto walked.

"My grandparents' place," she said. "Instead of a new house, we're building a covered arena and new barn for the riding school horses. How do you like that compromise?"

"If that's the way it is, then I've decided where we're going on our honeymoon." He snapped the reins and the horse trotted up the hill where he turned onto a pasture road. Within minutes, it seemed as though they were the only two people in the world as the lights and noise from the barn faded away.

"Oh yeah? Where's that?"

"My trailer," was his reply.

Lank hadn't expressed an opinion during the entire month of planning, but this was by far the best decision she'd ever heard. This time she let out the belly laugh.

Carli's heart was full. God really did want to give her the desires of her heart. Life might not be perfect and there would be trials and tribulations along the way. But when God gave amazing gifts of love—her husband, wedding, and reception, friends and new family—she would grab hold and treasure them for all time.

Acknowledgements

My endearing gratitude goes to my co-author Denise F. McAllister for her enthusiasm and work ethic. A new series with six books published in one year is a huge undertaking, and I wouldn't want to tackle this project with anyone else.

Credit also goes to my hometown of **Dimmitt, Texas**. There are so many memories that flood my mind and definitely inspired the Wild Cow Ranch series. Our next-door neighbor Mae offered her house for my wedding shower and forty-five women volunteered as hostesses. They all pitched in and gave us a microwave oven which we still use today, thirty-five years later, and microwaves were not cheap in those days. Small-town mothers can really pull together and go above and beyond for their kids. I remember themed proms, birthday party sleepovers, Friday night football and marching, and youth Bible studies at the First Baptist Church. And the home-cooked food! At the time, I could only think about leaving there as fast as I could, but now I realize the memory of those days are most precious and those faces continue to inspire me more than they'll ever know.

I would also like to thank the godly women who have crossed my path, both dear friends and family. I think we did a good job in this book depicting the influence that women can have on the people in their lives. From firsthand experience, I know the power of kindness and common sense, and how an unselfish attitude from one confident woman can alter the direction of an entire family for generations.

I hope you have found the plan God has for your life. There's nothing to do now but continue the journey and see where it takes you. Thanks for reading the Wild Cow Ranch series. Please find us on social media and connect. We would love to hear from you.

~ Natalie Cline Bright

Crafting a story (and series) like this is a painstaking process at times. Ultimately, it's a rewarding experience. My thanks go to my wonderful and talented co-author **Natalie Bright**. Without her all of this would not have been possible.

Many thanks to our friends with the **Western Writers of America**, **Wolfpack Publishing**, and **CKN Christian Publishing**. It's uplifting to be connected with encouraging folks like these.

We couldn't do any of this without our **Heavenly Father** who gives us many gifts including creativity, inspiration, perseverance, and friendship. We are grateful.

Thank you, Dear Readers, for following our stories. May they be a blessing to you.

~Denise F. McAllister

A Look At:
Wild Cow Christmas

Sometimes the quietest moments are the loudest in your heart.

Broken dreams, broken hearts, and even broken bones—God can fix it. A heartwarming Christmas story of faith, community, and finding true love.

Now that Carli and Lank got past the roadblocks trying to keep them from marrying, a whole host of other issues pop up for the newlyweds.

Carli is dead set on bringing back the Christmas traditions her grandparents set for the entire town of Dixon. But with her time being torn between various commitments, Lank isn't sure she can pull it all off.

New resident Mandy Milam wants to move on past the heartache and poverty of her past, and provide a safe home for her unborn son. After everything she's gone through, she doesn't want another man to rule her life. However, she can't help but wonder what it would be like to have someone to share the joy of a new baby, and the Christmas season, with.

Come on down to Dixon and enjoy a good old fashioned country Christmas with Carlie, Lank, Mandy, and the whole gang! Merry Christmas, everyone!

About the Author

Natalie Bright -

Natalie Bright writes stories that combine her passion for history of the American West and the unique people of the Texas Panhandle, where she calls home. She is a fifth generation Texan, and a fan of friendly people, a good story, Texas sunsets, and connecting with readers.

Follow Author Updates links above to read PRAIRIE PURVIEW, a Blog focusing on the amazing places and history of Texas, and the inspiration behind her work and featuring her photography.

THE WILD COW RANCH SERIES (CKN/ Wolfpack Publishing)

Find Natalie on Instagram @natsgrams, Pinterest, LinkedIn, and Facebook as NatalieBrightAuthor. If you like cows, the Texas sky, and all things Western, then you're in the right place.

Denise F. McAllister-

Lovers of the West can be born in the most unlikely of places. For Denise F. McAllister, her start was in Miami, Florida, surrounded by beaches and the Everglades.

But the marvels of television transported her to stories of the West—Bonanza, Gunsmoke, The Virginian, and many others—that she fondly recalls watching with her brother every Saturday morning.

After being in the working world for some years, Denise F. McAllister applied her life experience to study for degrees in communications and professional writing. She loved going back to college later in life and hardly ever skipped a class as in her younger years.